DOUBLE EXPOSURE

ANNE BARWELL

PŌNEKE SHADOWS, BOOK 1

Human or supernatural—no one escapes justice.

Cover design: © 2022 T.L. Bland
Publishing logo © 2019 T.L. Bland
http://www.thruterryseyes.com
Cover art is for illustrative purposes only and any person depicted on the cover is a model

Editing: Penny Tsallos
https://pennytsallosediting.com

Proofing:
Lissa Given Proofing
Maryann Kafka

ISBN: 978-0-9951466-9-3 (epub)
ISBN: 978-1-99-116210-6 (mobi)
ISBN: 978-1-99-116211-3 (print)

AUTHOR'S NOTE

Pōneke is a Māori name for Port Nicholson or Wellington.

ALSO BY ANNE BARWELL

Slow Dreaming

On Wings of Song

Prelude to Love

The Sleepless City

Shades of Sepia

Electric Candle by Elizabeth Noble

Family and Reflection

Shifting Chaos by Elizabeth Noble

Echoes Rising

Shadowboxing

Winter Duet

Comes a Horseman

CO-WRITTEN WITH LOU SYLVRE

New Zealand Romance

Sunset at Pencarrow

Magic in the Isles

The Harp and the Sea

To my readers

ACKNOWLEDGMENTS

To Elizabeth, my shared universe partner in crime, who alpha and beta read, brainstormed, and was a huge support throughout. The characters in this story were originally developed for our co-written series *The Sleepless City*.

To Angela, Gillian, and JJ for alpha and beta reading.

Naomi for the series title and tagline.

To my writing and reading communities for your support and friends, in particular RWNZ, and my Facebook group Anne's Books and Brews. A special thanks to the New Zealand Rainbow Romance Writers group—you guys rock.

Gillian, Emma, and JJ for all their support, friendship, and awesome accountability.

T.L Bland for her wonderful cover art.

Penny for editing.

Lissa and Maryann for proofing.

To my family. Love you.

CHAPTER ONE

"You're taking too many risks." Ben Leyton yanked at the top of Simon's newspaper, nearly ripping it in two.

"We've already had this conversation. I'm a vampire. I can take care of myself." Simon Hawthorne raised an eyebrow. "And I've been doing this for a very long time."

"You mean, you've already stated your opinion. The last time I looked, it takes two for a discussion."

"I thought we had discussed it." Simon flinched at the anger he felt through their shared soulbond. He folded his morning paper while it was still relatively intact and laid it on the table. "And don't think I haven't noticed the risks *you've* been taking either." He reached for Ben's hand. "You're still happy here in Boggslake, aren't you?"

"Yeah, of course. Why wouldn't I be?" Ben sighed and shuffled his chair around to sit next to Simon. He leaned in to kiss him, and Simon barely managed to duck out of the way in time. "Apart from the fact you're avoiding me like I have the plague."

"*I'm* contagious," Simon reminded Ben. "Not you." He shuddered at the thought of Ben's family's reaction to him becoming a vampire because they hadn't been careful enough.

Despite popular myth, vampires could only turn humans around the anniversary of their own turning. The length of that time depended on the age of the vampire. Simon had been turned in 1916 during the Battle of the Somme during WWI.

"I'm not going to catch vampire by sharing a bed with you or cuddling at night," Ben snapped. "And if I do, so what? I know you're worried about my family, but they'll be fine. Becoming a vampire isn't exactly a death sentence. The opposite, in fact. Our friends have had long productive lives, and so have you." He rubbed at his temples. "I'm not trying to be unreasonable and while I get where you're coming from, my family aren't yours."

"So, you keep saying." Ben's family might have accepted his sexuality, but becoming a vampire was a completely different scenario. Simon changed tack. "Watching loved ones grow old while you don't is painful."

"Don't you think I know that?" Ben bit his lip. "If I stay human, that's what you'll have to do. You've lost enough people you care about. We should be able to talk about this reasonably, but every time I bring it up—"

"You'll be late for your appointment." Simon cut Ben off. "What if we talk about this tonight, hmm?"

"You said that last year and the year before that. I'm tired of going in circles every time your anniversary comes around." Ben sighed. "I want to be a vampire, and I want to be one *with* you. I know what I'm getting into, and the downside of living a long life while my family doesn't. Isn't it better that we plan to do this on our terms, rather than waiting for something bad to happen to one of us and we've left it too late? Last I looked, big decisions were supposed to be something we discuss together, not avoid because you don't want to talk about it. This is frustrating as, especially watching you going after the bad guys. I worry something will happen and I don't want our last conversation to be an argument."

"Neither of us are going into the field alone."

Simon tried to smile reassuringly. Although it had been a couple of years since their friends had left to join the Vampire Guard, he and Ben had adjusted and added new members to their team. Anita and Charlie Coate—Lucas's sisters—had grown into their roles. The four of them, and Boggs, the castle ghost, worked well together investigating incidents connected to their city's supernatural community.

Living a long life meant change. Simon had lived at the castle for decades with Forge and Declan. Their family had grown after Lucas moved in, and years later, Ben and Blair.

"You did last week," Ben pointed out. "Just because I know you're more than just the mild-mannered history professor you appear to be by day, doesn't mean you have to prove you're a scary as hell arse-kicking vampire at night to everyone else."

"I have nothing to prove." Simon led Ben over to the sofa, where'd they be more comfortable. Frustration took the place of anger. "Both of us are on edge. It happens every year."

Their bond didn't like the enforced physical separation, and once Simon got past the anniversary of when he'd been turned, and the week long risk of contagion that came with it, they'd spend a couple of days fucking each other senseless and things would return to what passed for normal.

He trusted himself while they were both awake. He didn't trust the pull of their bond when they weren't. The last time they'd shared a bed when he was contagious had proved exactly how much that wasn't a good idea, and he'd only just woken in time to avoid ejaculating on Ben. Dream sex with

Ben might not be as good as the real thing, but it had the same results, especially when they were both horny as hell and wanting each other after days of enforced celibacy. Nevertheless, he'd watched Ben like a hawk for weeks afterwards to ensure he hadn't been infected.

Ben bit his lip. "I know we go through this every year, and we're both struggling with being physically apart." He snuggled into Simon, his head resting on Simon's shoulder. "I'm not asking you to turn me right now. Just that if we decide to go for it, we set a date and make a plan. We could have a special ceremony or something. Celebrate it with our friends."

"Like Declan's turning when he was with the Algonquin?"

Their friend Declan had learnt about vampires when he lived with the tribe and was later turned in a special ceremony by his lover, Kitchi. He spoke of his turning like a beautiful consensual thing, not the horror that Simon's had been.

"Yeah." Ben smiled. "I'd love that. The actual changing part would be private, though. Just between us."

"Definitely." Simon carded his fingers through Ben's thick, dark hair and held him close. They both knew that Simon would lose the control he'd fought so hard for if he lost Ben. "I'm sorry."

"I know, and I don't want to fight about it. Promise me we'll talk about it tonight?" Ben whispered. "Properly. If you still don't want to, at least it's *our* decision then."

"I don't want you to go through what I did. You're close to your family, and you need to hang onto that." Simon could feel Ben's anger and frustration through their bond. "I love you; you know that right?"

"Of course, I know that." Ben looked up in surprise. "I've never doubted that. Ever. I love you too. Just be careful, okay? If those Boggslake for Humans idiots found out who you really are—"

"I'm more worried about you if that happens." Simon didn't think for one moment that Ben wasn't more than capable of looking after himself. He'd seen him take down some scary supernatural creatures as part of their team. Yet this human group worried him more than the supernaturals ever had. He linked his fingers through Ben's. "Being on edge like this can be dangerous in a fight. One more day and I'll make it up to you, I promise."

"On edge doesn't come close to describing it." Ben caressed Simon's ring with one finger. "I've never regretted marking you as mine," he whispered. "Worry and frustration don't go well together, yeah? I guess we found the downside to being soulbonded when one of us is human." He sighed. "Damn shame jacking off doesn't work. I love watching you do that, but only if I can touch you afterwards."

Simon stopped himself from kissing Ben just in time. "If you still want to do that anyway, don't let me stop you."

"I'll take you up on that tomorrow once I've fucked you senseless. Good thing we've both got the day off. I don't intend to leave our bed apart from meals or to use the bathroom."

Simon let his eyes go completely brown. "I was hoping we could share a bath, too."

Ben groaned. "Oh fuck, yeah. I'd like that a lot." He glanced at his watch. "Bloody hell, I'll be late for my meeting with Daphne. I left a few of my photographs with her at the gallery last week."

Although Ben had intitally put his dream of becoming a full-time photographer aside, Simon had encouraged him to reduce his hours in the press liaison role at the Boggslake Police Department to focus more on his photography. His black and white photographs of locations around Boggslake were stunning, and Simon loved how he used shadow and light to give a glimpse of the area from a different perspective.

"I'm sure she will be very impressed with them. Daphne knows quality work when she sees it. She's had an eye for that kind of thing for as long as I've known her. Do you want me to drop you off on my way to work?"

Daphne Waterhouse was one of the vampire councillors on the Boggslake Supernatural Council. Simon had first met her when he'd settled in Boggslake after the war, and although they didn't mix socially, they'd always shared a mutual respect.

"Thanks, but I'll take my bike. Exercise kind of takes the edge off... you know, and the weather's decent today, so I won't need my car to get home if you get held up at work." Ben stood, then blew Simon an air kiss. "I'll meet you for lunch and let you know how I get on, okay? Do you want to go out or should I come by your office at the uni?"

"I'll take you out to celebrate."

"I'd like that." Ben paused at the doorway. "And don't think I don't know you changed the subject. We're still talking about this tonight after we get home."

Immediately after Ben had left the room, Boggs appeared in front of Simon. "He made several valid points, and that change of subject wasn't subtle. Avoiding this conversation won't help the other thing you're putting off."

"I'm waiting for the right moment." Simon closed his hand around the small box in his suit pocket. He'd marked Ben as his as part of their soulbond, and Ben had marked Simon in return with a ring because a bite from a human would heal over. Simon's mark was on Ben's inner thigh and hidden. A ring wouldn't be. "I worry about him out there with those Boggslake for Humans people upping their game. Asking him now will make the bullseye on his back even bigger. They've already killed humans they know are friends with supernaturals. If someone figures out what I am, and we're married—"

"Someone only needs to see you together to figure out you're more than friends," Charlie said from the doorway. "I worked it out in under a minute." She grinned. "Besides, he stinks of vampire."

"Charlotte has a point." Boggs had called her by her full name ever since she'd moved into Lucas's apartment on the top floor the year before. He was one of the town's founders, the original owner of the castle, and had been a ghost long before he and Simon had met.

"You have werewolf senses," Simon reminded her. "Humans won't have that advantage."

"The BFH killed Lily's cousin Jasmine a couple of weeks ago," Charlie said. "She didn't know any supernaturals, and it's only a matter of time before they go after one of us."

"We're harder to kill," Simon said. The line in the sand between them and the B—he stopped himself from using Charlie's acronym in time—had already been drawn. "We haven't been able to prove to the council that they were responsible for her death." Charlie started to protest, and Simon held up his hand. "We both know they were, but the council refuses to act until they have proof."

"Or one of us is killed." Charlie snorted. "You're not the only one with human friends or loved ones. Sometimes, my father is so stubborn." She shrugged. "But then he's not talking to me at the moment, so it's a waste of time trying to get him on our side. Anita tried, but he's ignoring her too. Uncle Jasper's trying to stay neutral, but we'll see how long that lasts."

"Your father is only stubborn *sometimes*?"

Jacob Coate was head of the Supernatural Council in Boggslake. He and Simon had moved past barely tolerating each other into an uneasy friendship of sorts. Still, he hadn't been impressed when Simon and Ben had taken his daughter under their wing and offered her a home at Boggs' Castle. He hadn't been happy when his son Lucas had soulbonded with a vampire and now one of his daughters had a *human* girlfriend. At least he hadn't discovered that Charlie had told Lily about the hidden side of Boggslake. Werewolves weren't supposed to share their secret with humans, but Charlie had refused to be in a relationship built on lies.

Simon could understand that one. He supported her decision and half expected a summons from the council when the truth came out.

"You could always join the council," Charlie said. "I overheard that one of the vampires wants to step down, and that Marion is keen for you to join her and get some long-overdue changes made."

Simon shuddered. He preferred to keep his distance from the council as much as possible, despite their continually expecting favours that weren't returned. Marion had joined them because it was easier to keep an eye on them from the inside, or so she claimed. At times, Marion could be tarred with the same brush as Rupert, her ex-husband, although he would have made himself scarce long before any hint of a council invitation. It was one of the reasons he'd survived so long.

"That's never going to happen." Simon made a show of checking his watch. "Oh, is that the time? I need to head out for work, and don't you have a lecture you're meant to be attending?"

Ben's phone rang immediately after he parked his bike. "Hey, Blair."

"Any luck?" Blair Turner had worked with Simon's team for years before coming to Boggslake and soulbonding with Jonas Forge, one of Simon's oldest friends. Blair and Ben had hit it off immediately and been friends ever since.

"It's Simon. What do you think?" Ben took off his bike helmet and ran his hands through his hair. "He's scared. I keep telling him my family aren't his, but all that does is bring back his memories of what an arsehole his dad was about the vampire thing."

"Forge says he'll talk to him about getting his head out of his ass if you want him to." Blair lowered his voice, although it would be a waste of time considering his husband was also a vampire.

"Yeah, nah." Ben hoisted his backpack over his shoulder. "I appreciate the offer, but this is something Simon and I need to work through." He heard a familiar voice in the background on the other end of the phone, although he couldn't make out the words. "I mean it about not ringing Simon, Forge." Ben raised his voice. "That goes for you too, Lucas."

"I wouldn't—" Lucas started to say.

"They mean well, mon ami, but I agree," interrupted Declan. He was Lucas's partner, another of Simon's oldest friends, and spoke in an undefined European accent. "This is something you and Simon need to discuss. He's a stubborn man, but so are you. I'm certain you'll be able to make him see reason, eventually."

"Yeah. I hope so." Ben grew quiet. He didn't want to be a vampire to live a long life, but so he and Simon could live one *together*. Not that being a vampire was any guarantee, especially with how dangerous their lives could be. But a guy could hope, right? Declan and Forge were centuries old. Ben wanted that for him and Simon. Or, at the very least, they'd go together so Simon wouldn't be left alone.

Damn this soulbond. What would happen to Simon if Ben went first? No one seemed to be able to give him a straight answer, and the only other human he knew who had been bonded to a vampire wasn't in a state to talk about any of it.

"Ben, you still there?" Blair sounded worried.

"Yeah, sorry. Just thinking." Ben mentally smacked himself on the forehead. "Bloody hell, I'm an idiot." He'd been trying to find out about their current problem instead of asking the one person he should have gone to in the first place. Charlie was a decent hacker, but Blair was way better.

"You love him," Blair said.

"Not about that. Geez. And yeah, I do." Ben took a deep breath. "I need some information about an organisation called Boggslake for Humans. We're calling them the BFH. Could you take a look and let me know what you find out?"

"Sure." Blair hesitated. "You're okay? That's not a great name for an organisation in a small town with a decent size supernatural population."

"Yeah, we're fine. They're causing a bit of trouble, that's all." Ben downplayed the situation. He wasn't about to worry or distract Blair when he was about to set out on a mission for The Guard. "We need to nip it in the bud before anyone else gets hurt."

"Or killed." Lucas took over the phone. "Charlie told me about her girlfriend's cousin. Her *human* cousin. Watch your back and Simon's. If these idiots figure out you're with a vampire, the situation could blow up in both your faces."

"Yeah, I know that, but thanks." So much for trying to keep secrets. Ben had been afraid their move away from Boggslake to join The Guard would change their friendship, but it hadn't. "I miss you," he said softly.

"Miss you too," Blair said. "We need to head out. Keep in touch and I'll send any info I find. I have some awesome

Nightwing merch I know you'll love, so I'll send that too when we get back. Bye!"

"Sweet as. Thanks."

Ben hung up and started walking towards the gallery. It looked dark inside. He checked the message on his phone to make sure he hadn't mixed up the time of their meeting. Daphne was a stickler for promptness, so he'd worked hard to make up the time on the way over. He felt better from the exercise, and the conversation with the guys, although he still wanted to scratch the itch at the back of his mind. It wasn't his and Simon's first time navigating his contagious period, yet each year it put him on edge, however much he vowed he wouldn't let it affect him. Unfortunately, their enforced chastity didn't slow down the other parts of their soulbond. Ben still felt Simon's emotions loud and clear, so double the frustration.

He shoved his phone into his pocket and took a deep breath. Another twelve hours and he and Simon could make up for lost time. The week was nearly over. He could do this.

The gallery didn't open for another hour, but Daphne had assured him she started her day early. Probably a leftover from when she'd been human before the days of electricity when everyone got up at the crack of dawn. Ben shuddered. He wasn't an early riser, and just thinking about getting up that early made him yawn. Nothing to do with the crap night's sleep at all.

He straightened his posture and knocked briskly on the door. To his surprise, it opened at his touch. Ben stepped over the threshold, his senses on alert, and then forced himself to calm. He wasn't walking into a supernatural crime scene. Daphne was a vampire, and the gallery had a sophisticated alarm system designed to protect its treasures.

Nevertheless, he helped himself to one of the carved walking sticks sitting in a rack by the counter. Hopefully, he could return it without her getting too cross he'd borrowed it. He read the price tag on the thing and swallowed. The worst she could do was make him pay for it. Right?

Any vampire or werewolf on the premises would have smelt him by now, so it was too late to back away. Odd, though, that Daphne hadn't come to meet him.

Suitably armed, he double-checked he'd left a clear path to the door in case he had to run for it and cleared his throat. Either he'd need to leg it, or make an idiot of himself.

"Ms Waterhouse?"

No reply. The hackles rose on his neck. The place was far too quiet. Daphne wouldn't have left her door open. He'd check behind the counter and then leave and hope like hell drawing attention to his presence hadn't been a huge mistake.

He heard a groan from behind the counter. A flash of red caught his eye. Gripping the stick with both hands, he crept over cautiously. Austin, Daphne's assistant, lay in a crumpled heap behind the desk, blood pooling at his head. Ben bent and rested his fingers on Austin's neck. No pulse.

Fuck. Who had he heard?

Where the hell was Daphne?

A woman screamed upstairs. Ben yanked out his phone and called Chief Sellers. "It's Ben Leyton. I'm at Waterhouse Art Gallery. There's been a murder, and someone's in trouble." He cut the call before his boss could tell him to get out. He'd never forgive himself if someone else died because he'd run.

Where the hell was Daphne? He could really do with a kick-arse vampire at his side about now.

Concern. Fear.

He felt Simon through their bond. His phone vibrated in his pocket. No doubt Simon telling him to get out.

Foot on the bottom step, he hesitated. He needed to leave.

Whoever was behind this had already killed. Let the police deal with it.

But what if he could save a life?

"Damn it." He sprinted up the steps, his footsteps almost silent on the carpeted stairs. A sole light burned in one of the offices on the far side of the floor. Daphne's office.

He tightened his grip on his makeshift weapon. He'd taken someone down with a bat before. He could do this. Or at least cause enough of a distraction to give whoever was in trouble in there a chance to run.

The woman screamed again, then laughed.

What the fuck?

Ben crept closer, wondering what the hell he'd walked into.

"I suggest you leave. The police will already be on their way." Daphne sounded calm, like she already had the situation under control. She raised her voice. "No one else is here apart from me, and neither myself nor my assistant will press charges if you leave now."

She knew Ben was there. Given the amount of blood downstairs, Daphne had to know Austin was dead. Ben's heart thumped in his chest, giving his location away to any supernatural in the building.

Why the hell hadn't she taken these idiots down already?

Something heavy crashed to the floor. Daphne hissed.

The smell of burning flesh made Ben instinctively wince, Simon's memories flooding his mind. His hand shook.

No, no, no.

He spun at the sound of footsteps behind him and swallowed. A blonde-haired woman dressed in red aimed her gun at him. "Bloody hell," he muttered, chastising himself for being distracted and caught like an amateur. "Where the hell did you come from?"

She grinned. "I figured if I screamed, it would bring

whoever else was in the building running to my rescue. The groan downstairs was a nice touch too, don't you think?" She gestured with her weapon. "Drop your stick, or I'll shoot you." Her grin morphed into a smirk. "We need you alive, Mr Leyton, but I'm sure a bullet in the leg or arm would still hurt like a bitch."

"You what—" Ben shut his mouth quickly. She knew who he was and didn't care that the cops would be on their arse for threatening one of their own. They'd already killed Austin, and they'd obviously subdued Daphne. *Please don't let this be about Simon.* Any hope that he'd managed to piss someone off on his own disappeared when the woman marched him into the office.

Two men stood by the heavily curtained window. One kicked at something by his feet. The other glanced up at Ben, then moved out of the way to give him a clear view of their prisoner.

Daphne lay sprawled on the floor, her hands cuffed in front of her, her ankles bound with silver-coloured ties to an overturned chair.

Her stockings hung in shreds, burnt and stuck to her flesh.

Not silver-coloured. Silver coated.

He gritted his teeth, determined not to react, to confirm he knew what they'd done. That he knew what she was.

Concern. Fear. Anger.

Simon's emotions gushed through their shared bond. Ben had never been any good at convincing Simon he was okay when he so totally wasn't.

One of the men grabbed Ben's arm and twisted it behind him. He winced in pain but said nothing. The man wrapped plastic ties around his wrists and then shoved him to his knees. Not silver. Plastic. They knew he was human.

Somehow, Ben doubted that was a good thing at this point.

The woman collected the duffle bag by the door and handed it to the man standing over Daphne. He pulled out a crossbow and armed it with a stake.

Ben started to struggle. "You can't—" The man holding him grabbed his hair, yanking his head up so he met Daphne's eyes. Ben bit his lip.

"I've lived a long time," she said calmly.

The man fired the crossbow. It hit Daphne in the chest. Her skin whitened, then crumbled to dust.

Ben retched.

"Your boyfriend's next," his captor whispered.

Ben slammed his head back, connecting with the man's groin. The grip on him loosened. Ben struggled to his feet.

Something hit him hard from behind.

Simon! He called through their bond frantically, desperate to warn the man he loved. Then everything went black.

CHAPTER TWO

Pain screamed through him. Simon swayed on his feet, his fingers white as he clutched the podium, staying upright.

Ben reached for him through their bond, anger and fear hitting Simon like punches to his gut in fast succession. Then darkness stained Ben's part of their shared soul instead of his usual light.

Ben!

Bloody hell. Simon forced himself to straighten. He kept his gaze averted away from a couple of concerned students who hovered a short distance away, and reached into his pocket, shoving his sunglasses on. He couldn't risk them seeing his eyes totally brown, or the vampire this close to the surface. His fangs descended and he bit down on a growl.

"I'm fine," he mumbled.

"Do you need to sit down, Professor?" One of his students —Macey—reached out to steady him.

He took a step back and raised his voice. "I apologise, but I'm cutting this lecture short today because I'm not feeling well." He winced at another shard of pain. "Migraine," he mumbled.

"Do you need us to go for help?" Macey asked. "I can—"

"No, that's not necessary." Simon gathered up his notes and jammed them into his briefcase. "However, I would appreciate it if you'd tell my assistant I'm leaving." He rushed out of the lecture hall at a speed that barely passed for human, pausing at the door to dry retch, and headed straight to his car.

Simon reached for Ben again. This time, he felt something groggy on the edge of their bond.

Ben?

He took a few deep breaths to calm himself and checked his phone. Still nothing from Ben. Simon rang Ben's number, his heart racing when it picked up instead of going to voicemail.

"Ben? Where are—"

"Simon, don't—" Ben's warning stopped abruptly. Simon heard the telltale click of a gun being cocked, then the phone went dead.

Simon growled. Ben's shaky psychic caress did nothing to calm him. Someone had Ben. His Ben.

He projected love and reassurance through their bond. *I'll find you. And then these people will pay.*

Ben had gone to see Daphne. Simon would start there.

Ben came to slowly, his head thumping. He tried to reach for the sore spot at the back of his head, only to find he couldn't move. Coarse ropes wound around his wrists and waist binding him to what felt like a heavy wooden chair. The skin around the plastic ties already felt raw, and the ropes over them weren't helping. His wrists stung, and any attempt to break his bonds sent sharp pinpricks of pain up his arms.

He opened his eyes cautiously, barely lifting his lashes,

careful not to draw attention to the fact he was awake. The two men who'd captured him sat around a table, talking in low voices. The room was decorated in an old-fashioned decor, the layers of dust suggesting it had been abandoned years before. A pile of dust cloths had been dumped in the corner of what looked like a living room. All but one of the curtains were drawn, and a poster was attached to one of the walls.

Boggslake for Humans.

Great, these were the BFH idiots their team had been trying to track.

One of the men glanced at him. Ben shut his eyes quickly, playing possum. Simon frantically reached for him through their bond, and Ben's phone rang with the theme of the TV show *Angel*.

The man who had killed Daphne picked Ben's phone up off the table and answered it.

"Ben? Where are—"

"Simon, don't—" Ben whispered, hoping no one else in the room would hear him, although Simon with his vampire hearing would. He froze at the feel of steel against his cheek. The woman from the gallery smiled and put her fingers to her lips.

The man who'd answered the phone smashed it under his feet.

Ben winced.

"Not very clever, trying to warn your vampire." The woman slapped him across the face.

He glared at her. "I thought you were all for keeping humans safe. I don't feel particularly safe at present."

They'd killed Lily's friend Jasmine. Her *human* friend.

"You're a traitor to the human race. You're consorting with vampires *and* werewolves."

Lady, you have no idea. Ben sensibly didn't voice his comeback aloud. If they found out he was soulbonded to a vampire, he and Simon would be totally screwed.

He took a deep breath. If one of two soulbound vampires died, the other one followed soon afterwards. If he died, he couldn't take the risk Simon might too. He needed to stay calm and not aggravate them. For Simon's sake.

"Simon's a good man," he said quietly. "You have no idea what you're—"

This time she punched him in the stomach. He hissed in pain.

"You're the one with no clue." She levelled her gun at him.

"Stop it, Sable! We need him alive for now. Once we have his vampire, and he's watched him die, you can kill him. But not until then."

Simon would come to him, but he already knew he'd be walking into a trap. He would have picked up enough through their bond to know.

That wouldn't stop him. These idiots hadn't seen Simon in scary vampire mode. Ben had a sudden image of Simon, his eyes entirely brown, his fangs down. Heat crawled up his skin, need and frustration quickly doused with icy realisation.

Simon was still contagious. They were both on edge and off their game. Ben's stomach churned at the thought of Simon turning to dust in front of him.

The woman yanked at Ben's restraints. The rope dug into his skin, blood swelling up to trickle down his fingers.

"Oh, crap." He whispered the words aloud before he could stop himself.

Simon would come to Ben's rescue, angry as hell. Then he'd get a whiff of Ben's blood, and all bets would be off.

These guys expected a bad arse vampire with a taste for blood, and that would be exactly what they'd get.

They'd be lucky if any of them survived.

~

Simon glared at the police officer guarding the taped off area around the gallery. "I need to get in there," he said, struggling to keep his tone even. "My partner—" He'd caught the scent of human blood when he'd got out of the car. Not Ben's, but still human.

"I'm sorry, Professor Hawthorne. I can't let anyone through." Susan Lincoln sounded polite but firm. "I can get the detective in charge to contact you later."

"Could you at least tell Detective Larson I'm here to see him? I have information about the case." Simon usually kept a low profile in such matters, but to hell with that. He'd worry about damage control later. All that mattered was finding Ben.

She hesitated. "This is very—"

"It's fine, Officer. The professor is helping us with our enquiries, so you can let him through." Anson Larson pulled up the tape to allow Simon access. He lowered his voice so only another vampire could hear. "I figured you'd be here when you could. Did the council send you?"

Anson had helped their team out on numerous occasions, although he'd turned down an offer to officially join them. He had no intention of being the Supernatural Council's "pet vampire on call on the force" despite Simon's pointed assurances that wouldn't happen. Jonas Forge and Lucas Coate had both worked for the Boggslake PD, in the roles of head detective and medical examiner respectively, and all of their team had told the council at some point where they could shove it. Despite risking his life for them several times over, at the end of the day, Simon was well aware of where he stood with them.

Useful *and* disposable.

"The council?" Simon frowned. "No. Ben's in trouble. He... called me."

Mindy O'Shea looked up from her conversation with the medical examiner when Simon passed the front desk. She'd joined the local force as a detective a few years ago. Despite being a werewolf, she'd come from a pack in Indiana, so she was thankfully not connected to the Coate family and their internal politics. She and Anson made a good team.

He politely returned her nod, retreating into social niceties to mask his relief that the human blood he'd noticed outside had come from the poor chap on the floor.

"After he called us, I hope." Anson continued their conversation while he led Simon up the stairs to Daphne's office.

The smell that hit Simon when he walked into the office was very different, and difficult to ignore, considering it had been spray-painted in large letters on the walls.

Simon wrinkled his nose. "Pig's blood. Lovely." He sniffed, his nostrils flaring when he recognised a very familiar underlying scent. Although cured of John's bloodlust virus, it had left Simon with the ability to recognise the smell of Ben's blood and the temptation that accompanied it. He pushed past Anson and knelt on the carpet, running his fingers along the rough fibres. His fangs descended, he brought his finger to his lips and stopped himself in time from licking it.

"Give us the room," Anson said sharply to the two human police officers guarding the crime scene. "Human blood," he said once they were alone. "I noticed it earlier. It's not Austin Sumison's. They killed him downstairs."

"It's Ben's," Simon said flatly. "Luckily for whoever did this, there's not much of it." He wiped his fingers on the carpet, trying to rid himself of the addictive smell. Giving in to the forbidden taste now wouldn't help him find Ben, and the little control Simon had would disappear until he'd sated his thirst. "He called you?"

"A very brief call to the chief's direct line," Anson said, "but the place was deserted by the time we got here. Sumison has been dead at least a couple of hours."

Simon started to stand, then noticed the chair and the pile of dust next to it. "They killed her." Damn them. Daphne hadn't been a close friend, but she'd been a part of their community for a long time. She'd be missed.

A thin strip of metal barely peeking out from behind the curtains caught the light with a tiny glimmer. Simon straightened and walked over to it, pulled out a handkerchief from his pocket to avoid touching it directly, then bent to retrieve it. "They were careless when they cleaned up. I doubt they knew this was missing."

"Silver?" Anson winced. He hadn't been a vampire that long and had been turned after joining the Boggslake police force as head detective to fill Forge's position after he'd left.

"It must have sprung loose from whatever they were using and landed here."

Anson peered at it closely. "Silver can restrain us, yes?"

"Yes, and it burns." Simon had experienced it firsthand when he'd been kidnapped by his psycho maker, John, shortly after he and Ben had soulbonded. "The arseholes would have tortured her first, and then Ben—"

Ben still had nightmares about staking John and seeing him turn to dust.

"We'll find him, Simon." Anson placed his hand on Simon's shoulder. "The council will act now that one of our own has been killed."

Simon shook it off. They wouldn't be so worried about a missing human. "I'll find him," he muttered.

No point in tracking Ben's phone. It would be destroyed by now. But whoever was responsible had still overplayed their hand. There would be witnesses, and CCTV would have caught them somewhere. Everyone left a trail. He just needed to find its end and yank it tightly until they fell out.

"This is police business, and he's one of ours," Anson said firmly. "I know he's your partner and you're worried, but I assure you we'll find him for you. We'll keep in touch, okay?"

"I'm sure you will." Simon reached behind his back, picked up one of the photographs from Daphne's desk and slipped it into his coat pocket. If one of Ben's abductors had touched it, Simon would trace them that way. He had resources at his disposal and intended to use them.

"Simon?" Anson moved at vampire speed to block the doorway before he could leave. "Don't take this into your own hands. We want them alive, okay?"

Simon smiled thinly. "Oh, so do I."

"That should do it."

Ben blinked against the sudden flash of light. Arsehole One, who he decided to call Tom, had taken his photo. "What the hell was that for?" His head thumped, his mouth felt dry, and his arms and legs were stiff, with pins and needles travelling up and down his nerves. "And can you loosen these ties? You're cutting off my circulation." If he could get free, he wasn't sure if he'd be able to run if he stayed like this much longer.

Sable brought over a water bottle and held it to his lips. "I suppose we should keep you alive until your boyfriend arrives. You can't watch him die if you're dead already, right?" She laughed. "I bet you're regretting he hasn't turned you into a soulless monster like himself yet, so you could get free. He seems like a bit of a wimp for a big bad vampire. Or perhaps he hasn't had the balls yet?"

Ben hesitated. "How do I know you haven't drugged this?"

"Yes, how do you know?" Arsehole Two taunted. Ben decided to call him Harry.

"I'll pass then, thanks." Ben muttered. He could still sense Simon through their bond, so Simon would be able to feel him too. He couldn't do much to help Simon find him, but that would drop to zero if he lost consciousness.

"Suit yourself." Sable yanked away the bottle. "It's such a shame that you're wasting your time on a vampire. A good-looking guy like you could have found a nice girl and settled down by now."

Ben blinked. "I'm gay, so finding a nice girl wasn't going to happen anyway."

"Sent the photo to your boyfriend, so let's see how much he loves you, then, huh?" Harry leaned in closer. "Perhaps he'll decide his life is worth more than yours, so we'll have to find another way to trap him. Still not a good outcome for you, though."

"Wanker," Ben muttered. "Get off on spouting about things you know nothing about, do you? Simon's worth way more than you'll ever be."

Harry balled up his fist. Tom pulled him back. "He's winding you up. Leave him. Fucking vampire lover isn't worth it." He wrinkled his nose. "Put on some coffee. We'll need our wits about us."

"Yeah, you will," Ben said. "Good luck with that." Simon felt pissed and growing more so. He wouldn't want to be them by the time Simon arrived.

"And you can shut the fuck up, too." Tom forced an old rag between Ben's teeth and gagged him.

Ben retched at the stink of beer and sweat. He glared at Tom, then decided the guy wasn't worth his energy. He closed his eyes and focused on Simon.

I'm still here. I'm alive. I love you.

"Ben. You're Ben, right?" The girl sounded young and curious rather than concerned.

Ben opened his eyes. A little girl no more than ten stood in front of him. She was dressed in a pale blue dress in a style of at least a hundred years ago.

He started to reply, then remembered the gag, so he nodded. The BFH gang had their backs to them and were discussing werewolves. Their knowledge was way off.

The girl smiled. "I'm Violet. Simon told me to tell you he'll come to get you soon."

Ben made a relieved choking noise, catching himself too late.

Sable turned, glanced at him, then returned to the conversation.

She can't see you. You're a ghost.

Violet put a finger to her lips. The air around her shimmered, then she disappeared, leaving Ben alone again.

Simon was coming.

Ben's hope sparked, then fell.

They'd killed Daphne.

What if they killed Simon too?

He stilled, biting back tears. He couldn't ask Simon not to come for him. He wouldn't, any more than Ben would abandon him.

Damn it. He wanted a long life with Simon by his side. They'd only lived a few years together. It was too soon for this. They should have had more time.

CHAPTER THREE

Simon quietly lowered the man's body to the ground. Leaving three men outside very obviously guarding a house was like putting a large sign in front of it proclaiming, "Bad Guys Here." These BFH people hadn't trained their disciples well.

Taking them out had been child's play. Finding them was suspiciously looking like they'd wanted to be found.

His telephone vibrated in his pocket. He ignored it. Anita would have discovered he'd already taken matters into his own hands and ignored her advice to wait for backup. She could clean up what was left of the bastards who had taken Ben after Simon had finished with them.

His telephone vibrated again. Simon took it out of his pocket so he could put it on silent, then frowned, not recognising the number texting him.

He opened the text, growling when he saw the image attached to the message and dismissed any thoughts that he might show them *some* leniency. They hadn't worried about Ben's welfare. Why should Simon be concerned about theirs?

Ben's face looked bruised, his expression barely hiding

the pain Simon was already far too aware of through their bond.

Any doubts he'd had about whether they wanted to be found disappeared. They'd sent him an open invitation, along with the address.

If you want your boyfriend back in one piece, be here an hour after dark.

The sun felt warm on his shoulders. This was one of those times where the misconception that vampires couldn't walk in sunlight definitely worked in his favour.

He'd have to find a way into the house, though. Unfortunately, that particular myth was true.

One of the guards stirred. Simon smiled. Right on cue, a human who could ensure he was invited in.

The little girl ghost Violet materialised on the front porch. "I talked to Ben. He knows you're here."

She'd stood on the porch and waved to him when he'd first arrived, and helpfully told him where the guards were posted.

"Thank you."

"I don't like mean people in my house," she said. "But you and Ben can visit me afterwards if you like."

"We'd like that, thank you." Simon frowned. "Do you have somewhere else to go?" Although she was a ghost, she was still a child and he didn't want her to witness any violence.

"I want to help."

Simon opened his mouth to argue, then froze when he caught a familiar scent. Ben was bleeding. He took a step forward, drawn to the smell, his fangs descending, and salvia forming in anticipation of the delicious taste.

"Simon?" Violet yanked him back from the edge.

"I'm fine." Simon clung to his sanity with everything he had. He couldn't lose control. Not yet. He needed to get inside.

"Tell Ben he needs to invite me in."

"He can't talk." Violet frowned. "But I'll go tell him." She vanished before he could protest.

He can't talk?

Bollocks, they must have gagged him. He hoped for their sake that was what she'd meant. Simon narrowed his eyes. If... He reached for Ben and got an answering caress. Definitely a gag. He'd have to do something about that.

The guard started to sit up. Simon grabbed his collar and yanked him fully upright. He deliberately let his eyes go entirely brown, then spoke in an even tone.

"I need to get inside. *Now.* You will go tell them I'm here." He chuckled. "You've made a mistake. You've seen me in sunlight. I'm only human. I'm harmless."

"You're human. You're harmless." The man's speech slurred.

"You'll remove Ben's gag."

"I'll remove Ben's gag." The man blinked, shaking his head like he was clearing it.

Simon let go of him and moved out of sight at vampire speed.

The man stumbled into the house.

Now Simon just needed to wait. He took several deep breaths and forced the outward signs of his vampiric nature to recede. He could play the part of a harmless history professor for Ben. He only needed the role to get inside. Then he'd show them exactly what they'd expected.

Violet materialised in front of Ben again. "Simon's outside. The guards are taking a nap. He needs to be invited in."

Ben nodded grimly. If he and Simon were going down, it wouldn't be without a fight. Hope surged within, this time sparking and taking hold. He'd heard enough to know his captors had no idea what a vampire was capable of. They knew less than he had before he'd met Simon. Although the silver bullets and wooden crossbow terrified Ben, these idiots thought garlic and a crucifix would work too.

They'd taken Daphne by surprise. Simon knew what he was walking into.

"These people are silly. They won't know he's a vampire." Violet sat on the floor in front of Ben. "He knows you're bleeding, though."

Crap. Double crap.

"They already know!" Ben tried to yell through his gag, but only managed a few choking noises. Fuck, he needed to get rid of this bloody thing.

One of the outside guards walked into the room. "We've made a mistake," he drawled. "He's not a vampire. I saw him standing in sunlight!"

Sable frowned. "But we've done the research. He's got to be, and his boyfriend never denied it!"

Yeah, go me. Ben groaned.

Sable stalked over to Ben and whipped off his gag. "What the fuck are you playing at? Do you want your boyfriend to die?"

They don't know about the sunlight thing either.

Someone knocked at the front door.

Ben's yell came out like a croak. "Simon, come in." Stupid bloody rule. If Simon heard him, he could cross the threshold. With any luck, he also knew Ben's big mouth had levelled his plan before he'd had a chance to use it.

Sable's eyes widened. She pulled her gun and held it at his head. "Explain yourself, and now."

The guard from outside dropped to the floor. Simon stood behind him.

"Put down that gun. Now," Simon ordered.

"Oh, I don't think so." Sable pulled out a knife and quickly sliced through the ropes holding Ben to the chair. She yanked him to his feet, using him as a shield, and dragged them both through Violet, who disappeared.

Harry and Tom exchanged a glance. Harry strode towards Simon, garlic around his neck and holding a crucifix.

Light streamed through the one open curtain, illuminating Simon in its glow.

"He can't be. Why isn't he burning?" Sable lowered her gun.

Ben shoved her with his elbow and dived out of her way. "They're armed! Look out!"

Simon sniffed the air. His nostrils flared. His eyes changed. "Not for much longer." One moment Simon was bathed in light, the next behind Harry in darkness, his arm around Harry's neck.

One squeeze and Harry slumped to the floor. Simon bent over him and ran his fangs over his neck, drawing blood. "He smells so good. But you smell better."

Ben shivered. He forced himself to his feet. "Simon, please." He couldn't let Simon go down that path again. "Don't kill anyone else. You don't—"

Blood from Harry's wound dribbled onto the floor. Simon caught a drop with one finger and instinctively brought it to his lips.

"No!" Ben tried to run towards Simon to stop him, but his legs were too stiff. He stumbled and grabbed onto the chair for support. "Don't. It's not worth it. You're not that person anymore."

"He's not dead," Simon said in a flat voice. "Merely unconscious." He slowly licked his finger. "He tastes better warm, and what's the point of a meal that makes you violently ill afterwards? This way, he'll be a decent dessert once I've had the main course."

"Main course? I'm not your bloody main course," Ben hissed. Fuck, if only he had a Taser. He reached for Simon through their bond, desperately projecting love, desire, and memories of the good times they'd had together.

Sable laughed. "Oh, this is brilliant. He'll kill you for us, then we'll kill him."

"Like hell." Ben dropped to the floor, grabbed the chair, and used all his strength to throw it at her.

She ducked out of the way.

"You're not my main course." Simon smiled, yet his expression was far from comforting. "They hurt you and they're going to pay, and then we can be together the way we're meant to be. I'm looking forward to tasting you properly. Finally."

"I don't want to be turned like this," Ben muttered. "You don't want to do this. We talked... we were going to talk about it. Remember?" Darkness flared at the edge of their bond. Fuck it. He'd felt this before. Once, when they bonded, and he'd seen Simon's memories. And later, when Simon had attacked him when he'd been under the influence of John's bloodlust virus with Ben as his target. "I want *you*. Simon, please. I want this to be something we do together when we *both* want it."

Finally recovering his wits, Tom fired his crossbow. Simon blurred out of the way, grabbed the crossbow from Tom and threw it to one side. He wrapped his fingers around Tom's throat. "You hurt Ben. He's mine." His fingers tightened.

"Simon! Stop!" Ben forced his legs to move, ignoring the pain shooting through him.

Simon hesitated. "You're..." He glanced at Ben. Tom dangled nearly half a metre off the ground, desperately trying to get free. Simon's expression softened for a moment.

"I can feel your pain. You're hurting." He returned his attention to Tom. "You did this to him."

Sable raised her gun. Simon grabbed a heavy book off the nearby table and threw it at her. She grunted and hit the floor, then was still.

"Simon." Ben reached through their bond again, felt the glimpse of the man he loved, and held on. *Hard.* "Listen to me. You don't want to kill anyone. I'm not Albert. I'm not dead. You're a good man. I know you are. This is the bloodlust messing with you."

Simon froze. He turned to face Ben, yet didn't loosen his grip on Tom. "I'm not a good man. I told you who I really was. But you never believed it." He bit his lip. "I have to keep you safe; don't you see that." He groaned. "Fuck, I want you so much."

Lust surged through Ben. He staggered. A light bulb went off in his head.

"This isn't just bloodlust. That need you're feeling. It's this damn bond. Another couple of hours and it won't matter. I promise it won't matter."

"It won't matter." Simon dropped Tom with a thump. His eyes returned to normal. He stared at his finger in horror. "I... I don't do this anymore." His nostrils flared. "I can smell your blood. You smell so good."

"I'm sorry." Ben felt another surge of anger at John and the legacy he'd left them. "I love you. We'll get through this. Just like we did last time." He wished he could pull Simon into his arms, but that didn't seem like a good idea. Ben wouldn't let the taste of his blood send Simon over the edge again. "Trust me, please."

Simon nodded slowly. "I'm so sorry. I..." He looked and sounded normal again, the darkness within Ben's mind fading to a pinprick. He let out a slow breath. "I'm not... we're all right." He frowned. "We *are* all right, aren't we?"

Ben turned at the sound of the gunshot. Simon crashed into him, pushing him out of the way, but not in time.

Pain screamed through his shoulder. Ben's vision blurred.

Simon stepped backwards, immediately putting distance between them. "No," he cried. "I can't..."

The front door smashed open. Ben heard footsteps, but they sounded far away. Someone grabbed him, holding him.

"It's okay, Ben. I've got you." Anita turned to someone behind her. "Arrest the cow who shot him. Charlie, grab Simon. Quickly!"

"Anita?" Ben closed his eyes. "Simon. I need..." He'd just rest his eyes for a moment and then everything would be okay.

Ben came to slowly, his first sensation the firm, cool touch on his hand, the second the low-level pain in his shoulder. He snuggled down into the blankets until the steady machine beeping caught his attention. "Hmm? Simon, turn off the bloody alarm. Still sleepy."

The grip on his hand tightened. "Ben? Oh, thank God, you're awake." Simon's worry and relief were rolled into one tight ball of emotion.

"Simon, what—" Ben opened his eyes with a start, taking in the hospital room and the IV attached to his arm. He struggled to sit, but Simon shook his head.

"You don't need to sit up for me." Simon leaned over the bed and kissed Ben softly on the lips. He looked like crap, with his tie loosened and his usually immaculate clothing rumpled. He was unshaven, and his eyes were red like he'd been crying.

Memories flooded back. "That bitch shot me!" Ben bit his lip. "I'm so sor—wait, how are you okay being here?" There had to still be the smell of blood where he'd been wounded, right?

"Vicks under my nose." Simon avoided Ben's concerned gaze. "Lucas's idea. He's used it to disguise the smell in some of the nastier autopsies."

"Simon hasn't left your side since you came out of surgery." Anita poked her head around the door. She looked tired, like Simon, although she managed a smile for him. "I'm glad you're awake. I'll make sure you're not disturbed for a bit. You two need to talk." She shot Simon a glare. "Don't tire him out, or I will sic the nurse on you. The *werewolf* nurse who will send your vampire ass home to rest if you step out of line." Anita turned to leave, then paused. "I'll phone Lucas too and update him, so you can focus on that conversation you need to have."

"Thank you, I'd appreciate that. I promised Forge I'd let him know when Ben was awake."

"She's scary when she's worried," Ben said after she'd left.

"You have no idea." Simon flinched. "Once she realised the bullet hadn't done any permanent damage to your shoulder, and assured me you'd make a full recovery, she scolded me for going after you without backup." He faltered. "She was right. I got a whiff of your blood and I couldn't think about anything else. I nearly got you killed."

"I'm still here, and I'm not going anywhere." Ben squeezed Simon's hand. "You scared me, though."

Simon yanked his hand away. "I... I didn't handle that very well. I lost control." He got up and started pacing. "I haven't done that in years. Not since... You were in trouble, and I couldn't think straight. I had to do what was necessary to save you. If you hadn't stopped me, I would have killed those men, and enjoyed it." He stilled. "I was going to turn you. God, if I'd done it like that..."

Ben used the remote to put the bed up to a sitting position. "Simon, come here." Grief and self-loathing poured off Simon like an intense waterfall. "Simon! Please?" He shuffled across the bed and patted the empty spot he'd made.

Simon sat down slowly but didn't take Ben's outstretched hand.

"Oh, for fuck's sake." Ben grabbed Simon, pulled him close and held him tightly. "I love you, don't ever forget that. It's not your fault you have to deal with that crappy part of yourself. You came for me, despite the risk, and you pushed me out of the way of that bullet. If you hadn't been there, I could have died."

Simon gently laid his head on Ben's good shoulder. "I couldn't hold you when you'd been shot," he murmured. "I was so scared I was going to lose you."

"If I'd died, you might have too," Ben pointed out. "That scared *me*."

"Never be scared of that." Simon straightened. He caressed Ben's face with his fingers. "I've lived a long time. More than I ever expected to. If something happens to you, I take comfort in the hope I won't be without you for long and that your lifespan is mine now. I want..." He cleared his throat. "I want to enjoy what we have, not focus on how long that might be." He glanced away, then met Ben's gaze full on. "If you'll still have me, after what happened."

"Geez, like I wouldn't?" Ben wished Simon would stop beating himself up about stuff he couldn't control. "We've had this conversation how many times, and my answer will always be the same. I love *you*, all of you. And yeah, I know you're a kick-arse sexy as hell vampire who is over a hundred years old, but so what? I'm not perfect either." He winced. "I aggravated those guys by shooting my mouth off. And you know I'll probably do it again, despite all my intentions not—"

Simon silenced him with a long kiss. "Yes. You will, but I

love you, quirks and all." He grew silent, nervous. "Although I wish I could, I can't blame our enforced separation for this either. I knew I was off-kilter, but I didn't wait."

"When have I *ever* waited?"

"That's true." Simon chuckled. "The doctors said you'll probably be left with a scar, but apart from that, there shouldn't be any long-term consequences. I was thinking once you're up to it that—"

"Yes," Ben said. "We have a week of lost time to make up for when I'm up for it, even if I have to tie you to the bed to make sure you don't go anywhere."

Simon flushed. Desire rushed through their bond. Ben grinned.

"Come here." He yanked Simon's tie, pulling him close again and captured his lips in a searing kiss. When they broke apart, Ben lowered himself carefully back onto his pillow. "And that's my energy gone for now. Raincheck for the rest?"

"More like a promise." Simon still seemed nervous. He reached into his pocket but didn't take his hand out. "There was another reason I've been on edge. I've had something on my mind, but it didn't feel like the right time." He looked down. "Then I was scared I'd left it too late. I'm an idiot."

"You're *my* idiot. It's never too late for whatever." Ben frowned. "You're okay, right? You'd tell me if you weren't. The police aren't—"

"I'm fine, and you stopped me before I seriously hurt anyone." Simon smiled grimly. "All the members of the BFH organisation have been arrested. I'm not sure what Anson said to them, but they've given up the locations and names of their other cells in the city. They've also been charged with murder, kidnapping, and assault. They won't be causing trouble again for quite some time. Although..."

"Although what?" Ben didn't like sentences that began with that word.

"I'm not sure Boggslake is the only city with this... problem. According to Charlie's research, it's more widespread than we thought. I'm worried we haven't seen the last of them."

"We'll be careful, then, and watch our backs, like we always have. I asked Blair to look into them too." Ben tried to sound reassuring, then decided he sucked at it, so he changed the subject instead. "You were saying something about leaving *it* too late? What's it?"

Simon licked his lips, then swallowed. "I marked you as mine when we soulbonded, and you gave me a ring to mark me as yours."

"You *are* mine."

"Let me finish, please." Simon slipped off the bed and got down on one knee.

Ben's breath caught in his throat. Oh God, did this mean what he thought it did? He opened his mouth, then shut it again.

"Ben Leyton, will you marry me?" Simon opened the small black box he'd retrieved from his pocket, to reveal a simple, yet elegant gold ring that matched the one he wore.

Ben stared. He swallowed.

"Ben?" Simon got off the floor and bent over Ben. "Are you all right? I've left this too late, haven't I? You don't want this. I didn't—"

"Yes. Yes. Of course, I want to marry you." Ben laughed. "I... for once in my life, I'm speechless, that's all."

Simon rolled his eyes, then looked smug. "I like you loud."

"What kind of fiancé would I be if I disappointed you? Once we get home, I intend to be very loud, don't you worry about that." Ben held out his left hand for Simon to slide his ring on, then held his hand next to Simon's. "Perfect," he said.

A thought struck him. "Oh God, we'll have to plan a wedding. Mum's going to kill me if she can't—"

"That's the other proposal I have for you. How do you feel about two ceremonies? One here in Boggslake with our family at the castle, and another in New Zealand with yours?"

"You'd come to New Zealand with me to get married?" Ben let out a low whistle. "Wow. I don't—" He'd suggested a trip back to Wellington before, but Simon had always changed the subject. He'd talked to Ben's parents on the phone, but he worried about their reaction when they found out the truth.

"Yes. They're your family. It's the right thing to do." Simon looked sheepish. "Besides, your father suggested it when I asked him for your hand in marriage."

Ben raised an eyebrow. Simon would probably never completely shake the Edwardian gentleman he was raised to be. Ben didn't want him to, either.

"I telephoned him when I bought the ring," Simon continued. "Then he said that your mum would be on the first plane over here if we didn't, and I figured given how we'd already tried to hide the truth from someone you know when they came here, and failed—"

"It will be fine, I promise." Ben smiled. His family would accept Simon for who he was, of that he had no doubt. But if not, they'd have to deal with it. Simon was his present and his future and Ben wouldn't have it any other way.

CHAPTER FOUR

"You're sure you're okay?" Ben placed his left hand over Simon's and squeezed it.

"I'm fine." Simon massaged his temples and took a sip of his tea. He never enjoyed using thrall to hypnotise someone for an extended period, but in this case, the expected headache was worth avoiding any problems with security to get them through New Zealand customs. "It's only a headache and it will go soon enough."

"The people we're meeting with know where to find us, right?" Ben looked more than a little jet lagged despite getting some sleep on the long flight from the States. Although it had been a couple of months since he'd been kidnapped and shot, Simon still kept a close eye on him.

"Yes," Simon reassured him. "They're used to this kind of thing, and it's a little difficult to miss a well-labelled coffee shop in the middle of an airport." He'd deliberately booked them a flight with a decent layover before their final Wellington destination, so he had time to obtain a flask of blood. Meeting Ben's family would be nerve-wracking enough without being on edge because he hadn't fed in over twenty-four hours.

Ben nodded, drank his coffee, yet kept hold of Simon's hand. "I haven't been to Auckland in years. I flew out through Christchurch when I came over." He grinned. "Flying business class is so much more comfortable than economy."

"Long flights have improved somewhat since the last time I took one." Simon lowered his voice. "And before you ask, I have used domestic flights around the US, but the last long one was when I came to Boggslake."

"I figured my idea of years ago and yours would be a little different." Ben chuckled. "At least they had flights back then."

Simon rolled his eyes. "I'm not *that* old. I moved there in the late '40s and my flight was the best money could buy at the time."

"Of course, it was." Ben glanced around again, then at his watch

"We have plenty of time before our flight." Simon brought their joined hands to his lips and kissed Ben's ring.

Their wedding in Boggslake had been perfect, and they'd said their vows surrounded by the friends they considered family. Forge had stood as best man for Simon, and his husband, Blair, for Ben. They'd insisted on a small affair, and for once they'd had a day without someone causing trouble or trying to kill them. Declan had presented them with a family wedding portrait that would pass for a photograph.

Simon wasn't sure how they were going to convince Ben's family not to take photos of their second ceremony with them.

"I miss the guys," Ben said quietly. "I know they're doing important stuff and all that, but it's not the same with them gone."

"I do too." Simon finished his tea, but it didn't quench his thirst. "It's not the first time Forge, Declan, and I have spent time apart. I didn't see them much at all in the '20s or '30s, apart from that incident in Paris."

Forge had found Simon after John had turned him and taught him what he needed to survive as a vampire. Declan had helped him through a very dark period of his life during World War Two when he'd embraced his dark side after the murder of the man he'd loved.

"Twenty years feels like a long time." Ben grew silent for a moment.

"Life still seems too short no matter how much of it you have." Simon stilled, catching low conversation in the distance. "I definitely arranged to just have one person deliver. The idiots have sent three."

Ben shuffled around in the booth to sit closer to Simon. "Do you think this is more than just a delivery?"

"It better not be. A vampire, werewolf, and a human," he warned Ben in a low tone. Simon smiled politely when two men and a woman walked over to them.

"That sounds suspiciously council-like." Ben didn't look impressed.

"Doesn't it just?"

In most cities, Boggslake included, the Supernatural Council was comprised of three vampires, three werewolves, and three humans. The council in New Zealand had decided to spread its resources. The country and its population were small, so Auckland, Wellington, and Christchurch had a sub-council of three, with all nine counsellors meeting when needed.

The vampire helped himself to a chair from another table and positioned himself opposite Simon, the others on either side. "Good afternoon, Mr Hawthorne." He extended a hand, which Simon shook politely. "I'm Tyson Dalgleish, and these are my colleagues Olivia Wayland, and Giles Torrance." He introduced the werewolf and human in turn.

"It's *Professor* Hawthorne," Simon corrected him. If the council insisted on making their presence known, they could at least get their introductions right. "This is my husband, Mr Leyton."

Torrance held out his hand to Ben, who followed Simon's cue and shook it. He didn't look much older than Ben, perhaps in his mid-thirties, if that.

"My apologies, Professor," said Dalgleish not looking sorry in the slightest. He sounded local, although that didn't always reflect a vampire's origins. Not everyone kept their original accents as Simon had.

"I believe you have something for me?" Simon wasn't about to engage in conversation while still hungry.

"Of course." Dalgleish pulled a flask from his messenger bag and handed it to Simon, who took it, drained it, then placed it on the table in front of him.

Ben moved closer, caressing Simon's thigh with his own. Simon appreciated the silent support. He disliked having to drink blood in public, but at least the council could be discrete when it suited them.

"We're on our honeymoon." Ben got straight to the point. "We're not in New Zealand to work for you."

Wayland raised an eyebrow. "I'd heard that you were outspoken, but I expected some degree of manners first." To an outsider, she appeared to be the oldest of the group, but although werewolves aged more slowly, appearances, in this case, were very deceiving.

Although he'd hoped to avoid the New Zealand Supernatural Council during their stay, Simon had found out what he could about them before leaving Boggslake. He'd worked with their local council long enough to know it was always wise to be prepared.

"*We* expected some warning that the council was handling the delivery I requested," Simon said icily, placing a warning hand on Ben's knee. He'd ordered the blood through the usual underground channels. This kind of business transaction rarely required the presence of the council.

Torrance smiled. "We figured it was easier to talk to you directly, than contact you once you reached Wellington. This situation is a little... delicate... and you being in the right place at the right time was too serendipitous to ignore." His heart sounded steady, yet a little elevated. Whatever this was, the council hadn't approached them lightly.

"We're not—" Ben started to say, but Simon shook his head.

"We'll listen, but that doesn't mean we're going to work for you." Simon looked at his watch. "You have fifteen minutes, and then we have a flight to catch."

"We've lost contact with the council in Wellington," Dalgleish said.

"Have you asked anyone there to look into it?" Simon asked. Although Wellington didn't have a team like theirs in Boggslake investigating supernatural cases, the city had a thriving supernatural community. "I'm sure Rupert—"

"Professor Milne has made himself scarce." Wayland sounded unimpressed. "Naturally, he was the first person we tried to contact about the matter. The local pack doesn't involve itself in council business."

"Of course, it doesn't." Simon didn't believe that for an instant.

"Needless to say, they're looking for their werewolf representative," Wayland added, ignoring Simon's response.

"Have you contacted the police?" Ben shrugged when the council stared at him in disbelief. "Hey, they might be supernaturals, but they're still missing persons, right?"

"Obviously, Erik's disappearance has been reported," Torrance said stiffly.

"He's the human councillor?" Ben asked.

Torrance nodded. "Yes."

"Now, how did I know that?" Ben muttered.

"We would be very grateful if you made some enquiries for us," Wayland said smoothly. "Very grateful." She smiled and leaned in closer. "It can be so difficult to travel these days unless you know the right people. Especially for *vampires* who don't show up on camera."

"Are you threatening me?" Simon asked evenly.

She patted Ben's hand. Simon growled, and she pulled her hand away quickly. "I'm sure your husband's family knows everything about their new son-in-law."

Ben glared at her. "They wouldn't give a shit if they found out. Try something else, and if you threaten him again... We've gone up against some nasty shit over the past few years, and they've come off second best. We know a few of the *right* people too."

"We'll look into it while we're there," Simon said quickly before Ben said anything else they'd both regret. "And for future reference, asking nicely gets you a lot further than threats ever will."

Dalgleish slid a card toward Simon. "That's my direct number. If you find something, call me." He retrieved the blood flask, then he and his colleagues stood and left the table.

"Arseholes," Ben muttered. "Why did you give into them so easily?"

"Firstly, I don't want to spend my honeymoon inside a cell, and secondly, if supernaturals are disappearing, we need to find out why." Simon kissed Ben softly on the cheek. "They don't have anyone with our experience they can call on in Wellington. I know you're angry, and so am I, but we'd both feel bad walking away from someone who might need our help."

"I guess." Ben sighed. "You're a better man than me. I was ready to tell them where to go."

"Oh, I've told our council where to shove it on more than one occasion." Simon shrugged. He'd make sure the case didn't encroach on their holiday too much. "If I can find someone else to take over, I will."

"Simon?" Ben waited until they'd left the coffee shop before he spoke again.

"Yes?"

"Their threat was an empty one. You know that, right? My family will accept you for who you are. They won't care you're a vampire." He bit his lip. "That wasn't the real reason you took the case, was it?"

The loudspeaker announced, "Air New Zealand Flight 564 to Wellington is ready to board. Please make your way to gate 25."

Simon slipped his hand into Ben's. "Come on, we need to hurry. We have a flight to catch."

~

"They're *all* here?" Simon wondered if it was too late to catch the next flight out. "Your whole family?"

"Except for Granddad." Ben skimmed through another text. "According to Ange he debated coming to the airport to give you some moral support then decided it would be easier for you to deal with the in-laws first before seeing an old friend for the first time in... a while."

"That sounds like him, and I appreciate it." Simon felt torn about seeing Frank again. They'd met over fifty years ago in Boggslake and although he'd seen photographs of Ben's grandfather and spoken to him, he never enjoyed the reminder that his friends had grown old while he still appeared young. Frank had been Ben's age when they'd met. One day...

Ben put his arm around Simon and held him close, ignoring the bustle of people walking around them while they headed through the busy gate. "It will be okay, I promise. If anyone causes you grief, they'll have to answer to me."

"You can't put me before your family."

"You're part of my family now, and I love you." Ben kissed Simon's forehead. "They'll love you too."

"You sound so certain." Simon bit his lip. He'd taken on some terrifying foes and stood his ground, yet all of that didn't even rate compared to meeting Ben's family.

"They're not your parents," Ben reminded him softly. "Times have changed, and my family has always been really accepting of everything. They supported me when I came out."

"Coming out is a little different than what I'm hiding." Simon wished he could have Ben's faith and rid himself of the nightmares that had plagued him since he'd booked this trip. He'd never had the chance to tell his parents he preferred men after they'd turned their back on him when they learnt he was a vampire.

"Granddad's in your corner too." Ben moved his hand down Simon's back in a caress, then took his hand.

"You're sure he's fine with us staying with him?" Simon had suggested they could stay at a hotel, but Frank wouldn't hear of it.

"Definitely. I've told Mum and Dad you might need some space, so we'll be disappearing there if we need to."

Simon doubted Ben had told his parents his grandfather had stocked his garage fridge with blood either. He blew out a breath, grabbed Ben's excitement, and let it trickle through their bond.

They still needed to talk about Ben's wish to become a vampire, and the chances of him backing down were slim to none. He missed his family, so Simon was determined to give him this time with them, and some happy memories. Hopefully, they'd get through the ceremony before Ben's family discovered the truth.

"If anything, your mum will stop asking when she's going to meet me," he murmured.

Ben rolled his eyes. "Stop being so determined this won't work." He lowered his voice so only Simon could hear him. "There's a time and place for being an angsty vampire, and this isn't it."

A familiar voice caught Simon's attention before he had the chance to deny Ben's comment.

"Ben! Simon! Over here." Ange Duncan, Ben's friend, waved, then ran towards them. She caught Ben in a hug, then grinned at Simon.

He took a step backwards when she let go of Ben and held out his hand.

"No, sorry. You're getting a hug this time." Ange pulled him close. "It's good to see you again. AbenChat's not the same when you don't show up on camera," she whispered.

Ange had visited Boggslake after Ben settled there and was dropped into the mess with the werewolf plague. She also, like Frank, accepted Simon for who and what he was.

"It's good to see you again too." Simon hoped he didn't look as awkward as he felt. He'd never been good at showing his emotions in public unless he was with Ben. Although he detested how he'd been raised, it still dictated far too much of his behaviour.

"Marriage looks good on you, son." Ray Leyton, Ben's father, grinned at him before giving him a brief hug. "Pleased to meet you at last, Simon." Ray looked like he was about to hug Simon too, then thankfully held out his hand instead.

"Thanks for taking such good care of Ben while he's been away." His grip was firm like Ben's, and he had the same dark hair and eyes.

They hadn't told Ben's family that he'd been in hospital recovering from a gunshot wound. Or about the other times he'd been nearly killed because of the world Simon had brought him into.

Ben glanced at Simon, sighed, and shook his head very slightly. "Simon makes me happy. I'm very pleased you've finally met."

"Your photographs don't do you justice." Abby Leyton, Ben's mother, smiled at Simon. "You don't look your age either." She chuckled. "If I didn't know better, I would have thought there were at least ten years between you."

"Simon gets that a lot," Ben said quickly. "He's always complaining that he's getting carded, although he's older than me."

"It's very annoying," Simon added.

Abby opened her arms like she was about to hug him, then looked embarrassed, and held out her hand instead. "It's nice to finally meet you." Her grip was firm like Ray's and Ben's.

Simon wondered how many hands he'd shake before the day was over.

A werewolf couple with their child walked past, and the woman glanced at Simon and whispered to her partner, "I didn't know there was another vampire in town."

Simon flinched. Abby quickly let go of his hand. "It's not you," he said quickly. "Sorry. It's been a while since I've been part of a big family gathering. My mother—"

"You're part of this family now," Abby said firmly, "and don't worry, we'll get out of the airport as quickly as we can."

Two women had Ben in a group hug, the three of them talking over each other. Ben grabbed Simon's hand when

Abby let go and pulled him over. "Maddie, Tash, this is Simon. Simon, my sisters, Maddie and Tash."

Maddie was dark like her brother and father, while Tash had their mother's blonde hair and blue eyes. He could see more of Frank in Abby and Tash in person, especially with how their eyes crinkled when they smiled.

Before he could stop them, Ben's sisters pulled Simon into their group hug. To his surprise, he found himself relaxing, and even enjoying it a little.

"Plenty of time to catch up with everyone while we're here." Ben broke the hug and shot Simon an apologetic look. His tiredness bled through his excitement and something else.

Contentment.

"Yes, there will be." Simon had a worrying thought. "And you're not telling Lucas about that group hug. I'd never hear the end of it."

Ben laughed. "Would I do that?"

"Yes, you bloody would."

Lucas had teased Simon enough on his wedding day about his reluctance to accept hugs in payment for persuading Forge and Blair to visit Declan's tailor. Given she kept stakes in a basket by her door, Simon reluctantly agreed Lucas was right. Not only that, but Ben did look amazing in his suit.

Simon pulled Ben close, kissed him soundly in front of his family, and then realised what he'd done.

"I'm already yours, but if you want to go all possessive on my arse to prove it in front of my family, I'm not going to stop you," Ben murmured.

Tash wolf-whistled. "You go, big brother."

Simon flushed. "I apologise. I..."

"It's fine." Ray smiled. "You love my son and you're not afraid to show it. That's a good thing. Now let's go find your luggage and get you home. You must be tired after your flight." He and Abby headed off, with Ange and Tash following behind, talking non-stop. Ben hadn't mentioned that Ange and his sister were close friends, but Simon expected he'd learn a few things he didn't know about his husband's family and life during the next few weeks.

"What Dad said," Maddie murmured. "Welcome to our family. Hope you enjoy the experience. We can be a little overwhelming at times. Just ask my husband, who sensibly decided he'd come around later."

As she walked past, Simon heard something he'd missed during the earlier noise. He smiled, and Ben caught his arm once his family were out of earshot.

"What was that? I felt... something when Maddie talked to you."

"Your sister is pregnant."

"Yeah, we know that already."

"She's having twins."

Ben raised an eyebrow. "Oh, wow."

Simon enjoyed the drive along the waterfront to Ben's family home. The scenery was gorgeous, and Ben pointed out all the places he'd talked about since they'd met. His family lived in a suburb on a hill with views of the harbour. Frank had a townhouse a street away. That way, he'd kept his independence but was still close enough if he needed help.

As they exited the motorway, Ben grew silent, snuggled into Simon, and closed his eyes. Simon put his arm around him, and listened to his steady heartbeat, pushing Abby and Ray's chatter in the front seat to one side.

"Simon?"

"Hmm?" Simon realised Abby was speaking to him.

"Sorry, it's been a long few days and I think it's finally caught up with Ben."

"You don't look as tired," she said, "although Ben said it's been a while since you left the States."

"It's been a while since I've travelled this far from home." Simon waited for her to continue, then realised she expected him to embellish. "I took a break in Paris when I was studying at Cambridge, and then... visited Europe with friends a few years later. I've mainly stayed around Boggslake since I moved there. Work keeps me busy."

"You must miss your friends since they left," Abby said. "Ange spoke highly of them after her trip, and I can tell from Ben's emails that the castle is a little quieter than maybe you're used to."

"We keep in touch, and they came for the wedding." Simon smiled at the memory of the "photo" of himself and Ben he carried in his wallet, courtesy of Declan. "Lucas's sister, Charlie, has settled in well, and Anita visits regularly." Although he no longer had to dodge Lucas's science experiments in the fridge, he missed over ten years of wondering about the contents of the plastic wrapped items. Not that he'd tell Lucas that.

"It's hard when friends you've known for a while move on."

"We've had... work... keep us apart for a substantial time before this. Boggslake is still their home."

Simon, Forge, and Declan had bought the castle between them. If something happened to Simon, Ben would inherit all his assets.

Not that he planned to do anything dangerous while they were here. They'd investigate for the council, then enjoy the rest of their holiday.

"When was the last time you had a holiday?" Ray's question took Simon by surprise.

"19—" They'd ended up in jail overnight during that trip to Paris in the '20s, so it didn't count. Still, it had been the break from his studies he'd needed. "A few years ago."

"This will be a good opportunity to relax then." Ray glanced in the rear-view mirror and Simon ducked out of his line of sight. The explanation about vampires not reflecting would come soon enough. "I hope you bought plenty of casual clothes with you. The beach is nice this time of year and not too hot or crowded."

"Umm…" Simon wasn't a huge fan of beaches and didn't like staying out in the sun for long periods. The sun taunted him with a reminder of why, when it streamed through the open window once they started the drive up the Maungaraki Hill. He turned away from it, reached into his pocket for his dark glasses and shoved them on without thinking. "My eyes are a little sensitive to sunlight," he explained quickly when Abby frowned.

Ben sat up and yawned when the car pulled into a long driveway. Tash parked behind them a few minutes later. "Leave the suitcases in the boot. I can drive down to Grand-dad's with them later, then return the car, and we'll walk back."

Simon got out of the car first and held the door for Ben so it wouldn't slam in the wind.

An old man stood at the top of the steps, outside the entrance to the house. Simon glanced up, then froze. "Frank," he whispered. He'd recognise his old friend anywhere, yet the photos and AbenChat calls hadn't prepared him for the reality. Although meeting people he hadn't seen in decades wasn't a new experience, it always left him trying to mesh his memory of young and old at first.

"Go talk to him," Ben said in a low voice only Simon could hear. "I'll stall my family so you can have some time alone."

Simon kissed Ben's forehead in thanks, then sprinted up the steps to meet Frank at the door. He grasped Frank's hand in his. "Thank you so much for sending Ben to me."

If Frank hadn't played matchmaker and suggested Ben go to Boggslake as part of his OE—overseas experience—they probably would have never met.

"You make him happy, and that makes me happy." Frank walked through the door, then turned to Simon. "Come in, Simon." He took a seat on the sofa by the window and gestured for Simon to join him. "We can talk more when we're not dodging family, but I'd hoped we could do this first, and now I've invited you in, you don't need to worry about that either." He looked Simon up and down, then whistled. "I always knew you wouldn't age, but actually seeing it is still a bit of a shock." His expression softened. "It must be hard on you. I've... changed a little since we saw each other last."

"It's never easy," Simon said. They'd spoken on the telephone and through AbenChat, but Simon always thought of Frank as he'd been in his youth. It was harder to ignore the truth in person. "You're looking well, though."

"I'm still active and living independently. I figure that's a win." Frank chuckled. "I haven't had any photos of you from Ben, apart from the ones he sent back with Ange. Declan still does great work, I notice."

"He's sent a wedding photo for you too. He and Forge send their regards," Simon told him. Frank hadn't lost the twinkle in his eye. His smile hadn't changed either. "Ben reminds me of you in a lot of ways."

"I'm presuming he appreciates your kisses more than I did."

"Frank!" Simon's cheeks heated. "I only did that once, and it was a mistake." He still felt embarrassed by how badly he'd misjudged that situation.

"I'm only teasing." Frank grinned. "When we get home, you can update me on everything else. I was sorry to hear about Hugh. I miss his regular letters, although we had to be careful about what we said." He'd visited Boggslake in the '50s with Hugh's cousin, but while Samuel had decided to stay, Frank returned to Australia and later travelled to New Zealand where he'd met Ben's grandmother. "Wouldn't have wanted them to fall into the wrong hands, you know."

"I appreciate that. We still visit Hugh when we can, but he hasn't recognised us for months. His dementia progressed rapidly once it hit." Simon tilted his head, listening to the conversation in the driveway, and opened the door for Abby before she reached the top of the stairs. "Sorry for leaving you so suddenly. Ben's talked about Frank so much and after all the conversations we've had, I couldn't wait to finally meet him in person."

CHAPTER FIVE

"It's been years since I saw Josh," Ben said as Simon opened the café door for him. They'd only known each other a few months before he'd left for Boggslake, but hit it off immediately and stayed in touch via email and Facebook. "This café next to the library is new too. It wasn't here when I left. Great idea though." He glanced around the small yet busy café. "Ange said they'd grab a table if they got here first. I hope they did. The place is packed."

"If not, we'll find somewhere else to meet," Simon said.

"Yeah, but this is convenient for Josh because he works next door, and we'd have less time if we had to go somewhere else. There aren't a lot of options nearby."

Pōhutukawa Grove Library, and the adjoining café, were only a fifteen-minute walk from Frank's. Ben had slept late, the travel finally catching up with him, and woken to an empty bed and Simon deep in conversation with Frank downstairs. Ben had taken his time in the shower to give them some privacy.

"Hey, Ben!" Ange yelled his name across the café and

waved frantically. She'd found a smallish table in the corner and pulled up a fourth chair.

"Hey." The café had a welcoming feel to it, which reminded Ben of Miller's, where he'd worked in Boggslake before it had been destroyed. "Where's Josh?" Ben was looking forward to catching up with his friend in person again. He, Ange, and Josh had been almost inseparable outside work in the months leading up to Ben leaving for Boggslake. *Almost.* Unfortunately, Josh hadn't been interested in joining their Dungeons & Dragons group, despite Ben and Ange's best efforts to convert him.

"He's at the counter grabbing his morning coffee." She grinned. "He's a bit like you, doesn't do mornings."

"Good morning, Ange." Simon took the seat next to Ben, leaving Josh the empty one by Ange. "I've already had my morning coffee, but another can easily tempt me. I expect Ben will want one too."

"Not my fault that you tired me out after we got back to Granddad's."

"You do realise he's not as hard of hearing as he claims to be, right?" Ange said.

Ben stared at Ange, mortified. "But I—"

"You're always loud." Simon chuckled. "And Frank is very polite when he wants to be. He's happy you're happy... and you were very happy last night."

Ben flushed. "I thought gentlemen didn't kiss and tell," he muttered.

"I figured out how loud you are when I stayed at the castle, so it's not news to me." Ange grinned. "And thanks for the offer to drop me off at Archives on your way to the uni this afternoon. I took the morning off, but I want to do a bit more on the project I'm working on with Ennis." She worked at Archives New Zealand, which was a good fit for her PhD in anthropology.

"Ah yes, the famous Ennis you've mentioned a few times." Ben figured a bit of retaliation teasing was in order. "Should I be expecting to meet him?"

Ange elbowed him. "He's a colleague, like Josh was when I worked at the library." She sighed dramatically. "I also think he's gay, so us getting together is never going to happen. Seriously though, Ennis needs to find someone nice." Ange lowered her voice. "At least Josh is finally dating."

Josh held a coffee mug in each hand and weaved his way through the crowd towards them. He looked the same as Ben remembered him, unruly blond hair, dark eyes, and a friendly expression. He'd bulked up a bit, so he had obviously been working out. It looked good on him.

"I see you couldn't wait for your coffee either?" Ben asked Ange, presuming the other mug was for her.

She shuffled over to make room for Josh. "The coffee here is excellent."

Josh ducked out of the way of a mother chasing an errant toddler, then froze, and sniffed the air.

At the same time, Simon looked up abruptly and caught Josh's gaze. "This could be interesting," he murmured.

Ben glanced from Simon to Josh, then back again, knowing he'd missed something, but there was definitely a *something* if the surprise he'd felt from Simon was anything to go by.

Josh slammed the mugs down on the table, hot coffee barely missing Ben when it sloshed over the side of the mugs.

Simon caught Josh's arm. "Sit down. This is not the place or time for politics." He sighed. "I had hoped our community here would be less bigoted about such things."

Josh yanked free of Simon's grip. His eyes glowed gold for a moment. "You didn't tell me you'd married *that*," he growled at Ben, his Australian accent broader than Ben remembered.

"You didn't tell me what you were either," Ben snapped. "And if you're going to insult my *husband* because of who he is, you can fuck off."

"We're in a crowded café. Keep your voices down!" Ange glared at both men. "Could someone please tell me what's going on?"

"Your friend Josh is the same as Lucas," Simon said calmly, "and traditionally, my kind and his are... not the best of friends."

"I knew it!" Ange grabbed her coffee and held it out of harm's way.

"You knew about Simon?" Josh said quietly after the other customers returned to their own conversations. "And about me? You have until I've finished my coffee to explain, and then I'm out of here."

Ben cleared his throat and kept his tone low. "Let's start again, shall we? And forget all the usual bullshit about who's what and whatever. One of my best friends is a werewolf and I'm married to a vampire, and you don't see me getting upset about any of it."

"You're human," Josh pointed out.

"And *married* to a vampire," Ben reminded him. "So, this kind of affects me too. And don't start with the 'you stink of vampire' thing either. I'm over that one too."

Simon squeezed Ben's knee under the table. "Hello, Josh, I'm Simon Hawthorne, Ben's husband." He held out his hand. "I've heard a lot about you from him and Ange."

Josh glared, took a gulp of coffee, then his anger seemed to deflate. "Josh McKenna." He shook Simon's hand. "No wonder you were difficult to research." He calmed and his accent shifted into something more neutral. "Vampires have a reputation for covering their tracks."

"With good reason. Perhaps I should order some coffee for myself and Ben while you catch up for a few minutes. I'm sure you can convince him I'm not in the habit of biting or hunting werewolves." Simon kissed Ben on the cheek before standing. He passed Josh and lowered his voice. "You owe Ben an apology. I hope for your sake he still considers you a friend, but do not make the mistake of insulting him again. Ever."

Ben rolled his eyes. "Possessive bloody vampire," he said affectionately.

"They tend to be about what they consider theirs." Josh ran a hand through his hair. "I guess I do owe you an apology. I just wasn't expecting... that."

"I wasn't expecting a werewolf either." Ben shrugged, willing to let the insult slide this time. If Josh tried it again, Ben wouldn't waste any more time on him. He turned to Ange. "You guessed, and you didn't think it might be important to tell me?"

Ange mirrored Ben's shrug. "I wasn't sure, but after spending time with Lucas, I figured the signs were there. Josh takes a lot of sick leave when the full moon doesn't fall on the weekend." She put her mug down. "And besides, it wasn't my secret to tell."

"Touché." Ben hadn't told her about Simon for the same reason, although he'd hated keeping it from her.

"I work evenings. It's that or going wolf in the middle of the library halfway through my shift." Josh took a gulp of coffee. "I didn't think our customers would appreciate it." He glanced at Simon, who was checking his phone and looking annoyed. "So, Ange, how did you find out?"

"Remember that trip to Boggslake to see Ben a few months after he moved?" Ange turned, her eyes widening for a moment, then turned her attention back to the conversation. "I found out then when a werewolf got stroppy about vampires, and the café I was in caught fire and exploded."

The story was a little more complicated than that, but

Josh obviously got the point because he winced, then followed Ange's gaze.

"You see them then?" Josh asked. "As we're putting all our cards on the table."

Ben looked around to see what Ange had seen. Two men in clothing at least fifty years out of date stood in the entrance to the café talking. One smiled at the other and kissed him softly on the lips. "The ghosts, you mean?"

"Bernard and Joseph are regulars," Josh explained. "Nice guys. Bernard passed away when the Wahine ferry went down in the harbour in the sixties, Joseph last year. They used to meet at the library regularly, so I guess that's why they stick around. There's an old graveyard at the back of the library, so we get a few ghosts hanging around from there too. They like the ambience of the library, and a few of them enjoy people-watching in the café." He raised an eyebrow. "Have you been holding out on me too, Ange? I figured out you could see them a while back, but not why. Most humans can't."

"I'm a mere mortal," Ange said. "I just happen to be able to see ghosts. I found that out when I visited Ben too. Turns out their landlord is a ghost."

"Mr Boggs isn't our landlord," Ben corrected. "He's a good friend." He glanced over at Simon, who was glaring at his phone. Ben had only managed to drag Simon into the twenty-first century to a degree, but Simon's reaction was more than frustration with technology. Whatever he'd seen had totally pissed him off.

"Ben, what's your excuse?" Josh asked.

"What? Oh yeah, the ghosts." Ben shrugged. He wasn't about to tell Josh about the soulbond. Not until they knew they could trust him, and maybe not even then. "I'm married to a vampire. I guess some of that *rubs* off."

Ange groaned.

"Thanks for that visual."

Ben grinned. *"My* pleasure." He slid over when Simon rejoined them with coffee. "Everything okay?"

"No." Simon shoved his phone at Ben. "My telephone informs me that I have a message from *them*, but I can't get it to reveal the information."

Josh blinked. "Does he always talk like he's about a century behind the rest of us?"

"I was raised in a time a little before yours," Simon said. "I am not a fan of technology despite Ben's constant assurances that it's not that bad."

"It isn't." Ben opened the email and read it. He'd already figured out who Simon had meant by *them.* "Wankers," he muttered. "When did you turn your phone back on?"

"This morning. Why?"

"They sent the contact details for the missing councillors before you told them we'd take the case." Ben handed the phone back to Simon so he could read the email for himself.

"Typical council arrogance." Simon skimmed through it, then shoved his phone back in his pocket. "They always ask, but on the assumption it's just a formality."

"That council?" Ange asked.

Josh glanced between Simon and Ben. "You're working for *the* council?" He pushed his chair back, like he was about to run.

"Yes, the Supernatural Council," Simon confirmed, "although under protest, as always." He studied Josh. "You're nervous, and your heart is racing. Is there bad blood between them and your pack?"

Josh stilled. "I don't have a pack," he said stiffly.

"Would you like a temporary one?" Simon asked. "Despite our initial introduction not being the best, Ben and Ange have always spoken highly of you."

Ben raised an eyebrow. Simon squeezed his knee under the table.

"I'm not interested in being around other werewolves, and they don't want to be around me." Josh started to stand.

"Sit down," Simon ordered. "I have a temporary proposition for you that will work in both our interests. At least hear me out. Please."

Josh shook his head. "I don't need a pack. I've managed by myself for years. You'll have to give me bloody good reason to change that."

"Packs aren't always just werewolves." Ben guessed where Simon was going with his offer. "When I moved in with Simon, he was working with three vampires, a werewolf, and a ghost. Now it's us, the ghost, and two werewolves. We're our own pack."

"Working with?" Josh's curiosity seemed to win over his fear. He sat down again. "This had better be good, or I'm walking out of here and keeping my distance while you're here. I don't want to get involved with the council. I know how they work."

"Our team in Boggslake works to solve supernatural related incidents," Simon explained.

"You're council lackies, in other words," Josh said.

"Let Simon finish," Ben said. "You asked for a reason. At least give him the chance to give it to you."

"Okay." Josh kept glancing around, his nervousness growing. "I do need to get to work in a few though, so keep it brief."

"I'm not a fan of the council or the way they do things, although they are a necessary evil at times." Simon kept his tone even and factual. "Ben and I were approached by them in Auckland and asked to look into the whereabouts of the Wellington Council triad. After our recent experience in Boggslake with some unpleasant individuals, I'm concerned that the council's concerns might be the tip of a very nasty iceberg."

Josh frowned. "You think there might be a group in Wellington targeting supernaturals?" He clenched his fist, and his eyes glowed gold, then he visibly calmed.

"I hope not." Simon's voice grew strained. He reached for Ben through their bond. Ben moved closer. "I think it's a good idea that we investigate and either make sure that isn't the case or shut them down before someone gets killed, don't you?"

"If they haven't already," Ben added. "We don't know what's happened to the councillors. It might already be too late for them." He'd prefer to think the worst and be totally wrong. Blair's confirmation that the BFH was part of something bigger hadn't helped either Ben or Simon's peace of mind on that front either.

Josh nodded slowly. "Okay, I'm in. But just for this, and no more." He took a deep breath, then blew it out slowly. "What do you need me to do?"

"I can help too," Ange said quickly.

"You're not putting yourself in danger," Ben said, although he knew he was wasting his time.

"Ben and I do not know the supernatural community here. Although you're a lone wolf, Josh, you'd at least know where to start looking. And you're a librarian, and I've already heard about your research skills." Simon chuckled. "You and Ange did come up with some interesting scenarios about me. You connected a few dots I wasn't expecting." They'd connected Simon's present identity with his original and were worried he was using a false persona based on someone who had died in 1916.

"Well, I could hardly tell Ange I thought you might be a vampire. She was worried enough about Ben, and I hoped I was wrong, so any conclusions I drew had to be from a human perspective." Josh pulled out his phone and made some notes. "I can do some research for you and point you in the right direction. Don't expect me to go talking to the local pack, though. That's a waste of time. Ben already has my email. Send me the names of the missing people and I'll see what I can find."

"Thank you. Ben and I are going to see an old friend of mine up at the university this afternoon whom I hope can shed some light on the matter." Simon's friend Rupert had moved back to New Zealand twelve years ago. "Perhaps you could start with the missing human? That way you can keep out of the way of the local pack."

"Sounds like a plan." Josh stood. "I'll be in touch when I have something. Won't be tonight, though. I have plans."

"With Cody?" Ange asked.

"Maybe." Josh grinned, leaned over the table, and kissed her cheek. "Welcome to Wellington, Simon. Hope you enjoy your stay." He headed off towards the door leading to the library, giving the ghosts a wave on his way through.

"Is your old friend at the uni the vampire who works there?" Ange still hadn't figured out who he was, although the hint Simon had deliberately dropped when she'd visited had driven her crazy for years.

"Yes." Simon sipped his coffee. "This brew *is* excellent. We might have to visit here again."

CHAPTER SIX

"How long have you known Rupert?" Ben asked.

His last name, Milne, seemed familiar, yet Ben couldn't place it. Professor Milne had taught a few of Ben's classes when he'd done his degree, but it wasn't that.

"We met in 1922 in London." Simon stopped at the top of the hill the university called home and looked around. "These old buildings are quite beautiful. Rupert told me a little about Wellington's history when we first met, and you've filled in some of the gaps, but there's still a lot I don't know."

Ben frowned. "Does Wellington have a mutual agreement thing like Boggslake?"

Simon had taught history at Lakeview University since the '50s, but no one had commented about him not ageing. Students did their study and moved on, while others kept quiet in return for the Supernatural Council's protection against stuff many humans preferred to pretend didn't exist.

"Not that I'm aware. Unfortunately, not all cities are enlightened like ours." Simon craned his neck, looking at the stained-glass windows. "He comes and goes and reinvents himself as his descendants. When I met him, he was teaching at Cambridge."

Ben itched to take his camera out of his bag and take photos, but had decided to focus on finding Rupert first. While he'd taken shots of the buildings with his modern camera, he wanted to try the antique Brownie camera Simon had given him, and explore the different aspects of shadow and light.

"I didn't have a clue when I was here," Ben said, "but I wouldn't have known what I was looking for then."

"Rupert's had a lot of experience in keeping a low profile." Simon opened the door to the building for him. "I'll follow you once you know where you're going."

"I *think* I remember where I'm going. It's been a while." Ben grabbed Simon's hand and stood for a moment, soaking in the place's ambience. A couple of the students glanced at them and smiled, but kept walking.

"You miss Wellington," Simon said softly. "Sometimes I wonder if it's fair that you've given up your life and family for me."

"Yeah, I do, but I love my life with you." Ben grinned to lighten the mood. "And it's not as though we can't visit again."

Simon's expression darkened.

"It will be all right, I promise. My family is not yours." Ben squeezed Simon's hand. "Enough with the memories. Let's find Rupert and see what he knows about the case."

Rupert's office was where Ben remembered. He knocked on the door but didn't get a response. "Do you know where he lives?" he asked Simon.

"Unfortunately, not, and the council didn't supply that information either."

"He's still not back?" A younger man spoke from behind them. He held a pile of books, with a couple of stapled, printed sheets of paper balanced on top. "Damn it. He gave me a deadline for this assignment and told me to leave it on his desk."

"Perhaps if the door is unlocked, you could still do that," Ben suggested, turning to face him.

The student's face brightened. He pushed his glasses back up his nose. "I hadn't thought of that. Hang on, let me check the door."

"He's not—"

"I'm sure if we don't touch anything, it will be fine," Simon said firmly. "Or I could pass it onto him if you'd prefer. I'm a... visiting colleague and an old friend of Professor Milne's."

"I'd prefer to leave it on his desk if that's okay, Professor...?"

"Professor Hawthorne," Simon said politely. "And completely understandable."

"Nice to meet you. I'm Liam, by the way." Liam tried the door, frowned, and then tried again. The second time it opened. A stack of papers sat on the desk in the corner. He added his to the pile. "Enjoy your stay in Wellington."

"Thanks." Ben didn't get a chance to introduce himself before Liam muttered something about classes and rushed out again. "Okay, that was weird."

"I heard the lock release just before Liam opened the door." Simon glanced at the wall behind Rupert's desk and smiled. "This map was on his wall at Cambridge too. It was old then."

"Yeah, it looks it. Wait... what?" Ben hadn't heard the lock open, but then he didn't have vampire hearing either.

"There are more than just supernaturals in this world." Simon began looking through the papers on Rupert's desk. "Some humans have talents too. I suspect our young friend is one of them. Bloody hell, Rupert, at least leave us some clue."

"Do you think we should be looking through his desk?" Ben didn't want to piss off an old vampire.

"Rupert has a habit of going to ground once there's any hint of trouble. It's how he's survived so long." Simon frowned. "The fact he's not here doesn't bode well for the seriousness of this situation. Have a look on the shelves. See if there are any books that catch your eye. He knew we were coming to Wellington, so he might have left a message."

Most of the books were old and well worn. Ben picked up a copy of *Tarzan of the Apes* and leafed through it. His eyes widened when he saw the inscription. "This is a signed first edition."

"Most of them are. Rupert collects them," Simon said absently. "He's a terrible name-dropper, too. It's quite tiresome after a while."

"So, all these Shakespeare plays are—"

"Signed first editions. Yes. Rupert and Will were friends at one point. Or at least that's the story he tells."

"Oh." Ben figured he'd better not touch any more books just in case he damaged one and got stuck with the bill. A stack that didn't look like it fitted in with the old and valuable vibe caught his eye. They were all by the same author. "Marion Milne. Milne, as in Rupert Milne. That's why his name sounded familiar. It's Marion's pen name."

One of the vampire councillors in Boggslake, Marion Cooper, wrote historical romance novels she claimed were her memoirs. Simon, Declan, and Forge had featured in three of them.

"Marion's his ex." Simon frowned. "Yes, that's right. I lose track. They've been married at least once since I've known them. They're one of those couples who can't live together, yet can't live apart, so they get married, stay that way for about fifty years, then divorce. Or one of them goes away for a while to reinvent themselves, and they marry again after a short courtship."

"Rinse and repeat?" Ben wasn't sure what he thought of that. He pulled down the latest in the pile and skimmed through it. "I figure Rupert's the main character in this one. It's set in Wellington at the turn of last century." He spotted a familiar volume. "He's got yours too."

"That book is *not* mine, and it's pure fiction." Simon started flipping through an old-fashioned Filofax. "Damn it. I thought he might have hidden something somewhere."

Ben couldn't resist picking up *The Aristocrat's Promise*, although he was already far more familiar with the story than he wanted to be. "You said some of this was true. Hang on. What if—?" He shook the book and a thin piece of paper fell out. "I think I found the message."

Simon was by his side in an instant, both of them reading the message together. "Well, that's useful. Thanks, Rupert."

"Don't call me, I'll call you?" Ben snorted. He slammed the book shut and returned it to its shelf. "What kind of message is that?"

"Typical Rupert." Simon tucked the message into his wallet. "Give me a moment to get rid of any sign we've been here, and then I'm taking you out to lunch. We should have time to still take in the rose gardens before we pay our missing vampire a visit."

"Do you think he's in hiding like Rupert?"

"I hope so." Simon blurred in a burst of vampire speed, then opened the door for Ben.

"Do you want to go there first?"

"The rose gardens are on the way." Simon smiled. "I doubt he'll be there, and tracking down his contacts is going to take time. This is our honeymoon, and I intend to at least be able to spend a romantic afternoon with my husband, despite the council's attempt to hijack our visit for their own agenda."

"What about the werewolf?"

"Tomorrow." Simon suddenly seemed nervous. "I have an important meeting tonight I can't afford to miss."

"Oh?" Ben raised an eyebrow. It was the first he'd heard of it.

"Your father wants to take me to your local pub for a drink."

~

"Mum reckons the rose gardens would make a lovely location for a wedding." Ben held up his hands in a mock show of defence. Luckily, they'd left it too late to book as a venue. "Her words, not mine."

"I thought we were exchanging our vows in your parents' back garden." Simon shoved his hands in his pockets while they crossed the street. "I did enjoy the roses, though. There were a few I haven't seen before. It's a shame I can't take cuttings back with me." He could be a little obsessive about his roses and, if upset, often retreated to his garden or played familiar pieces on his piano.

They'd parked the car a couple of streets away because they'd borrowed Frank's and didn't want to risk their investigation leading back to him.

"We are." Ben wasn't keen to draw attention to themselves any more than Simon was. "Mum's a force of nature once she gets an idea." He'd had a difficult time convincing her they wanted a private family ceremony and that they'd come home to share their vows with those they were close to, and no one else. "I told her you were a very private person, and she needed to respect that. She backed down then. At least until next time."

"I'll keep that in mind." Simon opened the front gate for Ben. "At least Victor lives in a quiet neighbourhood," he continued, not so subtly changing the subject like he always did when Ben tried to discuss his mother's views about what she thought their ceremony should entail. "We should be able to get in and out without too much fuss."

"Don't discard the power of the local Neighbourhood Watch," Ben murmured. "How are you planning to get in if he doesn't answer the door?" He doubted they'd just walk away when they'd no luck finding Rupert. Simon wasn't the only one who wanted this case solved quickly.

Simon knocked politely, then tilted his head to one side, listening. "There's no one home. I can't sense the presence of another vampire, or hear anyone else in the house." He dropped to a crouch in front of the lock and pulled on his gloves. "Watch the street. I won't be long."

"Another one of those things Declan taught you?" Ben deliberately turned away so he didn't see Simon pull out the lock picking kit Declan had given him. "You remember that my sister Tash is a police detective, right? I'm not going to lie to her if we get caught." She'd only just made detective, and Ben didn't want to jeopardise that by getting her mixed up with what passed for normal for him these days.

He also wasn't going to tell her that one of their friends was a cat burglar and con man. Or that another was a brilliant hacker.

"We're not going to get caught." The door swung open, and Simon straightened. "Or would you prefer I called the police, and we warn them they're in the middle of a supernatural crime scene, if this is what this is?"

"Yeah, okay, I get your point." Ben sighed and retrieved his gloves from his pocket. He'd figured their visit might come down to this, so he had grabbed them on their way out in case, although he'd hoped their missing vampire was holed up at home and ignoring the council. He'd sure as hell ignore the council if he could. "I miss Anson already. At least in

Boggslake we had a contact on the force who knew all about this stuff."

"If we do find something, I'll contact the council to deal with it." Simon stood back to let Ben enter first. Their information had already confirmed that no humans lived in the house, so Simon being able to enter wouldn't be a problem.

The house felt quiet, almost eerily so. Ben entered the kitchen while Simon checked the living room. The fridge contained a mix of food and blood bags, which he expected. Vampires still ate and enjoyed human food, but they needed to supplement it with blood to survive. He checked the date on the milk in the door. It hadn't expired, so the house had been abandoned recently.

The small freezer on top of the fridge had several frozen bags of ice cubed blood like the stuff Simon still added to milk occasionally, although thankfully Ben had convinced him to drink it from bags mostly.

"Come look at this," Simon called from the living room.

Victor Rochford was an accountant who had set up his own business ten years ago, but his colleagues hadn't seen him for a few days. They weren't worried, though, because he'd told them he would be taking some time off because of personal matters and would contact them when he was due to return, which was something he regularly did.

If he'd left the area, he should have told the council, or at least picked up his mobile when they'd called him.

A small, long, empty box sat on the coffee table in the living room.

Ben shivered, unable to shake the feeling he'd walked into a scene that would be forever frozen in time, although it had a weird juxtaposition of past and present about it. The furniture was old yet well maintained, and photos lined the wall. He studied them closely.

"These photos are all the same woman," he said slowly.

"They start when she's in her twenties, and in the last one, I'm guessing she's about ninety." One photo showed the woman in a wedding dress, but she stood alone.

"She's his wife," Simon said quietly. "He married a human. She aged while he didn't."

"That's so sad." Ben bit his lip, realisation hitting with a sick feeling in his stomach that this could be his and Simon's future too, if he couldn't persuade Simon to turn him.

"At least with us being soulbonded, I won't be left alone afterwards." Simon took Ben's hand and led him over to show him the photograph on the mantelpiece of the woman in her wedding dress standing with a man who looked the same age. They had their arms around each other and were obviously in love. "Someone painted this for them, the same way Declan did for us."

"Why would someone kill this guy?" Ben wondered. "Do you think it might be someone pissed off because he'd married a human? Or a human who figured out the guy with her wasn't her grandson, but her husband?"

"When you live a long time, you make a lot of enemies," Simon reminded him. "Sometimes people just kill for the fun of it, and it doesn't need to make sense. We don't know if he's dead yet. Let's hope he's not until we find proof he is, hmm?"

"There's no return address on this box," Ben turned it over. "That's weird. His wallet is sitting on the table too, and so is his laptop. Why would he leave that stuff behind?"

"I doubt he would," Simon said grimly. "I haven't checked upstairs yet. Stay behind me."

Ben wasn't about to argue about letting Simon go first. When they reached the top of the stairs, sunlight caught the air, a slight breeze moving through the house. Fine dust particles danced in the light. He held out his hand to catch one of them. "Not that small then, are you?" he murmured and studied it more closely. He swallowed. "Simon, I don't think this is—"

Simon stopped at the entrance to the master bedroom. He growled low in his throat. "I think we found our vampire."

Ben sprinted to catch up with him.

"Are you sure you want to see this?" Simon asked.

"I'm fine," Ben reassured him, already guessing what he'd found.

A pile of grey dust lay on the bed. In the middle of it sat a long silver knife.

Ben's stomach churned. "Oh, crap." Although he'd expected it, he never dealt well with seeing the dust remains of a vampire, and the reminder that this might be Simon one day.

"I can deal with this if you don't want to." Simon sounded much calmer than Ben felt, although he could feel the turmoil of emotions underneath Simon's outward reaction.

"It's fine." Ben distracted himself by examining the crime scene. "My guess is that someone's set this up to look like a suicide, but I don't get it. His wife died years ago. He's not going to kill himself in a fit of grief now. And besides, if he's as old as the council said he is, he would have lost a lot of people he loved." He winced. "Sorry, that sounded much colder than I meant it."

"It's the truth." Simon peered at the knife but didn't touch it. "The knife doesn't explain why he turned to dust. I doubt it's sharp enough to decapitate a vampire, and I don't see a stake anywhere, do you?'

"Silver is poisonous to vampires, but it doesn't kill you instantly." Ben picked up the knife with his gloved hand and cautiously ran the edge of his glove across the blade. "Definitely blunt as. And why would a vampire pick up something silver? It doesn't make sense."

Simon moved around the room, then froze at the doorway to the ensuite. "Human blood," he murmured. "Very faint, but definitely there."

"You don't want to get near that," Ben said sharply.

"It's faint, and I'm fine." Simon gave him a reassuring smile. His eyes still looked normal, and his fangs hadn't dropped. "See?" He pulled out his phone. "I think you're right and we're looking at a murder set up to look like a suicide. I'll telephone the council so they can hand this over to the authorities, and then we'll leave. We can't do anything else for him now."

"Apart from finding the bastards who did this," Ben reminded him. "I'm going to go downstairs and check if there are any clues on his laptop while you phone them."

"Be careful," Simon said. "Whoever did this is long gone, but they might have left some kind of calling card."

"Yeah I will be, promise." Ben felt better once he'd left what remained of the body. Whatever this guy had done with his life, no one deserved to die that way.

Simon's annoyance bled through their bond before Ben reached the stairs. His voice rose, his British accent becoming more clipped. Also, never a good sign. Contacting the council tended to do that.

Ben busied himself looking through the laptop. Victor had actually used the word 'password' for a password, so getting into his files took little effort. He had a few meetings in his Google calendar that Ben noted, but nothing over the last couple of days.

"The council is sending someone and wants us to wait for him." Simon leaned over Ben's shoulder. "Although they claimed they didn't have anyone who handles these things in Wellington, apparently they do."

"Then why ask us?" Ben closed the laptop, having got everything off it he was going to.

"Fresh eyes?" Simon shrugged. "Given Josh's reaction to me, I don't think the supernatural community is very impressed with the Treaty, so having someone investigate from outside the area might have factored in too." He glanced at his watch. "We're going to end up in the middle of traffic, and late for dinner if this takes too long." His expression brightened. "Perhaps I'll have to put off my meeting with your father."

"Simon!" Ben sighed. "If I know Dad, he'll be looking forward to some quality time with you. I wouldn't be surprised if he's also roped in Trent." He'd got a text from his mum while they were at the rose gardens asking if he'd like to spend the evening with her and his sisters, so he expected he'd get his own version of what Simon was looking forward to. "Granddad's been invited too."

"I should expect a proper family inquisition then?" Simon didn't sound like he was joking.

"I doubt it's going to be like that," Ben said, although he figured that was exactly what it would be. "I mean, how bad can it be? And you've had practice at this kind of thing. You're really good at covering your tracks for an old guy."

Simon rolled his eyes. "Far too much practice, although family is different. I don't like pretending to be—"

Luckily, a sharp rap at the door interrupted whatever he'd been about to say.

"That didn't take long." Ben had thought they'd have to wait at least an hour before anyone turned up.

"He was in the area." Simon got up to answer the door. "Apparently." He sniffed the air. "A werewolf. Interesting."

The man who walked in had dark hair and eyes, and a runner's build. His expression was nothing less than suspicious. Nevertheless, he held out his hand once they were inside. "Detective Garrick Frater, Wellington PD. You must be Hawthorne. The council warned me I was meeting a vampire."

Simon shook his hand. "Professor Simon Hawthorne. This is my husband, Ben Leyton. They neglected to tell me you were a werewolf."

"The council are a little... choosey about the information they decide to share."

"You're their liaison on the local police force?" Ben had heard the name Frater before but couldn't place it.

"Something like that. Any supernatural crime in the area, and I'm your guy. The only guy at present. So luckily, we don't get a lot of it. Or we didn't until recently." He shook Ben's hand too. "Just so you know, I don't hold with a lot of the traditional views about vampires, but not everyone around here is that... enlightened." He sniffed Ben. "There's certain parts of town I'd be wary of going into alone, especially with—"

"My husband's scent all over me?" Ben finished what he figured Garrick was going to say. "Yeah, well, if I had a dollar for every time I've heard that, I'd be rich."

Simon coughed. "Now that the niceties are over, we'd like to hand over the case to you, and be on our way."

"I hear you've got a meeting with the alpha tomorrow too."

"Yes. We have."

Ben raised an eyebrow. First, he'd heard of it.

"The council informed me when I telephoned them about this." Simon led Garrick up the stairs and explained what they'd found. "Have you any news about the missing werewolf councillor yet?"

"No, but I'll be in touch when we have now that I have your details to contact you directly." Garrick pulled on a heavy pair of gloves before touching the knife. Silver didn't play nicely with werewolves either. "I'll get this dusted for prints, but I doubt I'll find any apart from the victim's."

"You agree with us that it's a murder?" Ben asked.

"I knew Victor," Garrick said. "He was a friend, and definitely not suicidal. He'd taken last week off work because he was in his contagious cycle."

"The council said they'd lost contact with him," Simon said, "but I'm presuming you hadn't."

"When Erik Sedway and Kerwin Wayland disappeared, Victor didn't want to risk being out in public if something went down. He holed up here and let all his calls go to voicemail."

"So why send us when they could have sent you? And if your friend was ignoring their calls, perhaps the other councillors were too?" Ben doubted it would be that simple, but had to ask anyway.

Garrick studied what was left of his friend and sighed. "Erik and Kerwin enjoy their positions too much to risk them, so they'd never do that. Victor, on the other hand, doesn't—didn't—care what the other councillors thought of him, and had grown weary of their politics. Our friendship wasn't common knowledge, and we decided a long time ago to keep it that way. The council didn't know about it, and because I'd spoken to Victor a couple of days ago, I wasn't going to check up on him until later tonight. Yesterday was the anniversary of his wife's death and he wanted a couple of extra days to be alone with his memories. When I heard you were in the area, I changed my mind and was on my way over here to see him when I got their call." He glanced up at them. "I want to find out who did this and make sure justice is served. I'm hoping we can work together, and..."

"We'll keep your secret," Simon promised. "It never pays to let the council have any leverage over you."

"Okay, thanks." Garrick nodded. "I'm going to phone this

in as a missing persons report. Most of the people I work with have no clue there's anything supernatural going on in Wellington apart from that TV show, and I'd prefer to keep it that way."

"Works for us," Ben said. "We're here on holiday, so we'll be heading back home in a few weeks anyway."

He started to leave, and Garrick stopped him. "Ben?"

"Yeah?"

"You're Tash Leyton's brother, yeah?"

"Yes, but how—" Ben swore under his breath when his brain connected the dots. "Frater! You're that Frater."

Simon glanced between them. "What am I missing? How do you know Ben's sister?"

"She got the detective job about the same time you booked our tickets over here," Ben said slowly, anger burning through him as the dots became pieces in a much larger puzzle. "You would have filled in all those council travel forms, yes?"

"Jacob insists on it, yes." Simon growled. "Oh, I see."

"I'm her partner on the force." Garrick's expression reflected the realisation the truth was already out. "The council arranged it. She's got a lot of potential, and there's just me dealing with all the supernatural crime here. They thought with her brother married to a vampire, she'd be the ideal person to bring on board."

Simon glared at him, his eyes glinting dangerously. "Have you told her?"

"No, not yet, although now this has happened, I don't know how much longer I can put it off. The council will start putting pressure on now that one of their councillors has been murdered, and I don't have the resources to investigate on my own." Garrick took a step back. "And hey, this wasn't my idea." He frowned. "Are you telling me she doesn't know what you are yet?"

"No," Ben said quickly. "She doesn't, and we'd like to keep it that way at least a bit longer."

"And you have the resources now, so there's no need to tell her, is there?" Simon gave Garrick a curt nod. "Welcome to the team. I'll let you know when we're meeting with our colleagues, and we can trade information then."

CHAPTER SEVEN

"My treat tonight," Simon insisted.

"I'll get the next round then." Ray didn't seem impressed that Simon was offering to pay. "You're our guest, and we don't expect you to foot the bill for the evening."

"Let him pay." Frank laid a hand on his son-in-law's arm. "He's looking forward to spoiling us, and he won't get the opportunity again for a while."

"If you're sure." Ray still didn't look certain.

Simon had finally managed to get Ben to accept him paying when they went out, although his husband insisted on paying his way with other things.

"Very sure. You've opened your home to us while we're here, so it's the least I can do to say thank you." Once they'd each chosen their order, Simon went up to the bar. The pub had been named after the mythical water creature depicted in the huge mural decorating the wall behind the counter.

The man on duty smiled at him. "You're Ben Leyton's husband, yes? Could you tell him that we expect him to turn up for at least one darts match while he's here?"

"Yes, I am, and I will." Simon read the man's name tag.

"Thank you, Olly." He frowned, wondering how Olly had worked out who he was before he'd introduced himself.

"You're here with Ray, Trent, and Frank, and Ben's not." Olly leaned over the bar and lowered his voice. "We figured you'd get the invite to The Taniwha at some point or another." He held out his hand. "I went to school with Ben."

"Ah yes." Simon shook his hand. "Ben mentioned you might be on duty tonight. Pleased to meet you. I'm Simon."

"I hope you're enjoying your stay here, and his family aren't giving you the third degree."

Simon grimaced. "I'm sure that pleasure is forthcoming." He glanced back at the table and tried not to listen in on the conversation. "Could I have four of whatever beer you have on tap?" He repeated the order he'd been given, and then added, "and some snacks to go with them, please?" He couldn't get drunk, but at least this way he could drink a little and pretend the snacks had helped to keep him relatively sober.

Olly shook his head when Simon pulled out his wallet.

"Just pay when you're leaving. That's fine. It's not busy tonight, so I'll bring them over to your table."

Simon dropped a couple of notes into the tip jar. "Enjoy your evening, and I'll be sure to come back in a few days with Ben. I've heard about your darts matches and am looking forward to seeing him in his element."

"That's very generous, thank you." Olly's eyes widened when he saw the size of the tip Simon had left. He handed Simon a bowl of nuts and another of pretzels. "Those are on the house." While bar snacks were free in the US, they weren't here.

Simon smiled his thanks and made his way back to the table. He was looking forward to coming back with Ben to try their dinner menu one evening. The pub had an old-fashioned rustic feel to it, and Ben had told Simon they served good home-cooked food that would remind Simon of England.

Light pop music played on the stereo in the corner, loud enough to be background noise but not drown out conversation. He'd been concerned about mirrors, but none were in sight. If he avoided the restrooms, he'd be fine in that regard too.

"Olly is bringing over our drinks shortly." Simon placed the bowls on the table and took his seat. "This place has a very homely atmosphere. I can see why Ben enjoyed coming here."

"It's quite warm this evening." Ray took off his jersey and draped it over the back of the chair. "We're not formal here. If you want to roll up your shirt sleeves, that's fine."

"Thank you, but I'm quite comfortable like this." Simon wouldn't risk his silver scars showing and have them lead into another conversation he'd prefer to avoid. He cleared his throat. "I expect you and Maddie are looking forward to becoming parents, Trent."

Maddie and Trent had discovered they were having twins that morning at their scan appointment, and the entire family was delighted. Ben had done a great job feigning surprise and was relieved he no longer had to keep Simon's revelation secret.

"Yeah." Trent Oakley smiled. He was a few years older than Maddie, and had struck Simon as a gentle man comfortable in his own skin. They seemed a good match. "I don't have any siblings so I haven't had a lot to do with children, but I'm sure my in-laws will jump in and help."

"Abby can't wait to become a grandmother," Ray said. "If she oversteps, let her know, okay? Sometimes her enthusiasm to help can get the better of her."

"Having an extra pair of hands is always good even with one kid," Frank pointed out, "and you'll have two."

"Maddie's very capable," Trent said proudly. "I've taken parental leave for the first couple of weeks, so we can focus on getting into a routine and all that." He was an accounts manager for a national hardware chain.

"Tell us about your family, Simon." Ray gave Olly a nod when he delivered the drinks, and then took a sip of his beer.

"There's not much to tell," Simon said carefully. "I haven't seen my parents since I left England, and my brother and sister-in-law died in a... boating accident." He was hardly going to tell them that the boat in question had been the *Titanic*. "My niece, Clarice, and I stayed in touch for years though. She was young when her parents died."

"You're not in touch anymore?" Trent asked.

"No." Simon sampled the beer, which had a pleasant taste. Usually, he didn't see the point of drinking. "I've been away for quite a long time. Boggslake has been my home for years now."

"You must have left home very young." Ray sounded more concerned than curious.

"It feels like a lifetime ago." Simon helped himself to a handful of nuts. "If you'd like something more substantial to eat, please let me know. We didn't get home until late, so we had dinner quite recently."

"I passed through Boggslake when I was Ben's age." Frank, thankfully, diverted the conversation. "For a city, it's mighty small, but I found it very welcoming."

"It probably has changed little since then," Simon said. "Some of the people you knew are most likely still there, or their children are. We're still getting a lot of students each year too."

"I expect the university still looks the same." Frank smiled. "Ben's taken some great photos of the area. It was very good of you to give him your old camera."

"I wasn't using it, and my uncle would be happy that Ben

is getting such joy from it." Simon wished his uncle Edwin could have met Ben. He liked to think they would have become good friends. He sighed. His uncle had never had the chance to learn that Simon had survived the war. Uncle Edwin would have accepted him for what he was.

He hoped.

"You miss him," Ray said softly. "Sounds like a lot of your family has passed on. I'm sorry. It's difficult being alone in the world, although you're not alone now. You're part of this family."

For how long?

"I've had the company of good friends for a long time, and we've become a family." Simon drained his beer. Sometimes he really wished he could get drunk. "I'm going to have another. Does anyone else want one?"

"Good thing Trent's our designated driver." Ray raised an eyebrow. "I think we're fine for a while. I like to savour mine, and Frank can make a pint last all evening."

"I don't usually drink." Simon realised what he'd said too late. "Perhaps I'll wait a while or ask for a coffee." He really *really* wished he had a glass of blood, although he rarely drank it that way.

"Guess you're nervous with the wedding coming up?" Ray grinned. "You're already married, so it shouldn't be so nerve-wracking second time round."

"They didn't have my daughter there the first time," Frank murmured. "Small affair then too, right?"

"Right," Simon said.

Luckily his telephone rang. He checked the caller ID and answered it. "Excuse me," he murmured. "This is Simon. How can I help?"

Garrick sounded stressed. "I know I said I'd contact you in the morning, but thought you'd like to be forewarned."

Simon stood and walked away from the table, keeping his voice low. "They found one of the other councillors?"

"Yes. Kerwin Wayland's alive, but in a bad way. Looks like silver poisoning. The pack doctors aren't sure he's going to last the night."

"Any clues about who is responsible?"

"Nothing. He was dumped in the middle of Frank Kitts Park. Luckily, he was in human form and a couple of were-wolf teenagers found him." Garrett blew out a breath. "The alpha is not happy. I'm not sure what kind of reception you'll get tomorrow."

"We weren't expecting a warm one anyway." Simon glanced back at the table. The lack of conversation behind him wasn't a good sign. "Thanks for letting me know. Will you be at the meeting tomorrow?"

"Yeah. I'll see you there." Garrett paused. "And Simon? Watch yourself. I don't like this."

"Neither do I," Simon said grimly. "Watch yourself too. See you tomorrow." He pocketed his telephone and retook his seat. "Sorry about that. It was a work call, so I had to take it."

"Surely the university knows you're on holiday?" Ray didn't look impressed. "They need to cut you some slack."

Simon shrugged. He didn't want to lie, yet couldn't very well tell the truth either, so he settled for something in between. "Unfortunately, I've been asked to oversee something in Wellington while I'm here. We're hoping the problem of finding and authenticating this missing historical document will be resolved sooner rather than later."

"It's not always easy to say no when you work for someone," Frank stepped in to smooth over the conversation again. "That council of yours has a nerve," he said in a low voice that only Simon could hear.

He snorted. "That's a polite way of putting it."

Ray and Trent exchanged a concerned look.

"You'd tell us if you and Ben are in some kind of trouble, wouldn't you?" Ray bit his lip. "Abby has this crazy idea that we don't know much about you because you're in witness protection or something."

"I'm not in witness protection," Simon assured him. That was a new one he hadn't heard before. What was it with Ben's friends and family coming up with such inventive scenarios to explain his background? At least Ben's parents hadn't tried to find him online, although the digital trail left by the vampire network hadn't stopped Ange and Josh from drawing interesting conclusions either. "My job comes with a level of responsibility, and although I left it in very capable hands, it does tend not to be easily left behind." He managed a smile, and ignored the growing frustration he felt from Ben, who was most likely on the receiving end of questions he couldn't answer too. "Now, who would like some coffee? I spotted a lovely-looking apple pie at the counter that reminds me of a dessert I had at my grandmother's many years ago."

"We've got a problem," Ben said, backing out of his parents' driveway.

"More than your parents half convinced I'm in witness protection?" Simon raised an eyebrow. The frustration he'd felt from Ben earlier in the evening had grown into annoyance with a final burst of something he couldn't quite define. Not fear, or Simon would have left the pub and gone to Ben, and to hell with what anyone thought.

"I thought your plan to come here for a nice quiet holiday was a little too hopeful," Frank said from the backseat. "Especially considering your life seems to consist of fighting off bad guys."

"You don't know the half of it," Ben muttered. He'd toned down quite a few of the stories he'd told his grandfather to avoid him worrying.

"My point exactly," Frank said. "I thought you sidestepped rather well on several occasions back there in the pub, but I know my family. You're far from out of the woods yet. I think you need to come clean before someone else spills the beans for you."

"I'm not doing that," Simon said firmly, ignoring the fact that Frank agreed with Ben that their family wouldn't have an issue with Simon being a vampire. "What kind of problem?" he asked Ben.

Ben worried at his lip. "Tash has been following Garrick on her own time. She thinks he's up to something, at the very least, and possibly involved in something he shouldn't be. She's never been one to let a puzzle go unanswered."

"She sounds a lot like you." Simon sighed. "I have a bad feeling about where you're going with this."

"Yeah." Ben turned the car into Frank's street. "She saw Garrick go into Victor's house yesterday, and then she saw us come out. I... I'm not straight out lying to my family. I can't. It was bad enough sidestepping the truth with Ange when I first found out about you."

"What did you tell her?"

"I said I couldn't talk about it. Or at least not yet." Ben parked the car and turned off the engine. "She asked me whether we were in some kind of trouble and whether Garrick was bothering us. I told her he was helping, and not to worry." He gripped the steering wheel. "Of course, she's bloody worrying. Either we tell her, or she's going to find out!"

"It's probably better if you tell her," Frank said quietly.

"That girl is too much like her mother. And, as I said, the truth will be better coming from you, rather than have her build the situation up into something it isn't once she starts investigating and connects dots that aren't there. After all, the real facts of this case aren't going to be easy to find."

"No, they aren't, and we probably should." Simon wished they'd had more time. He'd started to enjoy being part of Ben's family. "I'm sorry."

"Hey, it's not your fault that the council are being dicks like usual." Ben opened the car door. "I'm not keeping secrets again, though. That's not open to debate."

He started to get out of the car. Simon grabbed his arm. "Wait!" He narrowed his eyes and focused. "Both of you stay in the car. There's someone in the house."

"You're not—"

Simon sprinted up the steps before Ben finished protesting. The front door was unlocked. Someone sat on Frank's favourite chair, nursing a drink. Simon sniffed, taking in the unmistakable scent of blood. He raised an eyebrow when he recognised the intruder.

"This is taking don't call me, I'll call you, a little far don't you think?"

Rupert Milne drained his glass. "I hope you don't mind me helping myself to your supply, but it's been a few hours since I'd partaken, and I wasn't sure what time you'd be home."

A low purring noise came from his feet. Simon startled when a black cat strode over to him and rubbed itself around his ankles. "You brought your cat?"

"She's not mine. I thought she lived here. She was sitting on the doorstep when I arrived." Rupert shrugged. "You need to improve your security. The lock was child's play." He glanced outside. "Aren't you going to invite your friends in?"

"Stay comfortably where you are, and I'll do that." Simon

switched the light on. He and Rupert could see well enough in the near darkness, but Ben and Frank wouldn't be able to. "It's good to see you again. It's been too long."

"Far too long," Rupert agreed. The cat jumped onto his lap and purred. "She's an interesting one, this cat." The cat turned towards Simon and studied him. He held out his hand and let her sniff him, then she licked it. "She likes you."

Simon stood in the doorway and gestured for Ben to bring Frank up to the house. "I'm going to make some tea. Would you like some?" When Rupert nodded, Simon added, "You still like Earl Grey, milk, no sugar?"

"You remembered." Rupert looked pleased.

"We drank enough of it in your study at Cambridge." Simon met Ben at the door. "Remember that note we found? This is what he meant by it."

Ben motioned for his grandfather to hang back a moment. He glanced at Rupert, then back at Simon. "How did he get in here without being invited?"

Rupert chuckled. "I'm a lot older than your Simon." Although he'd never admitted his age, and appeared to be in his early fifties, with grey creeping into the temples of his hairline, he was rumoured to be one of the oldest of their kind. "Some rules don't apply when you get to my age. Good evening, Ben. It's always a pleasure to meet one of my students again. I figured you'd go far with your enquiring mind and that attitude of yours." He gave Frank a nod when he entered the house. "Good evening, Mr Connell. I'm Rupert Milne, an *old* friend of Simon's. Thank you for the use of your home."

"An old friend?" Frank raised an eyebrow. "You're like him, then? A vampire?"

"I am a vampire, yes." Rupert started to stand, but Frank shook his head.

"Always nice to meet a friend of Simon's," Frank said, "but

don't stand on my account. I've had enough excitement for today, so I'm going to call it a night. I expect you have a lot to talk about that probably isn't good for my health to know too much about." He bent to pat the cat. "So, you're back then, are you? You don't live here, you know, though you think you do."

"It's not your cat, Granddad?" Ben frowned. "I thought she was when I saw the cat biscuits in the pantry, so I fed her this morning."

"I think she's a stray," Frank said. "I've reported her to Dr Quinn, the local vet, but she's not chipped. If her owner doesn't come for her soon, I'll need to find a proper home for her. I'm getting too old to worry about being owned by a cat." He hung up his walking stick by the door. "See you boys in the morning."

"'Night, Granddad," Ben called, "we'll try and keep the noise down." He grabbed the milk from the fridge and added it to the tea tray Simon had almost finished preparing. "So, Simon was your student, right?"

Rupert nodded. "I've had a lot of students over the centuries, but some are more memorable than others. He wasn't much older than you when we first met, but I have kept an eye on him from a distance."

"I'm sure Marion has been more than happy to keep you abreast of recent events in Boggslake." Simon handed Rupert his tea, retrieved the empty glass, and rinsed it in the sink. It wouldn't do to leave any evidence that someone had enjoyed an unusual beverage, especially given the risk that one of Ben's family might turn up unannounced.

"Marion did tell me about your run-in with the BFH, yes." Rupert settled back into the chair and balanced the cup and saucer on his knee. "They're amateurs compared to what's crawled out of the darkness over the past few decades."

"Dangerous amateurs." Simon put his arm around Ben,

pulling him close. He tried not to dwell on what had happened that night, but he'd never forget it. "Do you think they are connected to what's happening here?"

"That, I don't know." Rupert took a sip of tea. "Tell your mother she makes a beautiful fruitcake," he told Ben absently. "I sampled some earlier. But perhaps don't tell her that it goes well with my particular preference of red."

"Yeah, I'll definitely give that a miss." Ben rolled his eyes. "So, are we dealing with some kind of whack job organisation or something else? You don't think these disappearances—"

"One murder and one attempted murder so far," Simon interrupted him, "and we still don't know where Erik Sedway is."

Ben edged away from Simon slightly. "That's the other thing I need to tell you. I got a text from Ange tonight, and I thought you might have got one from Josh. He's tracked down a couple of Sedway's friends and they're going to visit them in the morning."

"Ange is going with him?" Simon shook his head. "No, he didn't contact me. Damn him. I'd hoped he knew better than to drag a human into this."

"Ben's involved," Rupert said mildly, "but then he's not just a human anymore, is he?"

"You know about that?" Ben asked before Simon could stop him.

"I know a lot of things." Rupert looked smug. "And Marion had heard rumours, which you just confirmed." He cleared his throat. "But, moving onto business. I doubt Sedway is in any real danger. He's human, and these people are more focused on ridding the world of the likes of us."

"The BFH's killed a human," Ben pointed out.

"Ah, yes, but they're not Human Destiny," Rupert said, "despite being tarred with a similar brush."

"That's what they're calling themselves?" Simon raised an eyebrow. "It's a little... pretentious, isn't it?'

"And there you have it," Rupert shrugged. "Don't let the name fool you. These people are dangerous. According to them, we're a threat to humanity, an abomination to their God, and they won't rest until they have wiped us all off the face of the Earth." He paused, apologetic. "Their manifesto, not mine, of course."

"So they're a cult?" Simon asked. "That makes them all the more dangerous. Is that why you went into hiding?"

Rupert looked mildly affronted. "I am not in hiding. The council were trying to get me involved, and I make a point of not getting mixed up in their politics, whatever the cost, considering that cost is usually too high for anyone but them."

"You're hiding from the council?" Ben asked. "I can understand that. They hijacked Simon's delivery at Auckland airport, then blackmailed him into helping them."

"If this is supposed to surprise me, you're a few centuries late with that titbit of information," Rupert said. "I have yet to meet a council I enjoyed doing business with. Though there was that group of werewolves in rural Japan a couple of hundred years ago that—"

"Why are you here?" Simon cut Rupert off before he could start on one of his stories. Although neither he nor Marion would admit it, they shared a predilection for embellishing stories about their pasts.

Rupert fished a large envelope from his pocket and handed it to Simon. "This is the information I have, but it's not a lot. They cover their tracks well, apart from that massacre in Brisbane nearly ten years ago. There is someone in Wellington who provides a safe haven to anyone in our community who asks for it. Nothing much happens in the area that Elard doesn't know about. You should talk to him."

"You're not going to help?" Ben asked.

"Heavens, no." Rupert raised an eyebrow. "At least Simon knows better than to ask that."

"Rupert's better at staying in the shadows and orchestrating things from afar. If we need help, I'm sure he'll be there..." Simon glanced at Rupert. "... but only on his own terms. I'd ask him to join our team, but it would be a waste of time."

"Totally a waste of time." Rupert grinned and nodded towards both of them in turn. "Now, I must be off. I'll be in touch. Watch yourselves, gentlemen. I don't enjoy funerals." He blurred towards the door. It opened, then closed behind him, and then he was gone.

"He's kind of how I remember him, but not," Ben said slowly.

"The not, would be because you didn't know what he was then. He's not hiding it now, though he's never completely upfront about anything." Simon emptied the envelope, took a pile of neatly typewritten sheets to read, and gave the rest to Ben to look through. "Rupert's always had his own agenda. It's how he's managed to survive so long."

"Uh-huh." Ben shook the papers he held. "There's something loose in here." A small card fell to the floor. He picked it up and his eyes widened. "It's a business card, so guessing it's Elard's."

"And?" Simon asked, knowing there must be an 'and'.

"He's a Catholic priest." Ben read the words on the card out loud. "Fr Elard Reith, St Ansgar's Parish, Newtown. We help those who ask." He groaned. "Oh great, I was hoping to avoid Uncle Martin while I was here."

"Uncle Martin?" Simon asked. Ben had mentioned him once or twice, but he'd got the impression Ben's father's brother wasn't that close to the rest of the family.

"Yeah. He lives across the road from St Ansgar's and always acts like he knows stuff the rest of us don't."

"Perhaps he does." Simon got up to pour some more tea.

"I hope not." Ben didn't look happy. "It's starting to feel like however hard we try to keep my family out of all this, fate is making damn sure they keep barging in."

CHAPTER EIGHT

"I hate that our world keeps trying to push its way into your family's." Simon kissed Ben's bare chest, then curled his tongue around a nipple.

"It's part of who we are, so we can't avoid it indefinitely." Ben threaded his fingers through Simon's hair and rolled them over in the bed so Simon was on top. "Less talk, more action."

"Frank's asleep across the hallway. Are you sure you can be quiet?" Simon scraped his fangs across Ben's skin, careful not to break it. Drawing blood hadn't been an option for a very long time. He reached down between Ben's legs, opening them gently while dragging his fangs down Ben's body toward his groin.

"Fuck yes. Just keep doing that." Ben's grip on Simon loosened when his breathing sped up.

Simon let his eyes go fully brown. "If you're not quiet, I *will* stop."

"I. Will. Be. Quiet." Ben gasped when Simon kissed Ben's soulbond scar inside his inner thigh.

"Hands above your head," Simon whispered. "No

touching either."

Ben opened his mouth as though he was about to protest.

Simon stilled immediately.

"Tease," Ben murmured, but obediently raised his arms and gripped the bed head. "Wait till it's my turn."

Simon raised an eyebrow and didn't move.

Ben sighed, but kept silent.

"I love you," Simon whispered. "Let me show you how much. Tonight's for you."

He lightly ran his fangs up Ben's leg, then flicked his tongue over Ben's balls. Ben shuddered but didn't make a sound. Simon hummed, and took Ben's cock into his mouth, alternating between licking and sucking. Ben bit his lip. His heart thumped, desire building through their bond, his skin heating in response to Simon's cooler touch. He gripped the wood of the headboard tighter, his fingers white. His hips bucked, and he groaned. Loudly.

Simon let Ben's cock fall from his mouth. He sat back on his haunches and licked his lips at the buffet in front of him.

Ben met his gaze with a defiant one of his own and jerked his hips. His cock was already leaking, his nipples standing up, his skin flushed with desire.

"You're so beautiful," Simon murmured. "I still can't believe you're mine."

"No point having someone if you don't touch them."

Simon chuckled. "I like you loud, but not tonight." He leaned over and kissed Ben slow and deep on the mouth, then broke the kiss. "Patience, my love."

"Not my strong point." Ben kept his voice low. "You know I can never resist you when you call me that." He eyed Simon up and down and licked his lips. "Hmm, hot as vampire."

"My love," Simon whispered. He only called Ben that when they were alone and intimate. "Still too much talk." He ran trembling fingers through Ben's dark chest hair, then lowered himself onto Ben, rubbing their cocks together, while he licked and nipped at Ben's neck and shoulders, kissing the skin each time Ben bit down on a groan. Ben's cock was hard against Simon's heated skin, their breathing both hard and fast against the thump of Ben's heartbeat.

Ben wrapped his legs around Simon, holding him against him, trying to match his rhythm. "Simon," he whispered, his voice ragged. "Simon."

"Not yet." Simon reluctantly eased Ben off him so he could move and reached for the lube. "Soon."

Ben gazed at him with desire fogged eyes, then parted his legs in clear invitation. Simon prepped him, then lowered himself again, pushing into Ben as quickly as he dared. Ben arched his hips up to meet him and reached for Simon through their shared bond.

Desire.

Need

Love.

Simon groaned loudly, Ben's emotions mixing and merging with his, a wave of passion smashing against his resolve to take it slowly and quietly. "Fuck this," he growled, and sped up his strokes. Ben met him part way and tightened around him.

He kissed Ben deeply, putting everything he was and wanted into the kiss. The two of them moved in tandem, one love, one soul.

Simon thrust hard and deep, then let go. They reached for each other, their emotions blurring together into one tangled whole. Ben threaded his fingers through Simon's, his grip tightening like iron, both of them falling together as one.

"Oh, God! Simon." Ben screamed Simon's name, then flopped back onto the bed, shaking. He kissed Simon's face over and over. "I love you. So much." He grinned. "I feel thoroughly debauched and fucked."

Simon kissed him again, although he didn't want to pull out just yet. He loved this part of sex, feeling Ben around him physically and emotionally. "You *are* thoroughly debauched and fucked." He heard a noise from Frank's bedroom and held a finger to Ben's lips. After a moment, the house went silent again. "What did I say about staying quiet?"

"Something about stopping if I wasn't?" Ben grinned and kissed Simon's cheek. "That didn't happen either, I notice."

"I fell prey to your charms," Simon deadpanned. He wrapped his legs around Ben, keeping them close. "Lucky for us, your grandfather's gone back to sleep."

"He's probably wearing earplugs."

Simon frowned. "Surely—"

"He threatened to after our first night here." Ben laughed. He rubbed his foot against Simon's calf. "I love that we're both here. Together." He kissed Simon's shoulder. "I'd started to wonder if I was ever going to convince you to come here so my family could meet you. I know you've been stressed and worried about it, and that you've faced your fears doing this for me." He kissed Simon again, this time lightly on the lips. "I also know it's not easy, but whatever happens, I'm here for you. Thank you." He rested their foreheads together. "They're my family, but so are you. You're my life now, and it will be okay."

"You're mine and I love you. I want you to be happy." Simon sighed. "I wish this was only about seeing your family. I feel like we're running out of time before our illusion of any kind of normal shatters around us." He pulled out of Ben and started to move off the bed.

Ben shook his head. "Stay there. I'll get the flannel and clean up." He walked over to the small ensuite and rinsed out a cloth under warm water. "Our life isn't normal. I went into this visit, like you did, knowing both sides of our lives would collide sooner rather than later. I had hoped it would be later." He turned to Simon. "You know what I see when I look at you?"

Simon swallowed. Although he'd heard Ben's words before, he never tired of hearing them. "I know what I see when I look at you." Simon smiled. "A sexy man who isn't afraid to stand up for anyone who needs help, or speak his mind in defence of the people he loves. You've risked your life for me on more occasions than I want to remember, and I'm humbled by that. And honoured that you love me and want me in your life."

"Hey, you stole my speech." Ben sounded husky. He sat on the bed next to Simon and gently cleaned him up, then himself. "I'll grab a towel for that wet spot, unless you want to change the sheets?"

"A towel will be fine." Simon waited until Ben had hung up the flannel, then moved at vampire speed so he was standing next to Ben in the bathroom. He put his arms around Ben, holding him tightly. "Come back to bed, my love."

"My vampire." Ben had tears in his eyes. He caressed Simon's cheek. "I know you've probably shortened your life being with me, but although I know it's selfish, it's also kind of a relief. If I don't... I don't want to abandon you to a long life alone."

They both knew the risk of that. And Simon's history. Last time he'd lost someone he'd loved... it hadn't been good. Even so, he wouldn't chance Ben's relationship with his family because of it. Especially now he'd seen that relationship up close.

"I wouldn't want that either," Simon whispered hoarsely. "Come back to bed, please," he said. "I'm feeling a little selfish too tonight, and I want to spend the rest of the night in your arms."

Ben smiled. "You never have to ask for that. It's what I want too."

~

Ben woke with a start to the sensation of a hand over his mouth.

"Quiet," Simon whispered. "There's someone in the house. Stay here while I deal with it." He removed his hand and quickly pulled on pyjama bottoms.

"Granddad?" Ben whispered back. Whoever was in the house must be human, or Simon wouldn't risk being overheard by another supernatural.

"Still asleep. I can hear his heartbeat, slow and steady." Simon paused at the bedroom door. "Stay put, but if you don't, please be careful."

Ben grinned. Simon knew him so well. He reached for some clothing, ready to follow Simon down the stairs. No point in calling the police until they knew what was going on, and whether it was something that needed reporting.

"I suggest you stop what you're doing right now." Simon's British accent sounded stronger than usual, a sure sign he wasn't impressed. "You're trespassing."

Two men dressed in black stared up at him, then exchanged glances with each other. "I thought we'd only have to deal with the old man living here," he hissed loudly.

"You were wrong," Simon said calmly. "What are you gentlemen looking for exactly?"

The man who hadn't spoken chuckled. "You're hardly more than a kid. Stay where you are, and we won't hurt you."

Ben winced. The idiot was going to regret that. Worse than underestimating Simon, he'd already added to how pissed off he was by presuming he was younger than he looked. He crept to the top of the stairs, wanting to see for himself how this played out.

"I told you to keep out of this," Simon said, not taking his gaze off the two intruders, although the comment was directed at Ben. "One day you'll actually do what I ask."

"Huh." Intruder One reached into his pocket.

"I wouldn't do that." Simon suddenly stood behind him, picked him up, and threw him against the wall.

The man slid down, not quite unconscious, but clutching his arm and groaning.

"I don't know about you, but I'm enjoying this," Frank whispered from behind Ben.

"Stay here!" Ben hissed and crept down the stairs.

Simon snorted and rolled his eyes. "Do what I say, not what I do."

Intruder Two swallowed. "Oh fuck, you're the vampire." He backed away, holding out his hands in a familiar pattern.

"How quaint," Simon said. "Is that meant to be a cross?" He closed the distance between them in a blur, grabbed Intruder Two by his collar, and held him up at arm's length. The man flailed against the grip that held him, and kicked at the air. "Who are you working for, and why did they send you here?"

Intruder One struggled to his feet. Ben grabbed the heavy antique iron his granddad kept on the shelf at the bottom of the stairs and brandished it at the man. "I believe my husband asked a question. I suggest you answer it before you really piss him off."

Simon shot him a smile. "Exactly." He let go of the man he held, who dropped to the floor with a thud and started backpedalling on his arse for the door. "Let's start with the easy question first, hmm? Who sent you?"

"If I tell you that, they'll kill me." Intruder One's teeth chattered. He looked around wildly.

Simon crouched in front of him. "And you think I won't?" He glanced at Ben and dropped his fangs at the same time his eyes went completely brown.

Ben took a sharp intake of breath. Fuck, he loved it when Simon did that. "The ninja vampire routine already turned me on," he said in a low tone only Simon would hear. "You didn't need to show your vampire just for me."

Simon grinned and turned his attention back to Intruder Two, who had started to crawl towards the backdoor. He wouldn't kill the intruders, but they didn't need to know that yet.

"I asked you a question," Simon growled, facing the man and helpfully giving Ben a clear view of bad-arse vampire.

The man Ben was guarding tried to move. Ben swung the iron, taking the man's legs from under him. These guys were total amateurs.

"It's our first assignment," Intruder Two babbled. "We were only supposed to break in and grab whatever information that other vampire left. It's past dawn, so you were supposed to be asleep. Or dead. Or whatever it is your lot do."

"My lot?" Simon's mouth twitched. "I was asleep until you idiots woke me. I don't appreciate my sleep being disturbed." He raised an eyebrow. They'd taken the envelope upstairs with them to read through before bed. "Who sent you? I'm not going to repeat myself again."

"We don't answer to your kind," the other man spat.

Ben sighed. "You're part of that Human Destiny crap, aren't you?"

The man's eyes widened. "How did you know about us?" He took a deep breath. "We won't let you and your kind take over the world. We're onto you and your nefarious plans."

"Nefarious?" Ben choked back a laugh. "Seriously?"

Simon shot him a warning glare. "Just because they're

incompetent idiots doesn't mean their employers are." He picked up the man he'd questioned and dumped him on the floor next to his companion. "Once you're released, you will go back to your employers and give them a message. Firstly, if they are responsible for the death or attempted murder of anyone in the supernatural community, they will be held accountable." He leaned in and bared his fangs. "And secondly, Frank Connell and his family are under my protection. If any harm comes to any of them, I will hunt you down and I will kill you." He smiled grimly. "Slowly."

The two men shivered. Now Ben could see the other man up close, he realised he couldn't be more than twenty. The other guy wasn't that much older either.

"But you're releasing us?" The older man said hopefully, almost begging.

"No, *I'm* not." Simon nodded towards Ben. "Find some rope or something to secure them with. Then call the police." He leaned in close. "Repeat any of this to anyone else other than your employers and I will deny all of it and make life very difficult for you and anyone close to you." He straightened. "Rope? Please? I'd prefer to get dressed before the constables arrive, and I suspect you would too."

"Of course, Professor Hawthorne." The police officer closed his notebook. "Are you sure you don't want to press charges?"

Simon shook his head. "I suspect they're more misguided than anything else, and this is probably the first time they were stupid enough to attempt a break-in when the owner of the house was home." He met the gaze of the perps in question and smiled, then wrinkled his nose when he caught a whiff of a familiar scent. "Oh dear," he said softly. "I think one of them just soiled himself."

The second police officer shook her head and handed Simon her card. "Contact us if you change your mind or think of anything else you want to tell us." She nodded towards Ben and Frank. "You and your family take care and stay safe." Her fellow officer led the two intruders from the house, then she followed behind.

"Are you sure that was a good idea?" Ben asked once they were alone. He'd been uncharacteristically quiet while Simon had spoken to the police.

"Yes. I've contacted Garrick, and he will keep an eye on them. Hopefully, they'll go running back to their employers, so we can find them."

Frank sipped his tea. "I might have to leave the earplugs out tonight in case they try again."

"Granddad!" Ben handed Simon a cup of coffee made the way he liked it. Being married to an ex-barista definitely had its perks. "What if we hadn't been here? Inexperienced guys like that are more likely to get you killed because they react rather than think."

"It's been a long time since I've seen Simon take down someone." Frank cradled his cup and grinned. "Those young men totally regretted underestimating you."

"They knew there was a vampire living here, but not that it was me." Simon shook his head when Ben offered him a slice of toast. "No, thanks, I'll eat later, so feel free to smear some of that disgusting vegemite on it if you want it yourself." He glanced at the door. "Unfortunately, they also now know who I am, but I'd prefer that than them making a mistake and hunting a human." He put down his cup. "Your sister's here."

"Maddie?" Ben frowned.

"No, Tash. She sounds quite... agitated." Simon got up and

headed for the door, but waited until she'd knocked before answering it. "Good morning, Tash," he said politely. "We're having breakfast. Please feel free to join us."

"Were you going to tell any of us you were burgled last night?" Tash got straight to the point, much like Ben always did. "Or that you caught them in the act?"

"The police have arrested them, and the situation is under control," Simon said calmly. "Ben's just made a pot of coffee if you'd like some. It's very good."

Tash glared at Simon. "They told me you didn't even press charges!"

"Sometimes that's not the deterrent that is needed." Simon carefully skirted around her comments. "Ben threatened them with an antique iron. Very impressive. I'm not surprised they surrendered so easily."

Ben choked on his toast.

"It *was* very impressive," Frank mumbled. "Come have a seat, dear." He patted the empty spot on the sofa. "Ben, pour your sister some coffee. She looks like she needs some."

"What I need is to know why they broke in here." Tash's heartbeat was elevated, and her expression a mix of anger and worry. "All my instincts are screaming at me that this wasn't a coincidence, rather than burglars thinking Granddad lived alone so he wouldn't be able to stop them taking his valuables."

Simon raised an eyebrow. "This?" he asked, keeping his tone even. He had hoped not to have to confront her about her suspicions until after they'd solved this case.

"Tash, this isn't the time—" Ben started to say.

"What are you involved in?" Tash kept watching Simon, although her question was directed at Ben. "You got lucky last night, but what if there's a next time?"

"You're thinking this is connected to you seeing us with your partner yesterday?" Ben shook his head. "We're the good guys here." He hesitated before continuing. Simon didn't interrupt. Ben knew his sister better and how she'd react, so he should take the lead in the conversation. "I've only met Garrick the once, but I got the feeling he is too."

"Garrick?" Tash took a gulp of coffee. "You're already on a first-name basis with him?"

"He's a colleague," Simon said quickly.

"You're a history professor! How could you be colleagues?"

"I think you need to calm down and listen." Frank put a hand on her knee and shook his head. "You always react with your heart rather than your head, and you have good instincts." His tone grew sterner. "But this is my home, Tash, and Ben and Simon are your family. Family is about trust, and listening. I had hoped I'd taught you that much when you were growing up." He shot Ben an equally disapproving look. "Both of you."

Simon felt a moment's panic. His, not Ben's. He wasn't ready to tell Ben's family the truth. They needed to exchange their vows, so Ben at least would have that memory. He swallowed, suddenly hungry for more than coffee.

He glanced at Ben.

Help.

Ben sat on the sofa opposite his sister, yanked Simon down next to him, and met Tash's gaze straight on. "Yes, we are involved in something," he said evenly. "But *we're* not in a position to tell you about it. When we are, *we* will." He elbowed Simon. "Won't we?"

"Umm..." Simon felt Ben's disapproval loud and clear after his incorrect response. "Yes, of course we will."

"Simon and I have helped the police with some cases back in Boggslake," Ben continued brightly. "Don't worry, we're fine, and it is a long story, but not one for today."

Frank nodded approvingly.

Tash didn't look convinced. "Why? Neither of you are cops. I know Ben works for the department there, but it's a liaison position, which isn't the same thing."

"When I met Simon, he shared his house with a police detective and the city medical examiner. Some of the cases they worked on ended up coming home." Ben shivered, and Simon put his arm around them. They'd had a few too many close calls, even before Ben had been shot. "He's also helped out with some antiquities thefts. I didn't tell you because I didn't want you to worry."

"In recent years, we've been working with Detective Anson Larson. I'm sure if you contacted him, he'd confirm it." Ben stared at her defiantly. "Unless you think I'm pulling all this out of my arse?"

"No, of course not." Tash's expression softened. "Look, I'm sorry. I'm just worried. You're family and families worry about each other."

"Yeah, we do." Ben smiled and threaded his fingers through Simon's. Simon squeezed his hand.

"We're helping Garrick find and authenticate a historical document." Simon repeated the story he'd told Ray.

"And the matter is a bit… sensitive… so we can't share any details," Ben lowered his voice. "Besides, can you imagine if Mum found out about what we've been doing before I told her?"

Tash shuddered. "Yeah, I totally get that." She looked at their joined hands and smiled, then her eyes widened, and her gaze fixed on Simon. "There's nothing else you want to tell me? About… Simon's past or anything?"

"His past is his business," Ben said coolly, "until he's ready to share it. Which he will very soon."

Simon followed her gaze and swore under his breath. The edge of his cardigan sleeve had slipped down and uncovered the scars on his wrist when he shuffled closer to Ben.

"Simon?" Ben elbowed him again.

"Yes," Simon said quietly. He didn't want to lie to Ben's family, although explaining those scars didn't mean he had to tell them *everything*.

Panic rose. He shoved it down.

"Don't you need to get to work, dear?" Frank took Tash's empty cup from her.

"Oh, shit, is that the time?" Tash stood and flashed Simon a look that clearly said he'd had a stay in execution, but she wasn't done yet. "Have a good day. Anything interesting planned?"

"Yeah, we're going to meet a friend in Wellington today, then take a look at an old church."

"Sounds like fun." Tash hugged Frank.

Ben stood and hugged her too.

"Be careful," she whispered. She glanced at Simon, who involuntarily took a step back.

"He's not really into hugs," Ben said quickly. "See you later, Tash. 'Bye."

"I thought you weren't going to keep the truth from your family," Simon said when Tash had gone.

"I'm not, but I don't want her getting involved in this. It's dangerous."

"She's a police detective," Simon reminded him, "and you've mentioned several times that she's good at her job. That position brings with it a certain amount of danger."

"Yeah, but for now, she's not involved in anything super-natural."

Frank glanced at both of them. "I'm off for my daily constitutional." He grabbed his walking stick, coat, and hat, and disappeared out the front door.

"I'm not sure we can stop her from becoming involved. She's too much like you, and that terrifies me."

"It should." Ben watched his grandfather bend to pat the

cat on the front step. "And I meant what I said. We *will* be telling her, and the rest of my family, the truth before we go back to Boggslake. It's just a matter of when."

CHAPTER NINE

"I still can't believe Wayland Real Estate is the pack business," Ben said in a low voice as Simon held the front door open for him. "Their firm has been around for years, and they have branches throughout the country. I think my parents bought their house through them."

"Not being obvious is rather the point," Simon reminded him, following Ben into the building.

"I've taken photos of this place too." Ben had noticed it immediately when he'd started university, and not only because he passed the brick building on his way up Salamanca Road every day. "It's always had an old and interesting vibe about it, like it has its own story to tell."

"It probably does. The Waylands settled in Wellington during colonial days, and built this in the early 1900s. This building has been their business premises since early 1913, shortly after the Land Agents Act came into effect."

"You've done your research."

"Of course," Simon said. "I'm a history professor. It's part of my job. *And* I like to know who I'm dealing with."

They made their way to the second floor, bypassing the

usual business front of the company, the elevator door opening onto a smaller reception area tastefully decorated with cream-coloured walls and photographs of older houses around the city. Some were in colour, others in black and white. One very old photo caught Ben's attention, and he couldn't resist taking a closer look at it.

"Very cool," he murmured. The caption confirmed it was an example of the glass plate photography in popular use until the 1920s. "I love the otherworldly effect it's captured. Makes it look like the house is haunted." Ben had long wanted to have a go at taking one himself but, given the process used silver salts, it wasn't worth the risk to Simon.

"We're here to see the alpha," Simon said politely to the receptionist. "He's expecting us. My name is Simon Hawthorne, and this is—"

"Detective Frater warned us you'd be coming." The receptionist glanced up at Ben and his eyes glowed gold. "He didn't tell us you were bringing a human to the meeting. He'll have to wait out here." He growled. "Or better still, he can leave."

"Hey, wait a minute..." Ben read the guy's nametag. "... Knox. Good thing I'm not a client, yeah? If you treated all humans like this, you wouldn't be staying in business very long."

A broad-shouldered, red-haired man strode over to the desk. He glanced at Knox and raised an eyebrow. Knox lowered his gaze immediately.

"I'm sorry, Uncle Holt," he murmured.

Given the way Knox had reacted, this guy must be the pack alpha. Ben had never thought much of the werewolf hierarchy, especially after how the pack in Boggslake had treated Lucas and Charlie.

Holt Wayland held out his hand to Simon. "The council insisted on this meeting, although I reminded them we have protected this city for years without the help of others in our community."

Simon shook his proffered hand. "It is not just the were-wolves in your community at risk, Mr Wayland. I'm hoping we can find out who is behind this and stop them before anyone else is harmed or killed by their actions." His displeasure with Knox's reaction to Ben came across loud and clear in his tone. "My husband and I are here to help. We have had some experience in these situations."

Wayland's gaze flickered over to Ben and back to Simon. His eyes glowed gold like Knox's. "Of course you have," he murmured, "although you're obviously completely unaware of this *situation*."

"Excuse me?" Simon asked.

"I'll get straight to the point, Mr Hawthorne."

"*Professor* Hawthorne," Simon corrected, "and we'd prefer you did."

"I'd prefer we handle this ourselves rather than work with vampires, but unfortunately, the council does have some authority over us." Wayland shrugged. "We did sign the Supernatural Treaty, after all. But the council ruling did *not* include working with humans, and it's becoming clear they're behind this—"

"My husband definitely is not a part of this," Simon said firmly, "and you owe him an apology at the very least." He glared at Wayland, and his fangs dropped.

Ben sighed. "You need to get this sorted, so we can stop the killing—"

"*Attempted* murder," Wayland corrected.

"Ben's correct," Simon said. "There *has* been a murder. A vampire was found dead yesterday." He dropped any pretence of politeness.

"Simon's right." Ben took a deep breath when Wayland shot him a look of pure disdain. "I had nothing to do with this. I might be human, but I'm married to a vampire if you hadn't noticed, so I'm hardly likely to cause any trouble in a community I'm very much a part of."

Wayland met Simon's gaze for a moment, then addressed Ben. "This is a sensitive situation, Mr Leyton. Perhaps it would be better if you waited out here, rather than igniting an already volatile situation with your presence."

"I don't think—"

Ben put his hand on Simon's shoulder. "Go have your meeting. You're not going to get any sense out of anyone if I'm here. I'll meet up with you later in town when you're done, okay?"

"It's not—" Simon's tone betrayed his concern.

"I'll stay safe, I promise." Ben squeezed Simon's shoulder, turned on his heel, and headed for the elevator.

"You still owe us both an apology," Simon said coldly to Wayland.

Ben wasn't sure if he should be relieved or disappointed that he wouldn't be privy to the rest of the conversation. Werewolves seemed to be the same the world over. They might have signed that bloody treaty, but they never hesitated to make it obvious that they'd done so under duress.

He dug out his phone once he walked out onto the street. "Hey, Ange," he said when she picked up. "You still in town? I'm at a loose end for a while and wondered how you and Josh are going with your investigation?" He grinned, nodding at her response, although she couldn't see him. "Great. I'm up by the uni and about to walk down to the city centre. I'll meet you there."

Simon watched the elevator close behind Ben and shoved down his anger. "If we are working together, we can't afford to give into any discrimination against the different factions in our community. The council is a representation of my kind, yours, *and* humans. Presuming that a radical sect is indicative of an entire species is not only foolish, but dangerous." He narrowed his eyes. "I had hoped your community here would be a little more enlightened."

"People are scared." Wayland led him down a short hallway. When they passed offices, werewolves working in them glanced at him, their eyes glowing gold for an instant. "The old teachings are not easily forgotten, especially when emotions run high."

"Your pack is not used to visiting vampires in their territory." Simon kept his tone polite, yet firm. If any of Wayland's pack thought Simon was a threat to their alpha, and attacked, he would be no match for them. Vampires might be more agile, but what werewolves lacked in that, they more than made up for in strength.

"And especially not vampires who stink so thoroughly of human, like you do." Wayland opened the door to the meeting room at the end of the hallway and ushered Simon inside.

A group of four werewolves sat around a table, Garrick being one of them. He glanced up when Simon took a seat opposite the alpha.

"Please bring Professor Hawthorne up to speed, Garrick," Wayland instructed.

"Kerwin passed away this morning from a combination of silver and aconite poisoning," Garrick said, "so we are hunting a murderer."

"One or more murderers," Simon reminded him, "considering the vampire councillor was also found dead at his home yesterday. Do you have any leads on Erik Sedway's whereabouts?" He hadn't received an update from Josh about their own investigations and, with the pack's current view on humans, wouldn't have shared that information anyway.

Garrick glanced at Wayland, who nodded. "We've been focusing our efforts on the supernatural community because we're more at risk," Garrick said.

"Is that an assumption, or do you have proof?" Simon raised an eyebrow. He'd talk to Garrick about that later when he wasn't in a meeting where he had to defer to the pack alpha.

"Information," Garrick said after a few moments. "I have a few leads I'm following, and I'm not at liberty to divulge my sources." Simon had already spoken to him about the break-in the night before, but it wouldn't do to let the alpha know they were already running their own investigation and, by doing so, give him the opportunity to shut it down.

"Our different communities exist side by side," Simon pointed out. "If someone is killing supernaturals, humans could get caught up in the crossfire. Sedway could be in hiding, or he might already be dead." The air of indifference about the fate of humans was beginning to annoy him. "This isn't just about keeping ourselves safe. If you're wrong about supernaturals being the only targets, it becomes much more difficult to hide our existence from the general population. Do we really want them knowing we're living among them, and risk the mass panic that would likely occur? Most humans believe the myths we've perpetuated over the centuries. They could easily be used against us as propaganda." He glanced around the table. The two younger werewolves kept their gaze locked on him, but didn't move. Were they merely observers, or there to ensure the vampire in their midst behaved?

One of the other werewolves cleared his throat. He looked older than Wayland, although that didn't make it any easier to judge his age. While werewolves aged more slowly than vampires, they still lived much longer than humans. "We have been keeping this city safe since we arrived here, and for the most part, without the inference of the council. There have only been two instances when vampires have stepped up to help against a threat. One of those vampires is now dead, and the other... I believe you know of Professor Milne's tendency to lie low as well as I do." His mouth turned up in a thin smile. "I suggested my son agree to this meeting because of a debt I owe to Victor Rochford, and I wish to see his killer brought to justice. If we find whoever is responsible for this first, they will face pack justice."

"If the killer is human, the law states—"

"The pack *is* law." The older Wayland cocked his head to one side. "Rupert Milne visited you last night. He would have told you about the group calling themselves Human Destiny." It wasn't phrased like a question.

"Yes, but—"

"The vampires on the council might have given us assistance in the past," Holt Wayland said, "but the same can't be said of the humans. To reiterate my father's words, we do not owe them anything."

So, the older man *was* Hedley Wayland. He'd brought his pack out from England when he was a young man, and it appeared he still had the last word in important decisions, despite his son being the alpha, at least in name. Usually a new alpha didn't take over until the old one died, but for some reason, Hedley had decided to buck tradition. All that meant, in this case, was that he'd retained his power by using his son as his mouthpiece.

Interesting.

Instead of unwisely commenting aloud on their pack structure, Simon opened his mouth to point out that many advances in science and technology, not to mention the arts, had come from humans, then decided to follow his better judgement. "Well, then, we'd better find whoever is responsible first, hadn't we?"

Holt growled. Hedley placed a hand on his arm and chuckled. "Rupert told me you were intelligent, although I had wondered when I'd heard you'd mated with a human. It appears I was mistaken." He exchanged a glance with his son before continuing. "Our traditions here in the colonies are a little different because our community is smaller and spread out across the country. Each councillor has a list of the supernaturals under their jurisdiction. We are concerned that all the Wellington lists may be missing."

"Bloody hell." Simon swore before he realised what he'd done. "My apologies for my language."

"I assure you, we all share your sentiment." Hedley stood and held out his hand. "Find these killers before they strike again. I suspect the councillors were targeted because of the information they are charged to protect. If Human Destiny has found those registers, this will most likely escalate and soon. I'd prefer that didn't happen." He gripped Simon's arm tightly when they shook hands and yanked him half over the table. "I know you and Garrick are already working together, and he *will* be relaying any updates back to my son. Try to protect any of these Human Destiny humans and things will not go well for you." He let go of Simon and met his gaze, his eyes flashing gold. "Or *your* human."

Simon's fangs dropped. He met Hedley's gaze straight on. "Threaten my *husband* again and things will not go well for you either."

The other two werewolves gasped and pushed their chairs back. One of them growled.

"I mean you no harm," Simon said calmly, "as long as no harm comes to what is mine." He paused and waited for Hedley's reaction.

As he expected, Hedley smiled. "Your reputation precedes

you, Professor. I suspect we will enjoy working together. Please keep me apprised of the situation."

Holt slid a business card across the table. "In case you need to contact me directly. We already know how to contact you... and your husband." He waited until Simon had picked up his card, then added, "if Human Destiny has detailed information about us, more deaths might be the least of our problems."

"Good morning, gentleman." Simon nodded politely, then turned and walked out of the room.

Garrick caught up with him out on the street. "You're either very brave or very stupid."

"Or perhaps a little of both?" Simon never reacted well when someone dared threaten Ben. "It does appear though that we'd better find these Human Destiny idiots first or we'll have a lot more to clean up than two, or maybe three, dead councillors."

Ben climbed the lane to the music shop, pausing at the second flight of steps to check that Powers, his favourite comic shop, hadn't closed down. He'd stop in there on the way back, although he probably wouldn't buy anything. He'd been spoilt by the cheaper prices in the States and would be heading back there in a few weeks anyway with a suitcase full of the few things his parents hadn't shipped over to him yet.

He'd forgotten how steep this street was and regretted choosing to walk down to Lambton Quay first and then up to the shop. At least the exercise had drained some of his anger. Bloody werewolves and their politics. The supernatural community mirrored their human counterparts in many ways, although they hated anyone telling them that. Still, it was a change to earn their distrust because he was human rather than stinking of vampire. He was totally over that one.

Unable to resist a peek in the window, he caught the eye of the owner and waved. Zeke Powis waved back and grinned. Ben hadn't been in there in years, but he and Zeke kept in touch through Ange. She'd dated Zeke for a while, and although it hadn't worked out, they'd remained friends. Ben still missed their group's monthly D&D games and hadn't got around to finding one in Boggslake. He'd thought about it a few times, then decided it mirrored his reality a little too much. He needed to revisit the idea. Roleplaying taking down evil supernaturals without the risk of being killed for real hadn't completely lost its appeal.

He missed his friends more than the game. Perhaps he should organise a time when Olly—their dungeon master—wasn't working at The Taniwha so they could have one last quest for old time's sake.

The thought of Simon playing D&D made him smile. He shook his head. Never going to happen. Simon still didn't get why Ben loved graphic novels and superheroes so much. He'd read a few of them and asked questions, but never caught the enthusiasm despite Ben's best efforts to convert him.

His phone buzzed with a text. Ange and Josh were running late, and at least ten minutes away. Finding somewhere to park the car in the middle of Wellington was still a pain in the arse. Ben hadn't missed that in Boggslake which, despite being a city, didn't have a lot of people. He only drove his car when the weather was too bad to bike, and when he needed to for work, and rarely got behind the wheel of Simon's Aston Martin.

The Right Note music shop was only a few steps down from The Terrace. Considering they sold pianos, that was probably a good thing. Ben shuddered at the thought of trying to shift one of those down several steep steps. He peered inside. The lights were on, and the sign on the window proclaimed they were open for business. Ange and Josh hadn't tracked down Sedway, but his shop had reopened the day before.

An old-fashioned bell jingled when Ben walked through the door.

A man in his late twenties looked up and smiled. "Hi, can I help you with anything in particular, or are you just browsing?" He was too young and the wrong build to be Erik Sedway. The guy met Ben's gaze and raised an eyebrow. His eyes were an unusual shade of dark green, and something about him made Ben uneasy, although he couldn't figure out why.

"Classical CDs," Ben blurted out. "I'm looking for classical CDs. Sorry for staring. I didn't mean to be rude. I was expecting Erik and seeing you here took me by surprise."

"Ah, so you're a regular here?" The guy nodded like that explained everything. "Uncle Erik's gone fishing. I was supposed to open for him last week, but my phone played up, so I didn't get his message until a couple of days ago."

"Fishing?" Ben didn't believe that for a moment. "And umm... I guess I used to be? I haven't been in the shop for a while because I've been overseas. Your uncle's been a fixture of the place for years."

Another man, around his own age, glanced up, watching their conversation, then returned to leafing through a pile of sheet music.

"No problem." Sedway's nephew shrugged. "I'm Ash." He lowered his voice. "I haven't been here for years either, so if you need anything I guess we'll be looking for it together."

"Your uncle didn't leave you instructions?"

"Yeah, somewhere, but I haven't found them yet." Ash shrugged again. "Unfortunately, he's down the Marlborough

Sounds somewhere and out of mobile range. He'll turn up again when he's ready, I guess."

"How convenient," Ben muttered. Either Sedway had taken off before the council had tried to get hold of him, or because of it. Ben didn't blame him for the latter. "Any idea when he'll be back?"

"You're a friend of his?" Ash didn't sound convinced. "He didn't mention that anyone might come looking for him." He eyed Ben up and down. "I can tell him you were asking after him if you'd like."

"Okay, thanks." Ben hesitated, sure the other guy in the shop was watching them with a little too much interest. Ash might be their only way to contact his uncle, so Ben couldn't afford not to give his details. "I'm Ben. My husband needs to talk to your uncle about some work-related stuff. Do you have some paper? I'll give you his mobile number so Erik can call him."

He was only stretching the truth a little, right? And if they weren't already too late and Sedway was next in line to be killed, better to tell a few white lies and save his life.

"Okay. I'm not sure when that will be, though."

"That's fine." Ben wrote down Simon's name and number, then returned the paper and pen to Ash. "Something urgent has come up and we're only here for a few weeks so the sooner your uncle contacts him the better."

"No problem." Ash shoved the paper into the till. "I'll message him tonight, so he'll get it once he's back in range." He raised his voice. "You still okay over there? I can check to see what else we have if you haven't found what you're looking for yet."

"I'm still looking," the dark-haired guy said, his accent sliding between Kiwi and Australian. "Thanks."

"So, classical music?" Ash asked Ben.

"What?"

"You said you were looking for classical music." Ash sounded amused at Ben's slip.

"Oh yeah. Umm, I just want to have a look through what you have." Ben grinned. "Simon's got so much of it I doubt I'd find something he doesn't have, but figured I'd look anyway."

"A fan, is he?" Ash led Ben to the back of the shop. "We have quite an extensive collection, best in the region apparently. Uncle Erik has several clients like your husband."

"Collectors who have pretty much everything, but still pounce on anything new?" Ben asked. Simon might not be into technology, but he still had a kick-arse stereo system and more classical music and jazz CDs than Ben wanted to count.

Ash chuckled. "Yeah, exactly." He indicated the bins on the rear wall. "Perhaps he'd like some of his favourites on vinyl."

"He's got an extensive collection of those too, and they'd take more room in our luggage." Ben would have an even harder job finding a vinyl Simon didn't already own. He'd bought most of them when they were originally released. "Thanks for the suggestion, though."

The door opened. "Ben!" Ange walked over to him. "Sorry, we're late."

The guy browsing the sheet music looked up at the sound of her voice, obviously recognising her. He returned the books he'd been looking at to their shelf and headed for the door. Ange turned, her eyes widening when she spotted him.

Josh collided with him on the way in. Both men stared at each other, then Josh broke into a grin. "Hey, Cody. I didn't expect to see you here."

CHAPTER TEN

Cody dropped his panicked demeanour between one breath and the next. "Josh, hey. What are you doing here?" He slipped his arm around Josh's waist and kissed him on the cheek.

"Meeting a friend." Josh glanced over at Ben, who shook his head, and nodded towards Ash.

"We're going out for coffee while I wait for my husband. Do you want to join us, Cody?" Ben not only wanted to meet Cody, but get Simon's opinion of him. Josh was a good guy, despite his earlier reaction to Simon being a vampire, and didn't need some idiot taking advantage of him. Not that Ben had proof of that, but something about Cody made his spidey sense tingle, and not in a good way.

Ange elbowed him and dragged him over to the doorway. "We should get out of the shop doorway. There's a café not far away that serves great coffee." She glanced at Ben. "It might even be up to your standard."

"Maybe." Ben stuck out his hand. "Ben Leyton. Good to finally meet you, Cody."

"Cody Prentice." Cody had a firm grip and an easy smile.

"I've heard a lot about you from these two." His accent sounded pure Kiwi, the glimmer of Australian vowels nowhere in sight. "And sure, that would be great."

Ange scurried ahead to lead the way to the cafe, taking Ben with her. "No go at the shop, hmm?" she asked.

"*Apparently* he's gone fishing." Ben glanced behind them. Josh and Cody had slowed down. Josh laughed at something Cody said, then ruffled his hair.

"That's convenient." Ange followed Ben's gaze. "Those two look good together, don't you think? Josh has been on his own for so long. He deserves some happiness." She lowered her voice. "Sedway doesn't have many friends, only acquaintances, and none of them knew he wasn't around. Who's the guy running the shop?"

"His nephew. Not sure he knows anything, but I'd like Simon to go pay him a visit to check."

"You think he's some kind of... you know?" Ange asked.

"I'm pretty good at picking people like Simon and Josh out, but... I don't know." Ben shrugged. "I'm a bit on edge since the break-in and getting chucked out of the meeting this morning didn't help. It's probably nothing."

Ange stepped in front of him to stop him in his tracks. "Break-in? What *break-in?*"

"Umm... I was waiting until we had coffee before I told you."

She frowned, and Ben could tell she wasn't buying his excuse.

"A couple of guys broke into Granddad's last night. Simon sorted them out really fast." Ben's face heated at the memory. God, he loved seeing Simon go all hard-arse vampire. "Then we called the police."

"You're both okay?" Ange relaxed after Ben nodded. "We need a proper team meeting. There's more you're not telling me, yeah?"

"Yeah," Ben plastered on a smile when Josh and Cody caught up. "Later."

Josh frowned. "Definitely later," he murmured in Ben's ear when he brushed past him on his way into the café. He would have heard their conversation with his way better than human werewolf hearing. "I've been here before. The coffee *is* great."

"Coffee's on me," Cody said when they found a table. "It's not that often I get to meet Josh's friends, so I insist."

"Okay, thanks." Ben pulled out his phone. "I'll have a flat white. Excuse me for a moment. I need to let Simon know where we are." From what he'd felt from Simon, the meeting had gone well. Not. While his and Simon's bond was weaker than one between two vampires, and Simon's had a stronger sense of Ben, the echo of any intense emotion from Simon came through loud and clear.

"I'll go help Cody order," Ange said. "You want the usual, Josh?" After Josh nodded, she followed Cody to the counter and distracted him with conversation.

"Sedway's gone fishing?" Josh asked Ben. "His letterbox at home is full of junk mail, and I saw a half-drunk cup of coffee on the bench when we peered in the window. Looks to me like he heard something or someone was heading his way and ran."

"That's what I figure too. His nephew said he was out of mobile range, but not sure I believe that. This guy's been on the council a while, so surely he's used to weird stuff." Ben shrugged. "I'm not sure that stuff is the problem, though." He could deal with supernaturals because they were easier to spot. Humans, not so much. Depending on how widespread the Human Destiny infestation is, anyone could be a part of them. "Watch yourself."

"I always do." Josh shuffled his chair closer to Cody's when he sat down.

Cody glanced between Josh and Ben, but fortunately didn't ask what he'd missed.

"So, how did you two meet?" Ben asked to fill the awkward silence.

"Work do." Josh flushed. "First time I've gone to one of those in years, but someone thought I should make an effort to be sociable once in a while." He shot Ange a pointed look.

"You're a librarian?" Ben asked Cody.

Cody chuckled. "No, I'm a sales rep. I work Sundays, so today's part of my weekend." He slipped his hand into Josh's and they linked fingers. "I play fiddle in a Scottish country music band." His voice softened. "I spotted Josh when he walked in, but we didn't connect at first."

"I went to their next gig," Josh admitted. "Couldn't stop thinking about the hot fiddler I'd seen. He asked me out for a drink, and six months later we're still together."

"I think they're very sweet together," Ange said to Ben. "Cody's a bloody good fiddler too."

Simon entered the café and approached their table.

"Simon likes music, right? His next gig is while you're still here. We could all go together."

"I'm not sure he—"

"I'd like to go." Simon bent to kiss Ben's cheek. "Hello, you must be Cody, Josh's boyfriend. I'm Simon Hawthorne, Ben's husband." He held out his hand. "Nice to meet you."

"I've never heard you listen to Scottish fiddle music," Ben said.

Simon smiled. "I have an extensive collection. It does take me a while to cycle through it. I knew someone once who played the violin, and yes, I know fiddle music is a little different. It's a beautiful instrument." He shook Cody's hand. "I need to order coffee. I'll be right back."

He headed for the counter and spent a few moments conversing with the barista. She smiled, then blushed. Ben rolled his eyes at her attempt to flirt with Simon, who politely rebuffed her, handing over his payment card with the hand that bore his wedding ring.

"Your husband seems like a nice guy." Cody watched Simon walk back over to them. "He's not what I expected."

"Oh, and what *were* you expecting?" Simon took the empty chair next to Ben's, and reached for his hand under the table.

Cody looked embarrassed he'd been overheard. "I'm sorry, that didn't come out the way I intended."

"Apology accepted." Simon chuckled. "I'm a little more... formal... than Ben. Our upbringing was rather different, and it shows on occasion."

"You're not the jeans and T-shirt guy I was expecting," Cody admitted.

"Simon doesn't own any jeans or T-shirts," Ben said. Although they were on holiday, Simon had still packed his usual trousers and shirts, despite Ben's insistence he might need to dress down a little. According to Simon, casual wear meant venturing out without his suit jacket. "He's improved my dress sense since we've been together, but I've had no luck degrading his. I think it's rather hot, actually."

Ange rolled her eyes. "Opposites attract and all that."

Their conversation paused when the waitress delivered their coffees. Simon had ordered his usual cappuccino, and Cody had ordered the same, much to Ben's surprise. He was generally spot on when figuring out coffee preferences, but he'd been way out with Cody.

"So, Cody, how long have you been in New Zealand?" Ben asked.

Cody coughed, his coffee going down the wrong way. "What makes you think I'm not Kiwi?"

"There is a hint of Australian in your vowels," Ben explained. "It's not obvious, but it's there. Grandad's

Australian, although he's been here for years and sounds Kiwi most of the time."

"His dad's Aussie," Josh said quickly. "Cody has gone to visit him every year since his parents split up."

"I guess I'm a bit of a mix with my mum being Kiwi." Cody turned to Simon. "You're definitely British."

Simon chuckled. "I never saw the point of changing my accent, although I know those who have. I do get ribbed for it on occasion, and for owning a right-hand drive car in the US, but I like to keep some reminders of my origins." He squeezed Ben's knee.

"What do you do for a job, Simon?" Cody asked.

"I'm head of the history department at Lakeview University in Boggslake." Simon sipped his coffee. "I enjoy lecturing, and we get a fair few students come from around the country for the courses we offer. Teaching them about the past is very satisfying. I think it's important we don't forget it, don't you?"

"Those who forget history are doomed to repeat it," said Josh softly.

"Exactly." Simon glanced at his watch. "I should call a taxi in about half an hour so we have plenty of time to get to our next appointment."

"Where are you heading?" Josh asked. "I need to drop Ange home and I could give you a lift. Do you need a ride, Cody?"

"Thanks, but I'm good. A work colleague is in town, so I have a meeting this afternoon I can't get out of." Cody drained his coffee. "And it's later than I thought. Great to finally meet you." He gave Ben and Simon a nod, then kissed Josh on the cheek. "I'll phone you about tomorrow, okay? Love you."

"Okay. Love you too." Josh watched him go, his gaze lingering.

"It's hard keeping secrets from people you love," Ben said softly. Despite his own misgivings about Cody, it was obvious Josh had fallen for him.

"Yeah it is," Josh said evenly. "He's a good guy, and I don't know how long I can keep holding out on him. He wants to take our relationship to the next level, and you'd have a fair idea how well that's going to go down."

Simon flinched. "He'll find out eventually, and it's not a good idea to build a relationship on a lie." He bit his lip. "A good friend told me that once, and I was foolish enough not to listen. Ben... I should have told him earlier."

"If Cody loves you, he'll accept you for who you are," Ben said.

Ange glanced between Ben and Simon. "You still haven't told Ben's family yet, have you?"

"No." Simon shrugged. "We have a case to solve first."

Josh snorted. "I see. Do what I say, not what I do. You got lucky with Ben. I need to find the right time to tell Cody." He clenched his fist. "Cody is my business, and I will tell him when I'm ready. Don't worry, I won't share any secrets that aren't mine to tell."

"I never thought you would," Simon said, "and you need to be the one to tell Cody. Don't leave it too late, so he finds out from someone else."

Ben kicked him under the table. "Practise what you preach."

"So..." Simon moved the conversation on smoothly. "I spoke to Holt Wayland this morning. It didn't... go well. He refused to include Ben in the meeting because he's human."

"The pack know everything that goes on in this city. They have their fingers in every pie that's worth having a piece of." Josh hesitated. "He wouldn't have been impressed that you're working with me."

"Either he doesn't know, or he didn't mention it," Simon

said. "I suspect the latter, although you're wrong about them knowing everything. They suspect the organisation behind the killings, but don't know who they are."

"Killings?" Ange asked. "I thought only the v... one guy had died."

"The pack councillor didn't survive his injuries." Simon lowered his voice still further. "Have either of you heard of a human-led organisation called Human Destiny?"

Josh paled. "They're here? Bloody hell." He took a gulp of coffee, his hand shaking.

"Who are they?" Ange took Josh's free hand in hers and squeezed it tightly.

"They're like the BFH," Ben said. "Earth for humans, and everyone else needs to go to hell."

"They warned me against protecting anyone associated with them," Simon said. "I reminded them that it's dangerous to judge a group on the actions of a few."

"Human Destiny is a fucking dangerous cult." Josh's voice rose. Simon growled low in his throat. Josh swallowed and when he spoke again, his tone was barely over a whisper. "I'd never protect anyone who had anything to do with them. *They* can all go to hell."

Simon met Josh's gaze and held it. After a few moments, Josh's eyes flashed gold, and he looked away.

"This is personal for you." Simon stated the obvious. "What happened?"

Josh swallowed again. He glanced around nervously, waited a moment, and then leaned in close. "Human Destiny killed my pack. All of them, women and kids too, no survivors. Except me."

"Oh God, I'm so sorry." Ange put her arm around Josh.

He pushed her away, then grabbed his jacket. "I'm sorry, I can't do this again. I've spent the last ten years running and looking over my shoulder. I'm so tired."

"Running isn't the answer," Simon said. "You're safer with friends than alone. We're your pack now and your family. We take care of each other."

"My family is dead," Josh said. "I can't lose another one."

"I used to feel the same way." Simon reached for Ben through their bond. "I went through a bad time eighty years ago. I turned my back on everyone and gave in to... things I want to forget. If it wasn't for my friends who were more like family to me than mine ever wanted to be, I wouldn't be here now. I would have never met Ben. Alone we're vulnerable, together, we're strong." His expression turned grim. "If we work together, we can find these bastards before they strike again. They need to be taken down. Running away from them gives them power they don't deserve."

"We had a run-in with a similar organisation in Boggslake," Ben added. Simon put his arm around Ben and held him close. "It... was bad, and one of the reasons we've come to see my family."

Simon growled low in his throat. "Those bastards nearly killed my Ben. I nearly killed them. Part of me still wishes I had, but Ben pulled me back in time. These kinds of organisations are like a noxious weed spreading through society. Leave them to take root and they're very difficult to eradicate."

"Family looks after each other. We know they're out there, and that gives us an advantage." Ange gave Ben a look that suggested he was going to have to come clean about the BFH incident next time they were alone. He'd downplayed what had happened because he didn't want her to worry. Big mistake. "Right?"

"Right." Simon said. "My friends and I have been doing this a very long time. We're not amateurs, and we will take down these people. You have my word."

"Can I think on it?" Josh still didn't look convinced. "I won't run. I... I just need to think on it first."

"Of course," Simon said. "Keep in touch and be careful."

Josh pushed back his chair. He stood and shoved his hands in his pockets. "Do you mind if I don't give you a lift home, Ange? I know I said I would, but I need to be alone right now."

"Of course not. I'll catch the cable car. It's not a problem." She caught his arm when he started to walk away. "Phone me if you need to talk, okay? And there's a spare bed at my place if you change your mind about being alone."

"I will, thanks." Josh walked away without looking back.

Ange sighed and sat down again. "Poor guy. I always thought he was hiding something, but I never guessed it was that." She turned to Ben. "And what the hell was all that about giving Cody the third degree about his accent? He's good for Josh. He's smiled more over the last few months than he has in years."

"He makes my spidey sense tingle," Ben admitted. "I'm not sure what's up with him, but something is."

"I was suspicious about Simon when you first met, and I was totally off base." Ange had gone all Lois Lane and researched Simon, then worried that Ben had hooked up with an axe murderer when the information she'd found didn't add up. "Unless you have proof, let Josh have a bit of happiness before all this Human Destiny stuff explodes in his face. And ours."

"Cody wasn't being completely honest when Ben asked about his accent." Simon didn't sound convinced. "His heart sped up when he was talking about his family."

"Everyone keeps secrets," Ange reminded him, "and they usually have good reasons. We're keeping a huge secret from him."

"He's human," said Simon.

"So are Ben and I. So?" Ange shrugged. "And as for keeping secrets, you've downplayed a *lot* of shit over the past few years. Some of it you haven't mentioned at all. Neither of you are good liars when it comes to something happening to either of you."

"I don't lie. I ... sidestep on occasion because I have no choice." Simon sighed. "I hope you're right about Cody. He might be hiding something, but he was definitely telling the truth about one thing. He loves Josh. When he said those words, his heart didn't waver at all. I hope that doesn't change when he finds out the truth."

"If he loves Josh, it won't." Ben wasn't the only human who had fallen for a supernatural before discovering their communities existed alongside his own. While his initial reaction hadn't been great, it hadn't changed his feelings for Simon. "He'll react and he might do something stupid, but in the end he'll realise Josh is who he's always been."

"You really think Cody will be okay with it?" Simon hadn't been able to keep any secrets from Ben once the soul-bond had kicked in. At least Josh would be able to introduce his world to Cody at a pace that worked for them.

"Yeah." Ben smiled. Whatever was up with Cody, if he loved Josh, that had to be more important than anything else, right? "I do."

CHAPTER ELEVEN

"What else happened at the pack meeting that you didn't tell us?" Ben pulled up the collar of his jacket after he and Simon got out of the taxi.

The temperature had dropped once the day progressed, although the mid-afternoon sun was still bright.

Simon squinted against the sun and retrieved his sunglasses from his pocket. "The sun feels brighter here. The air smells different too."

"Not so much ozone layer." Ben slipped his hand into Simon's when they started walking towards the church. Simon had instructed the taxi to drop them off a couple of blocks away so their destination wasn't obvious to anyone who might question the driver later. "And Ange is right. You're still really good at sidestepping."

"Old habits die hard. Sorry, I shouldn't be doing that with you." Simon stopped in front of a bakery and looked through the window while he collected his thoughts. "I didn't want to alarm Josh any more than he already is. You didn't find anything on Victor's computer that looked like a client list, did you?"

"No, nothing like that." Ben frowned. "Why?"

"You know all the red tape and forms the council is so fond of?" Simon didn't wait for Ben to reply. "Because of the council in this country being so spread out, each councillor has a list of the supernaturals in their constituency."

"So Kerwin would have a list of all the werewolves in the Wellington region, and Victor, all of the vampires?" Ben whistled. "Shit."

"Very much so," Simon agreed. "No one knows where those lists are hidden except for the councillor tasked with keeping them safe. If Human Destiny finds them..."

"They'd use the information to hunt everyone down?" Ben grimaced. "That's... fuck. What a shit storm. Is that why you asked me to check Victor's computer?"

"I didn't know about the list then but figured if his murderers were looking for something, that might be the first place they'd check if they didn't know the council mistrusts anything digital. Also of concern is that, given how old they are, these lists are a historical documentation of our history in this area."

"Hang on, so what about Sedway?" Ben frowned. "There's no point in him having a list of humans."

"We're not the only supernaturals in this world," Simon said. "Many of the others keep a much lower profile than we do, but they're still out there. I suspect Sedway's list is a lot smaller than the other two. Many of them stay well under the radar, so no one is aware of their existence, not even the council. There are also humans who have a few extra abilities, like the student we met briefly outside Rupert's office."

Ben gritted his teeth. "Hang on, let me guess. The council isn't just worried about the wellbeing of their councillors, but what would happen if these lists get into the wrong hands? It would be bad enough if Human Destiny had a hit list, but if the media found out and had proof that supernaturals are real? It could be like McCarthyism all over again."

"Which is why we need to find them before that happens." Simon moved away from the window. With the light shining through it, he could see Ben's reflection, but of course not his own. "I'm hoping this contact of Rupert's has a good idea where to start searching."

"Easy as, right?" Ben took Simon's hand again once they started walking. "Nothing is ever that simple, however much I wish it were." He grew silent, clearing his throat a few shop fronts later. "I got a bit of a weird vibe from Sedway's nephew, Ash. I don't think he's anything I've come across before, but... perhaps I imagined it."

"Do you want me to pay the shop a visit before we leave?" Simon doubted Ben was imagining anything. While he didn't have Simon's vampire senses, their bond had brought with it a few extras. Ben being able to see ghosts was one, even if they were often a little harder to recognise. His feeling someone wasn't entirely human could well be another.

"Yeah, thanks. At least it's a music shop, so you'll have a good excuse to visit." Ben paused in front of the church.

Simon opened the wooden gate and looked up at the church spire. "This building has been here a while. The design is quite old by local standards." He gave the woman tending the garden a polite nod. She glanced at them and smiled, then returned to her flowers, deftly pulling weeds that weren't there. Her clothing was out of fashion by at least seventy years.

"She doesn't have a shadow," Ben whispered.

"Of course not. She's a ghost." Simon ushered Ben inside the empty church. "I know you're there," he called out. "Come out and introduce yourself."

A brunet man wearing a priest's collar walked out of the sacristy. He saw Simon and Ben and headed towards them.

"Good afternoon," he said pleasantly. "You must be Professor Hawthorne and Mr Leyton. Rupert said you'd be calling by. I'm Father Reith."

Simon raised an eyebrow. "Rupert might have told you about us, but he neglected to tell us about *you*."

"Of course not. Rupert is careful about how much information he gives out at any given time." Reith chuckled. He appeared to be in his mid-thirties, but appearances were rarely accurate in Simon's experience. "I've known him longer than you have, and he never changes."

Ben glanced between them, then grinned. "I figured you were a vampire."

"Yes, but I'd prefer you didn't announce it to the world." Reith ushered them into a nearby pew, then took the seat in front of them, leaning over it so they could speak easily. "The church is usually empty this time of day, so we're safe to talk if we keep our voices down." He gave Ben a pointed look.

"Sorry," murmured Ben. "Umm… how do you avoid the silver chalice and all that stuff?"

Reith raised an eyebrow. "You do know that most of the so-called facts about us aren't true, don't you?"

"Well, yeah." Ben glanced at Simon. "I am married to a vampire."

"Chalices aren't always made of silver. I prefer pewter for obvious reasons, and I've always carried my own, so I know what's in the metal. It's safer that way." Reith nodded approvingly. "That isn't usually the first question someone asks when they find out. People get very hung up about how I can wear a cross and don't combust when saying Mass."

"I was raised Anglican," Simon admitted, "but I must admit I haven't been much of a churchgoer since I returned from the war. Mainly funerals, and far too many of those."

"Far too many of those," Reith agreed, "and from what

Rupert has said, we should expect more unless we stop these bigots."

"Can you help us find them?" Simon asked.

"It's more complicated than that, Prof—"

"Simon," Simon corrected. "My husband's name is Ben."

"Most of my parishioners call me Father Elard, although some of the older ones disapprove of the informality. I'm working on them. Whether you drop my title is up to you."

"You'd have a good idea of what goes on within your parish, though?" Ben asked.

Elard smiled. "That is part of my job, so yes." He sobered. "Although this... organisation has only recently surfaced in Wellington, I've been aware of their presence for at least a decade. At first, it was an insidious ripple of paranoia with people eyeing their neighbours with suspicion if they were a little different, but lately, it's been powering up. Unfortunately, it's human nature to be wary of someone who appears to be *other*, and it's not that difficult to play on common fears. Even good people fear what they don't understand, and the myths we've sown about ourselves are not going to do us any favours."

"They've been here that long?" Simon frowned. "Do you know anything about a werewolf massacre in Australia ten years ago?" The similar time frame was too much of a coincidence.

"The Brisbane Massacre?" Elard let out a long breath. "The council cleaned that up very quickly and paid off any humans who thought reporting it was a good idea. Very few people know about it. I'd heard rumours of Human Destiny through the years, and wondered if they were responsible, but they cover their tracks almost as well as the council. How did you find out about it?"

"Were there any reports of survivors?" Simon asked carefully. Rupert might trust Elard, but Simon didn't know him well enough yet. He'd come across clergy before who weren't the men they appeared to be, and it had cost him dearly.

"You don't trust each other." Ben shook his head. "I thought we were on the same side. If we can't work together, what chance do we have of taking these guys down? The werewolves are bad enough with all this political bullshit, but I thought vampires were past that, for the most part."

"For the most part." Elard met Ben's gaze. "My apologies. Rupert did say you could be trusted."

"He vouched for you too." Simon rested his hand on Ben's knee, a gesture they'd agreed on when they needed to be cautious. Their bond was empathic, not telepathic, and Simon's emotions didn't always reflect the message he needed to share. Besides, Ben was very tactile, and touch helped to ground both of them. "And to answer your question, I heard about the massacre from someone who might have witnessed it."

"Interesting, but not totally unexpected. Tread very carefully with the Waylands. I've known enough werewolves to know that very few turn on their packs." Elard held up a hand when Ben started to protest. "And yes, I'm aware of that incident with a werewolf working with a demon in Boggslake, but that was a complex situation. Pack and family are very important to them. It's why I think it's far more probable a human killed the Truaghs rather than their own kind."

"But?" Simon asked. He squeezed Ben's knee in a warning to stay silent.

"It wouldn't do for word to spread that humans had decimated a powerful pack, would it? There are rumours of a survivor, a young man who wasn't on pack property that night and came home to find his entire family slaughtered." Elard growled. "Instead of offering him sanctuary, the local council used him as a scapegoat. He fled the scene, which only made it easier for them to perpetuate the lie." He glanced at Ben. "I've suspected for some time that he's in the country, especially when a small group of hunters working for Human Destiny arrived here about the same time. They'll be tracking him, although I'm surprised they haven't already found him."

"He's probably been moving around a lot." Ben didn't give anything away.

"Ah, yes, but he's in Wellington now." Elard knew more than he was telling them. "And has been for a few years. No one can stay hidden forever."

"Even if no one believes him, it still sows doubt they can't afford." Simon shook his head. No wonder Josh was ready to run. "Bloody council. That's not how packs are supposed to work."

"The werewolf councillor was killed with his family," Elard pointed out quietly. "The vampires and humans on the council made sure they spread the misinformation before the other two werewolf councillors had time to recover from their shock and bring in someone from outside the area to fill their part of the triad."

"Arseholes," Ben muttered. "No wonder the werewolves here don't like humans and vampires." He frowned. "Hang on, I thought you said Wayland believes this bullshit."

"There can be a huge difference between what Holt, or rather Hedley, Wayland lets people presume is his perception of a situation, and the actual truth." Elard sighed. "Politics and half-truths will be part of the reason why Human Destiny has a good chance of success. Marry that with fear, ignorance, and preconceptions that have been encouraged for generations, and I worry about our future."

"Unfortunately, people haven't learnt from the past, or they've changed less than we'd like to think they have. I saw a lot of things I'd rather forget when I was with the Resistance in Europe during the last world war." Simon paused when Ben reached for him through their bond. "So, where do we go from here? You'll help?"

"From a distance, yes," Elard said. "I offer sanctuary here to anyone who needs it, both human and supernatural, so I need to stay neutral, at least on the surface. However, my offer doesn't extend to those like Human Destiny. Their hate-driven agenda could well destroy the peace and anonymity we've all spent centuries building between the factions of our own society, which includes the humans who are aware we exist."

"Fair enough." Simon fished into his pocket and gave Elard his business card. He'd changed the telephone number to the one he was currently using. "Contact me directly if you hear anything that might help us find them." Human Destiny most likely knew where to find him already, given the botched robbery, so he had no qualms in sharing his contact details with Elard.

"Thank you, I will." Elard glanced at his watch. "I need to prepare for early evening Mass soon. Is there anything else I can help you with today?"

"The councillor registries are missing. Do you have any idea where they might have been hidden?" Simon had heard enough from Elard to go out on a limb and trust him with that information.

"Bloody hell." Elard swore, then glanced up with a murmured apology. "If those are missing, we're all in danger." Momentary fear glinted in his eyes. "I might have an idea where Victor's is, but Kerwin and I didn't see eye to eye, so I can't help you with that one." He wiped his hands on his trousers and stood. "I'll be in touch when I have something for you. Meanwhile, it's been a pleasure meeting both of you. I hope to see you in church sometime."

"Not Catholic," Simon reminded him.

"Very lapsed," Ben added.

Elard chuckled. "God won't blame you for that, gentle-men, and my offer stands. Be careful. These are dangerous times."

"We'll look forward to hearing from you. I believe some of your congregation are a little early today. Good afternoon, Elard." Simon ushered Ben from the church, ignoring the curious looks of the two older ladies he opened the door for.

"Fuck, what a mess," Ben said once they were a distance away. "It does sound like Josh is the survivor Elard talked about. The council has a nerve, doing what they did."

"I believe Josh," Simon said, "and I'm very certain he is, or rather was, part of the Truagh Pack."

"What makes you think that?"

"To a werewolf, pack is everything, and although Josh lost his, he'd still cling to some kind of connection." Simon had made the connection immediately. "I suspect that's why he would have chosen McKenna as an alias. The McKenna family were originally from the Truagh area in Ireland."

"So that's why you wanted to stop by the university library? You wanted to research him?"

Simon raised an eyebrow. "Well, yes, of course. Although I had already invited Josh to join our team, I wanted to learn more about him, and whatever pack he might be affiliated with before I shared any further information with him."

Ben answered him with a kiss. "Of course," he murmured. "Although one of these days you'll figure out it's easier to Google."

~

"I never thought I'd see Simon like this. He's very relaxed around you," Frank said softly.

Ben smiled and caressed Simon's cheek. Simon leaned

into his touch, yet didn't wake. "He makes me happy too." Ben reached for his beer and took another sip, careful not to disturb Simon. They'd started watching a movie together, then midway through Simon had laid on the sofa, rested his head on Ben's lap, and fallen asleep. "And at least now we don't have to listen to his running commentary about the movie's inaccuracy."

Frank chuckled. "I was enjoying his comments, actually. I guess if you've lived it, it must be very frustrating watching something that gets so much wrong."

"Honestly, I enjoy his insight too, but you can't tell him that or he'd be insufferable about it." Ben didn't try to hide the affection in his voice. "I'm pleased you and Simon got to meet again. It must be weird for you seeing him still looking the same so many years later."

"Weird, and a bit disconcerting at times." Frank took another swig of Lemon & Paeroa, known locally as L&P, which was his drink of choice. "How do you feel about getting older while he ages more slowly? It is something you need to think about."

"I try not to think about it too much." Ben carded his fingers through Simon's hair. "We've only been together a few years, and it's not going to be long before he looks a decade younger." He hadn't talked about the ageing thing with anyone else but Simon. "To be honest I'd be more worried about growing old and leaving him alone, but at least that's not an option."

Frank raised an eyebrow. "It's not?"

"No. Apparently, that's one of the things about this bond we share. If I die first, he follows soon afterwards. At least we *think* that's what happens. But..." Ben's voice wobbled. "If he dies, I don't, given that Hugh didn't after his wife died. Though with all the dangerous shit we do, I expect to go first, which scares me. What if we're wrong and me dying first *does* leave him alone? Not that I want to think too much about dying either." He bit his lip. "Simon and I have... I want him to turn me, maybe not on his next contagious cycle, but soon. We do a lot of good together and I want a long life with him. You know I'm not going into this blindly." Ben swallowed. "If we're both vampires, we'll go together, whatever happens."

"Hugh always thought he'd die first, and although Cynthia offered to turn him, he decided against it. They had a happy life together until she was murdered." Frank shook his head. "I'm glad you got the bastard responsible."

"It's heartbreaking seeing Hugh now. He keeps calling for her, and doesn't remember she's gone." Ben shivered. He liked Hugh but had only known him for a short time before he'd started to deteriorate. "I'm sorry. He was your friend, and you probably want to remember him the way he was."

"I never knew he and Cynthia had a soulbond like you and Simon, or that was even possible until you told me." Frank moved the conversation on and took another swig of his drink.

"Do you think I'm doing the wrong thing asking him to change me?"

"If it's what both of you want, that's your decision, and although the rest of us might have opinions, at the end of the day, it's not ours that count." Frank had never been shy about saying what he thought. Ben admired him for that, and it was one of the reasons he didn't keep his opinions to himself either. "Simon's a good man, and you're well suited, like I knew you'd be. I suggested you visit Boggslake because I hoped the reason you were so restless after you'd finished uni was because you were missing something, or rather someone. I got to know Declan and Forge when I first met Simon. They've all lived long, productive lives, so why wouldn't I wish that for you too?"

"Would you have still told me to go to Boggslake if you'd known this could happen?"

"Yes, definitely." Frank smiled. "You're going to outlive me whatever you decide, and that's the way it should be." He paused before continuing. "One thing though, talk to your mum and dad first, okay? Don't spring it on them after the fact. It's high time they knew about Simon too. You can't keep that a secret forever. I guess what I'm saying is that you can't predict what's going to happen in life. We sometimes have to live longer than the ones we love, even us mere humans who aren't bonded to a vampire." His voice softened. "I miss your grandmother so much some days it hurts. We bought this place together and thought we'd have time to do all the things we wanted."

"She loved you." Ben had always envied his grandparents' relationship. His parents' too, and hadn't thought he'd ever be lucky enough to find someone he fit with as they did together. Until he met Simon.

"I still love her," Frank tightened his grip on his glass, the moisture trickling down the lines in his skin, accentuating the wrinkles and thinness of it. "Despite growing older together, I still saw her as the young, beautiful woman I'd fallen for on our first date." His expression softened. "If you decide to stay human, your Simon will do the same. He won't see you ageing. It's only the body that does that, not our souls, or the part of us that makes us unique." He grimaced. "Though I could really do without my body's reminder I'm getting on in years."

"Frank's right," Simon said. "You'll always be beautiful to me, whatever age you are." He sat up and put his arm around Ben. "I love you, and I'm content with living however long you do. I've lived a long time and seen a lot. Sometimes too much." He kissed Ben on the cheek. "And I'm sorry we haven't talked properly yet. Frank's right. Whatever the outcome, this is a decision we need to make together." He paused. "He's also right that we need to talk to your parents before we do anything. Tell them about me first, and let that sink in. Knowing I'm a vampire, and you becoming one are very different scenarios."

"How long have you been awake?" Ben didn't miss the shadow that fell over Simon's face. He was still worried about how the rest of Ben's family would react to the news that their son-in-law was a vampire.

"Long enough." Simon stilled. "Are you expecting company," he asked Frank.

"No," Frank said. "Do you think those Human Destiny people have sent someone else?"

Simon cocked his head to one side. "It's not them." He let out a breath. "It's Abby."

CHAPTER TWELVE

Ben opened the door before his mother had a chance to knock. "Hi, Mum, we weren't expecting you. Everything okay?"

"I hope this isn't a bad time?" Abby still wore her nurse's uniform, which meant she was on the way home from her shift.

"It's fine, dear. Come have a seat and tell us what's on your mind." Frank gestured towards the empty armchair. "Simon, come over here and join in. Whatever this is about, you're family now, so you're a part of this."

Simon was at the sink rinsing the last traces of blood from his glass. Thank God, he'd thought to move into the kitchen at vampire speed while Ben headed for the door.

"I got a phone call from Uncle Martin." Abby got straight to the point.

Ben groaned. "Of course, you did." He'd hoped that because they hadn't seen him, he hadn't spotted them. No such luck.

"He said he saw you leaving the church with a young man, and that you kissed on the street a few moments later." Abby flopped down on the sofa. Simon put the kettle on to boil for tea. "He then asked me if there was a family event coming up that he should know about?"

"He wants to come to the wedding?" Ben sighed. "We wanted the ceremony small and intimate. If Uncle Martin comes, the whole of Wellington will know all about it."

"You can't not invite him," Frank said. "Even though he and your dad have little in common, they're still brothers and he's part of this family."

"Were you going to mention you'd visited St Ansgar's?" Abby frowned. "I thought you wanted the ceremony at home. You don't even go to church. What happened to our long conversation that ended with me respecting your wishes?"

"We didn't go to the church because we're getting married," Ben said. "Could I have some tea too, Simon? Actually, make it coffee." He wanted a clear head for this conversation.

"Nothing for me, or I won't sleep tonight," Frank added.

"One of my colleagues is a friend of Father Elard's," Simon already had cups out and the kettle on, as though making tea and coffee was the real reason he'd been in the kitchen. "He thought Elard could help me with some research, so we arranged to meet with him."

"Oh." Abby looked part relieved; part unconvinced. "That's right. Ray told me you're working while you're here."

"I didn't plan to." Simon walked into the living room, handed her a steaming mug of tea, and put a cup of coffee in front of Ben. He hadn't brought a drink in for himself. "It was a last-minute request from some associates I'd prefer to avoid, but they made an offer that was somewhat difficult to refuse."

"You're on your honeymoon," Abby said. "That's very rude of them."

"Tell me about it," Ben muttered, sitting down with his coffee.

"I'm hoping it doesn't encroach too much on our plans." Simon put his arm around Ben. "You look tired, Abby. Long day at work?"

Abby nodded. "Thanks for noticing." She worked at one of the local hospices. "One of my patients is very close to death. Although I've lost so many over the years, it never gets any easier."

"No, it doesn't," Simon agreed. "I'm sorry."

"That sounds like the voice of experience." Abby met his gaze and held it for a few moments. "You must miss your family."

"They died a long time ago." Simon reached for Ben's coffee and took a long drink of it before returning it to Ben. Not that the caffeine would do anything for him, any more than alcohol did. "I've lost a few friends recently too."

Abby's gaze followed Simon's movements. "If you ever want someone else other than Ben to talk to, I've been told I'm a good listener."

"Thank you." Simon nodded. "So is he. You've taught him well."

Abby smiled. "Communication is—"

Simon's phone rang. He retrieved it from the table and frowned. "Excuse me. This is work related, so unfortunately I can't ignore it. I won't be long." He started walking into the kitchen while he answered the call. "Hello, Garrick, this is Simon. How can I help?" Simon let himself out the back door and closed it behind him.

Shit, what now? Garrick phoning when they'd already planned to meet in the morning couldn't be good news.

Abby leaned in close and lowered her voice. "Is Simon okay?"

"Yeah, just concerned about the work thing." Ben kept his voice light. "Why?"

"I don't want to intrude." Abby used the phrase that always meant she was about to ask questions he didn't want to answer.

"But?" Ben prompted.

"He's happy with his life now, yes?"

"Yes, we're very happy together." Ben wished his mother would get the point, considering Simon could still hear their conversation. "Why?"

"Those marks on his wrists don't look that old."

"They're—" Ben froze. *Shit.* No wonder she'd stared at Simon when he'd reached for Ben's coffee. He was usually very careful about keeping his wrists covered, but they'd been home and he'd rolled up his shirt sleeves.

"That's something personal I don't think you should be asking about." Frank spoke quickly. "Things aren't always what they appear to be, and if Simon wants to talk about it, he will in his own time."

Ben shot his grandfather a look of gratitude. The longer Simon refused to tell their family that he was a vampire, the more likely they were to find out on their own, and then any chance of making sure the truth they heard was the right one went out the window.

"Simon's okay, Mum, I promise." Ben bit his lip. "It's not what you think. He didn't... it wasn't self-inflicted. But Granddad's right. He'll tell you what happened if he wants to, and I'd appreciate it if you didn't ask. Don't worry about it, or about him. He can take care of himself."

"Bad people don't care how capable you are. They're dangerous for a reason." Abby didn't give up once she got an idea into her head. "I hope whoever was responsible got what they deserved."

Ben narrowed his eyes. "That bastard got exactly what he

deserved. I made sure of it. He won't hurt Simon or anyone else ever again." Silver was the only thing that left a vampire with a permanent scar.

Luckily Simon entering the room silenced the conversation.

Abby stood, then walked over to Simon, pulled him into her arms, and held him. "You're safe now, and with family," she whispered, loud enough so Ben could still hear her.

"Thank you." Simon's reaction seemed less awkward than usual. "I'm sorry," he murmured. "I *will* talk to you when the time is right." He glanced at Ben, concern and regret fighting a war he needed to put behind him. "I promised Ben."

"Good. I'll hold you to that too." Abby frowned. "Goodness, you're very cold. Make sure you put a jacket on next time you go outside."

"Yes, ma'am... er... Abby."

"It's late and Ray will be sending out a search party." Abby's grin didn't cover her worry. "You boys are still coming for dinner tomorrow night, yes? I thought it would be good if we had another family get together before you exchange your vows next weekend." She gave Ben a hug. "I'm so glad you brought him home to meet us. You should have done it sooner."

"Love you too, Mum," said Ben.

"I'm running out of time." Simon made a beeline for the fridge once Abby left and poured himself a glass of milk. "Not just with this case, but with your family too."

Ben eyed him suspiciously. "You're not putting blood ice cubes in that, right?" It had taken him far too long to dissuade Simon from that disgusting habit.

"Maybe." Simon bit his lip, then slammed the fridge door. "Bloody hell. Your mother saw my wrists and thought I'd tried to kill myself?" He banged the glass down on the counter.

"She means well, she's concerned, and you heard us tell her not to worry and to back off." Ben walked up behind Simon and caught him in an embrace. "The longer we don't tell them you're a vampire, the more likely she is to try and figure things out. My mum has an overactive imagination. You don't want to go there." He kissed Simon's head. "What did Garrick want?"

Simon leaned back into Ben. "There's been another murder. Two more werewolves. Teenagers, this time, and killed the same way. They were dumped in front of Wayland's building, already dead."

"Oh God." Ben turned, so they were facing. "This is escalating, isn't it?" He swallowed. "Do you think—?"

"Yes." Simon glanced over at Frank. "If we don't catch these people, and soon, they'll come after every supernatural in the area. We can move out if—"

"This is your home for however long you're here. And for the record, I'm proud of what you're doing. Very proud." Frank stretched, then winced. "If I were younger, I'd be out there helping you, instead of heading for bed." He paused at the bottom of the stairs. "My Abby means well, but she pushes until she gets answers. You know the type." He grinned. "You did marry my grandson after all."

"Hey." Ben couldn't resist grinning back.

"I like him that way," Simon murmured, "and thank you." He waited until Frank was out of earshot. "Garrick thinks—and I agree with him—that they've found the werewolf list. We're just hoping like hell we can stop them before they kill any more werewolves."

"If they don't have the other lists, and only the wolves die, you know what's going to happen, don't you?" Ben had seen enough of the animosity between supernaturals to guess what might come next.

"Yes, that's what I'm afraid of. If only werewolves die, and

Wayland refuses to admit humans are responsible, the pack will draw their own conclusions. And then the people we're after won't need to track down anyone else. The werewolves will do the job for them."

~

"Mum's going to push for taking photos next weekend at dinner tonight," Ben said when they pulled up in the car outside a non-descript house in Naenae. "She doesn't get why we don't want any at our ceremony here. She loved what Declan gave us, but I can hardly explain they're not actual photos."

"Yes, I know. I need to tell her sooner rather than later." Simon tried to sound less irritable than he felt. "I... wanted to get past next Saturday first."

"I think we need to come clean before that or she'll find out when you don't show up in the photos." Ben turned off the engine, then squeezed Simon's knee. "I know I sound like a broken record, but it will be okay, I promise."

Simon bit his lip. "I wish I could believe that." He brushed his lips across Ben's cheek. "Your family is important to you. I don't want to screw that up." Like most vampires, he'd become very good at avoiding cameras, but it was getting harder with people having them on their telephones now.

"They're your family now too." Ben captured Simon's mouth in a long kiss. "We've come a long way in the last century. My parents were fine when I came out. They'll be fine with this."

"Telling them I'm a vampire isn't the same as them finding out you're gay." Simon's parents wouldn't have accepted that either.

"I wasn't prepared to keep that a secret either, so yeah, it is. Sometimes you've just got to do something and hope for the best." None of Simon's arguments would sway Ben. "And besides, with all this supernatural shit going down, isn't it better they hear the truth from us instead of some Human Destiny idiot spiel?"

"Anything is better than that." Simon couldn't shake the feeling that their two worlds would collide head-on, no matter how hard he tried to stop it.

"Exactly my point." Ben got out of the car and peered at the house. "Any idea why Garrick wanted to meet at his place?"

"Probably because it's private." Simon opened the gate for Ben and waited for him to enter the property before shutting it behind them. At least with it being a werewolf's home, he didn't need to be invited in. "With this situation escalating, we don't want any supernaturals overhearing our conversation either. We have enough of a time bomb ticking without deliberately lighting a fuse."

"True." Ben raised his hand to knock on the front door.

Simon caught his arm. "Garrick's not alone. I can hear voices inside." He listened for a moment. "Oh hell."

"What?" Ben glanced at him. "You've gone pale. What's wrong?"

The door opened before Simon could answer.

"You'd better come in," Garrick said.

"Good morning." Simon scowled, "Could you tell us what the bloody hell you're playing at *before* we come inside?"

Ben took a step back. "Who's in there?"

"The Auckland and Christchurch councils contacted me late last night." Garrick ushered them both in. "And I don't want to talk about this on my doorstep. My neighbours spread gossip like you wouldn't believe."

"Oh, I can believe it." Ben nudged Simon when he didn't move. "Come on, this can't be that bad. Maybe they've actually sent us some help."

"That's exactly what they've done," Garrick said.

Ben stopped at the open living room door. "Tash? What the hell are you doing here?"

His sister rolled her eyes. "Good morning to you too. I'm guessing you know more about why I'm here than I do." She sipped her coffee and leaned back on the sofa.

Simon swallowed, his fists clenching. He had a horrible feeling about why the council had been in contact. "Garrick? Is this some kind of joke? We can't—"

"The council has the final word in situations like this." Garrick looked apologetic, at least. "Even over the pack. We both know the details of the Supernatural Treaty."

"Of course, they do." Simon growled.

"That coffee smells good," Ben said. "What say I grab us both a cup and then we talk about why the council thought it was a great idea to involve my *sister* in all of this."

"I love how you've made me feel so welcome," Tash murmured.

"How much does she know?" Simon perched on the edge of the sofa opposite her.

"Nothing." Garrick confirmed Simon's suspicions. "I thought it was better to wait until we're all here and tell her together."

"So, she doesn't know about you either?" Simon asked.

"As I said, nothing." Garrick grimaced. "This isn't just your secret. The council has put us both in this position. I'm not happy about it either."

"Hey, I'm still here." Tash lowered her coffee mug. "And I'm guessing you're not referring to the local city council."

"Those wankers have some nerve." Ben handed Simon a coffee, waited for him to sit on the sofa properly, then took the space next to him. "I'm sorry, Tash. I didn't want you dragged into our world like this. We were going to tell you at the dinner tonight."

"We were?" Simon regretted the words immediately after feeling Ben's annoyed reaction. "Oh yes, we were." He sipped his coffee, remembering all too well Ben's reaction when he'd found out. At least, thanks to their soulbond, Ben had been able to see the truth for himself through Simon's memories. But, on the other hand, without it, he had the option to skip over all the not-so-great highlights of his life.

"Your world?" Tash stared at both of them. "Right, I'm waiting. I knew there was weird shit going on, and you did already promise to tell me sooner rather than later. You're involved in some undercover crime thing, aren't you?"

Simon bit his lip. "Do you want to go first?" he asked Garrick.

"Not particularly." Garrick gave Ben a pointed look. "She's your sister, and I'm not in the habit of telling humans. Especially when we're usually not supposed to." He shrugged and settled into the lone chair in the room. "The council thinks we need the help now, not later, so they've decided to up the timetable. For the record, Wayland's angry with them too, and I would have loved to have been a fly on the wall for that conversation."

Ben squeezed Simon's hand in a silent signal of support.

Simon put down his coffee and took a deep breath. "We're helping Garrick investigate a series of murders in Wellington. Ben and I are part of a team in Boggslake, so the Supernatural Council asked—"

"Blackmailed," Ben interjected.

"Asked us to look into it," Simon finished.

"Supernatural?" Tash's eyes widened. "You're serious, right? Like ghosts and stuff like that."

"The supernatural council is made up of a mix of vampires, werewolves, and humans." Simon shuffled closer to Ben, then rushed out with the words before he could take them back. "I'm a vampire. Garrick is a werewolf."

Tash glared at him. "Haha, not funny. Come on, what's really going on?"

"What is it with you and your family not believing me?" Simon asked.

"Sorry," Ben murmured. He cleared his throat. "It's true. I didn't believe it either when I found out. And before you go there, Simon and Garrick are the good guys. A lot of that stuff you think you know isn't true. Like humans, there are good and bad supernaturals."

"You're all crazy." Tash stood and glanced between them and the door.

Simon moved at high speed to block her way. He let his eyes go completely brown and dropped his fangs. "I *am* a vampire. I'm sorry. There is no easy way to tell you." Dropping it into casual conversation didn't work. He'd tried.

"Shit." Tash flopped back down on the sofa. "I knew you were hiding something, but I wouldn't have guessed it was this."

"That's kind of the point." Simon sat back down next to Ben. "I wish your brother had been easier to convince. I showed him my eyes and fangs and he still didn't believe me."

"So how old are you?" Tash leaned in, curious, rather than scared. "And how does it all work? I've seen you in sunlight, so guessing that part of the myth is bullshit."

"You're taking this well," Ben said. "I ran off and ended up in a werewolf bar."

Garrick raised an eyebrow. "That must have been fun, especially with how much you smell of vampire."

"Thanks." Ben shrugged. "I was lucky. Lucas saved my arse and filled me in on the important stuff. I hadn't guessed he was a werewolf either."

"You love each other, and Simon makes you happy." Tash shrugged. "You're my brother and I trust your judgement. I wish you'd trusted me, and not just told me because you had to." She twisted a strand of hair around one finger. "That bit hurts, you know. We've always shared stuff. Then after you met Simon, I got the feeling you were more closed off than you used to be, but I couldn't figure out why."

"I'm sorry." Ben averted his gaze. "It wasn't my secret to tell and... you'd worry if you knew all the stuff that's happened since we met. We've been up against some seriously freaky and dangerous shit."

"It's my fault, not his," Simon said. "The thought of your family finding out and rejecting him because of it terrifies me."

Tash gave him an incredulous look. "Why the fuck would we do that? Ben's my brother." She rolled her eyes at Ben. "And telling me you don't want me to worry and then hinting that I probably should isn't the way to go."

"My family disowned me when they found out." Simon winced. The memory always hurt, no matter how much he tried to put it behind him. "I came back from the war no longer human, and..."

Ben pulled him close. "It was a different time, and his family isn't ours." He kissed Simon's forehead. "He was turned in 1916 when he was twenty-two. That's why he looks younger than me, although he's way older." He turned to Garrick. "Simon's done enough soul-bearing for today, and we've got murders to solve. He's shown her his fangs and stuff, now it's your turn, and then we can get onto why we're here."

"Whatever." Garrick's eyes turned gold, and fur sprouted over his face. "I'm not doing a full transformation just to show her my wolf. That's not how this works."

"I believe you, and you don't have to." Tash's eyes glinted with interest. "I will be asking lots of questions though, and I expect you to answer. All of you. There's got to be some payback for keeping this from me. Right?"

"Right." Simon relaxed. She'd taken it well so far. Much better than he'd thought.

Ben grinned and poked Simon in the side. "See, told you it would be okay."

"You haven't told Mum yet," Tash pointed out. "And I'm guessing Granddad knows?"

"Yeah." Ben groaned. "Dinner tonight is going to be so much fun, isn't it?"

"Make sure you bring her favourite chocolates and loads of flowers," Tash suggested.

"Another good reason for not telling humans our secrets." Garrick smirked.

"Don't get too comfortable, Garrick," Tash said. "You kept this from me too, and *you* don't have the excuse of being family." She drummed her fingers along the side of her cup. "And don't think I didn't hear what you said earlier about upping the timetable. Did this council of yours pull some strings to get us partnered together?"

"Yes." Garrick met her gaze directly. "I've been running supernatural ops in this city on my own for years, and they figured I needed a partner. And with your brother married to a vampire, you were the obvious candidate. Welcome to our world."

CHAPTER THIRTEEN

"So I got this job because my brother is already knee-deep in all this supernatural stuff? And they presumed I'd find out about it anyway?" Tash glared at Garrick. "What happened to the fact I'm a damn good detective and already knew you were up to something?"

"It's better not to think too hard about the council and its ideas," Ben said hastily. His sister had a temper on her once she got going. "They wouldn't have set you up in the job if they didn't think you were capable. That would be a waste of their time and yours."

"I suppose." Tash didn't seem convinced.

"If this is turning into a full team meeting, we need everyone in on this." Simon changed the subject. "Excuse me a moment while I telephone Ange and Josh."

"We were going to meet up with them for lunch," Ben added, "so they should be local or close to it."

"Josh McKenna?" Garrick asked.

"Yeah," Ben confirmed as Simon was already on the phone. "You know him?"

"I know of him." Garrick looked like he'd tasted something unpleasant. "He's that lone wolf. Word is he helped Human Destiny kill his pack."

"Bullshit." Ben rolled his eyes. "Last I looked, surviving something like that doesn't mean you're in league with the arseholes responsible. The name is a bit of a giveaway. *Human* Destiny. I saw his reaction when he found out they're here. He's a victim in all this, same as your dead werewolves."

"You've been talking to Elard." Garrick's response was a statement, not a question. "That's his theory too."

"Yeah, well, Elard's been around a while and seems to know his stuff." Ben narrowed his eyes. "And for the record, being human doesn't automatically mean we're part of their cult. If you're determined to believe the crap your alpha is spouting, then perhaps we'll solve this one on our own."

Garrick raised his hands in mock surrender. "Hey, I haven't met your friend, Josh, yet. And given the last few days, I'm not sure what to believe. The alpha has his own agenda, always has, but he does have the pack's welfare at heart with every decision he makes."

"If Josh does stick around, don't scare him off because of some stupid preconception, okay?' Ben said. Jacob Coate had convinced himself that banishing his son, Lucas, from their pack was necessary to protect it.

"Josh is a werewolf?" Tash asked. "And who's Elard? Another one of your pack?"

"He's a priest." Ben hesitated, unsure how much he should be saying.

"And a vampire." Garrick finished the explanation for him. "He's a good guy. I've known him a while, and he tends to have a good handle on things. But if we're going to be upfront, we'll have to tell Wayland we're bringing in yet another human. He's not going to be happy." Given Garrick's response he already knew who Ange was, but that wasn't surprising. Tash and Ange had become friends shortly after she'd met Ben, and the council would have researched everyone connected with his sister before considering bringing her onboard.

"We need to work together if we're going to stop these people, not argue politics," Simon shoved his phone back into his pocket after he re-entered the room. "I've already had my fill of bigotry from Wayland. From both Waylands." He sat down beside Ben. "If we're arguing about such things amongst ourselves, hasn't Human Destiny already won?"

"They sound like complete tossers." Tash didn't say whether she was talking about Human Destiny or the pack. "Poor Josh. I never knew his family had been murdered. And for the record, I've met him a few times, and he's always struck me as one of the good guys."

"I think he is too," Ben said. "Are Josh and Ange on their way?"

"Yes. They're only about ten minutes away." Simon was more relaxed than he'd been when they'd arrived. Hopefully Tash's reaction would help with his nervousness about telling the rest of the family. "We can bring Tash up to speed while we're waiting."

"Sounds good, thanks." Tash took out a notebook and pen.

Simon nodded his approval. He still took notes the old-fashioned way too. "We've had four deaths so far, three werewolves and a vampire. We have no proof this organisation is behind them, but it's looking increasingly likely they are. They were also responsible for the break-in at Frank's the other night. A colleague left some information they wanted."

"I figured that was probably tied into this." Tash scribbled a few notes. "Anything else I should know that's directly connected to this case? I'll grab the details about each victim and how they were killed once you've filled me in on the current situation."

Garrick got up, retrieved a folder, and laid it on the coffee table between them. "We also have a missing human. I've been in touch with my associates in Picton and they confirm that Erik Sedway hired a boat a week ago, and headed out to a bach in the Marlborough Sounds."

"Bach?" Simon asked.

"A holiday home," Ben explained.

"Ah." Simon had picked up a lot of Kiwi slang since they'd been together, but the odd word still threw him.

"They're sending someone to take him into protective custody. He's the only surviving local councillor so, despite him not being a supernatural, I'm not prepared to take any chances." Garrick paused. "We need to find his list before they do."

"Each councillor has a partial list of supernaturals in the region," Simon added for Tash. "Have there been any more werewolf deaths since those two teens last night?"

"No, but the pack has sent out a warning to be vigilant and not out alone. Our community is on edge, and tempers are already rising. Unfortunately, we have a few factions who are very quick to point fingers. Many of our elders remember the last time we came under siege." Garrick sighed. "Equally unfortunately they've conveniently forgotten that vampires helped us at the time. I wasn't aware of that until Wayland mentioned it at our meeting."

"Werewolves are always very quick to blame vampires," Ben pointed out.

"There's good reason for that," Garrick retorted. "At least we don't need blood to survive."

"*Animal* blood," Ben said. "Are werewolves all vegetarians, then?"

Garrick glared.

"Yeah, didn't think so." Ben missed Lucas and his happy-go-lucky attitude. He'd never been bothered that his friends were vampires. His sisters were good value too.

Simon pinched the bridge of his nose. "Can we please keep to the subject at hand? Ideally, we need to learn from the past, not repeat its mistakes."

"Excuse me for sticking up for you," Ben muttered.

"I can fight my own battles. Although I do appreciate the sentiment,' Simon added quickly. "So, Garrick, any luck in tracking those young men who broke in the other night?"

"They were squatting in a house in Newlands," Garrick said. "Although it was empty by the time we got there."

"*They* were the guys who broke into Granddad's? They left a bit of a mess behind them, but no clues to their identity." Tash frowned. "Hold up. Wayland, as in Wayland Real Estate?"

"Yes. The firm is owned and managed by the pack." Garrick confirmed. "The empty house the perps were squatting in is managed by the firm, but I—"

"What if there is a connection?" Tash asked slowly. "Otherwise, it's a hell of a coincidence."

"In my experience coincidences are usually anything but," Simon agreed. "Did Kerwin work for the pack?"

"Yes, he is... was... one of their senior agents." Garrick cursed under his breath. He opened the folder and flipped through a few documents. "The pack is still old school for the most part. Like the council, they prefer to keep most of their paperwork off any server that might be able to be hacked."

"Real estate stuff is online these days," Ben said, "so it would be easy enough for someone to figure out what properties are managed by the firm, and not that much more work to find a few empty houses. It makes sense to fly under the radar that way and avoid rental agreements that can be tracked. It wouldn't be the first time someone's found a way to tamper with an electricity meter to hide that a house is occupied."

"Hmm." Garrick sounded distracted. He scanned the paper in his hand. "The morning before he died, Kerwin had a viewing. He sent a text to say his clients weren't interested and he'd show them something else, and that was the last anyone heard from him. Until he was dumped several hours later."

"Anyone can send a text." Ben shrugged. "And if his phone was already unlocked, or the password wasn't that hard to crack, maybe that's our clue right there. What better way to entice a real estate agent than with a possible sale or new rental agreement? There are several new subdivisions with nearly finished empty houses in the region. I'm guessing their contact number was probably a burner phone, and they gave a fake address."

Garrick looked up and sniffed. "There's a werewolf and a human approaching the front door. We have company."

"Probably Ange and Josh." Ben stood. "I'll get it so you can keep looking through those papers."

He opened the door as Ange was about to knock. Josh looked pale, and his eyes were red. He gave Ben a shaky smile.

"Hey."

Ben pulled him into a hug. "Glad you're still with us."

Josh let out a long sigh. "Yeah, well, I almost wasn't. Ange and I had a long chat this morning. I've been running for far too long. I'm tired of looking over my shoulder, scared they're going to come after me. They're already killing werewolves here. I'm not going to sit and wait for them to finish what they started ten years ago. So yeah, I'm in. Whatever it takes. Let's stop these bastards."

~

"So, is your PhD real?" Tash asked. "And are you okay to make this the last property for today?"

Simon looked up from his telephone. "Yes, and yes." He raised one eyebrow. "I assure you my qualifications are quite authentic. I studied at Cambridge, although of course very little of the history I teach had happened then."

"That must give you a unique perspective." Tash frowned. "How many properties do Wayland's firm manage? It's going to take us a couple of days to get through this lot, even with Josh and Ange doing their bit tomorrow."

"It does, along with far too many unpleasant memories. I've seen two world wars, and the deaths of far too many people I care about." Simon scrolled down the list of properties on his telephone. "It's a shame we can't investigate these properties remotely, but it would be too easy to miss something that way."

"I'm sorry. I hadn't thought about that side of immortality."

"Very few do." Simon hesitated, then added, "I'm not immortal. I age a lot slower than you do."

They'd left Ange at Garrick's looking through the online listings for Wayland Real Estate. She'd already sent them several dozen addresses before calling it a day. Josh had received a call to fill in at the library after someone had gone home sick. Despite Simon's initial misgivings, he'd agreed to Garrick's suggestion that they split their resources, with someone from the police force in each search party. He and Tash were looking at properties in Wellington suburbs while Garrick and Ben focused on the Hutt Valley area.

Tash parked the car a couple of houses down. Fortunately, she hadn't asked Simon to elaborate on his last comment. "I'm now looking at Wellington, wondering what else I'm missing. How large is your supernatural community?"

"You outnumber us by a substantial number."

Many supernaturals had stayed closer to home rather than immigrating to New Zealand and Australia, although that had changed in recent years. Simon hated flying, and spending weeks at sea. Rupert, on the other hand, wasn't fazed by any of it, although Simon suspected some of that was because he was hungry to try anything new.

"Most people aren't going to see it that way." Tash picked up her speed. "We need a break on this case, and quickly, before things escalate. Once a journalist gets hold of what looks like a serial killer working in the area, people will panic."

They'd checked the house Kerwin had shown first, but whoever had been there had already cleared out. Simon had noticed the underlying smell of blood immediately. Although the stench of disinfectant and bleach had masked it, the blood was werewolf, not human, so this was definitely the crime scene. He'd alerted Garrick so he could let Wayland know.

"I suspect the pack is working on that but, in my experience, all dams eventually break and when they do, the fallout is far worse than if they'd been left to trickle." Simon caught Tash's arm when they approached the next property on their list and put a finger to his lips to signal quiet. Apart from the first house they'd checked, none of the others had revealed anything out of the ordinary. Hopefully, this one would be the break they needed. He listened intently, dismissing the bird noise, and heard the distinctive click of a door closing.

Not the front. Definitely the back.

Simon sprinted to the fence and jumped it without slowing down. He crept around the side of the house, missing the Taser he usually carried when hunting prey. Not that he needed one, but it did negate the need for violence which he preferred to avoid. Movement caught the corner of his eye. He moved at top speed to block the path and stood in front of the man fleeing the scene. "Going somewhere?"

"Who the hell—oh shit." The man paled, and his heart sped up. He averted his gaze. "If you're looking for the owner, he's not here."

"This property is empty apart from you." Simon took a step closer. He inhaled, and caught a chlorine scent, with an underlying odour of werewolf blood. "You're a little late cleaning up."

"I'm not cleaning up." The man started to shake.

"You're lying." Simon smiled. The man's heartbeat jerked unsteadily. "Let's try this again. Who do you work for?"

"You can't do this. I know my rights. I'm calling the police."

"I am the police," Tash said from behind him. She was breathing heavily. "Or, if you'd prefer, I can turn you over to one of the other authorities in the city." She showed him her badge.

"You can't do that!" The man didn't bother pretending ignorance.

"Being arrested is the better option. I've seen what the other... authorities do to people who cross them. It's not pleasant." Simon took a step closer, took his sunglasses off, and let his eyes go brown, then gripped the man's chin so their gazes met. "You know what I am. I know who you are. Give us at least some information and I'll be sure to tell them you cooperated."

The man shivered, then tried to shake his head. Simon kept a tight grip on him. The man would bruise, but considering he'd attempted to mask the smell of werewolf blood, Simon didn't care.

"Detective," Simon continued in a low voice. "This house

was the scene of at least one murder. This man has blood on his hands." He made a show of sniffing the man's hands. "Or he did quite recently." He smiled again, and let his fangs drop. Human Destiny hadn't hidden they knew he was a vampire, so he didn't see why he shouldn't use their knowledge to his advantage. "Blood has quite a distinct smell that is almost impossible to mask, don't you think?"

"So I've heard." Tash took a pair of handcuffs from her pocket. "I'm arresting you for suspicion of murder. You have the right to remain—"

The sun glinted off something metal to their right.

"Get down!" Simon yelled, shoving the man onto the ground as a shot rang out. Simon rolled, scanning the area, while the man tried to crawl towards the fence. Simon turned too late after another shot followed the first. The man jerked, then lay still. "Bollocks!" Simon reached for him, then recoiled at the inviting smell of blood. He scooted back well out of temptation's way. "I'm going to find the shooter."

He took the tall fence in a single bound at the same time a motorbike roared down the driveway. He'd almost caught up to it when the passenger on the back turned and fired a pistol. Simon ducked and hit the nearby grass verge. He spluttered, spitting dirt from his mouth. "Bloody hell," he cursed, too late to catch them. Vampire speed only worked for short bursts, and they now had too much of a head start. He wiped the dirt off his trousers and headed back to Tash. Unfortunately, at the speed he'd been moving, Simon hadn't been able to read the registration plate although, given what they knew of this organisation, the bike would soon be abandoned.

"He's dead. He was going to tell us what he knew, and they made sure he didn't." Tash glanced at him. "You okay? And that was damn impressive."

"Not that impressive. He's dead." Simon bent to pick up

the small object that had rolled out of the man's jacket. Luckily it was a decent distance away, so it wasn't covered in blood. "I didn't think they'd kill one of their own." If they had no qualms killing another human, that meant no one was safe.

"I've called the ambulance. They'll be here soon. I told them no rush."

"We should check the house. He'd recently cleaned up werewolf blood." Simon got another whiff of human blood, and his fangs dropped again. His hands shook, and he dropped the pen.

Tash picked it up. "Fawke Security," she read aloud.

"I'd say at the least, that's a clue, wouldn't you?" Simon's voice sounded more strained than he'd anticipated. The bullet struck its victim in a major artery, so there was a large pool of blood around the body.

His phone rang. He didn't need to look at the caller ID to know who it was. "Ben. Don't worry. I'm fine. I'll talk later, okay?" He smiled when Ben responded both by voice and through their bond. "Love you too."

Tash studied him intently. "So, how did Ben know to ring you right now?"

"Coincidence?"

She rolled her eyes. "But neither of us believes in those. Remember?"

Ben trudged up the hill. He'd asked Garrick to drop him partway up so he could walk the rest of the way and clear his head. Despite his side of their bond not being as strong, Ben had picked up on Simon's struggle with his reaction to human blood, loud and clear. The last few months had been a rollercoaster of emotions he hoped wouldn't become the new norm. Ben was used to the vague hum of Simon's presence that brought with it the reassurance he was okay. While he mostly loved being able to feel Simon's emotions, he was exhausted by the increased barrage since their encounter with the BFH. Why wasn't Simon constantly overwhelmed by his side of their bond? After all, this was normal for him.

Once they'd told the rest of his family about Simon, and brought down Human Destiny, things should return to normal. Though their definition of that wasn't anywhere near everyone else's standard. He kind of liked it that way, and didn't regret their life together despite the dangerous situations they ended up in on what seemed like a daily basis. He was crazy thinking their trip here would be any different.

He paused at the entrance to the dairy across the road from the library, tempted by the goodness of a chocolate-driven sugar rush. None of the addresses he and Garrick had looked at had checked out, resulting in the afternoon being a futile exercise. Most of the new builds had sold signs on them and were waiting for their owners. The rentals either had tenants still packing up to leave or were occupied by new arrivals surrounded by piles of boxes. Houses didn't tend to stay on the market long especially if they were priced to sell, and rentals had a long list of people waiting to move in.

His stomach rumbled. Stuff it, that chocolate had his name on it and, once he left the country, he wouldn't have easy access to the local brands.

"Ben, what are you doing here?" Abby stood at the counter, a plastic milk bottle tucked under one arm. "Long day? You look tired. I'm sorry I can't offer you a lift, but I walked. Needed to clear my head before dinner."

"It has been a long day," Ben admitted. "I'm walking for the same reason."

Abby studied him for a moment, then grabbed a peanut

slab chocolate bar and put it on the counter with the milk. "To get your blood sugar levels up."

"Thanks." Ben waited for her to pay, then followed her out of the shop.

Abby smiled, then ruffled his hair like she'd done when he was growing up. "I'm proud of you, and I need to tell you that more often. You've made a life for yourself in another country, which isn't easy, and with someone you love and respect. It's hard to get a good feel for a relationship from half a world away, but I immediately relaxed when I saw you together at the airport."

Ben swallowed, blinking back tears. "Thanks. I'm happy with Simon. I wanted you to like him."

"He's very sweet." Abby hugged Ben. "Although I still think there's something going on that you boys aren't telling me."

Ben groaned. "Tonight, over dinner, okay?" He unwrapped the chocolate and started munching.

Something cold crawled up his spine, and he shivered.

"Ben!"

He turned at the unfamiliar voice but couldn't see anything.

"What's wrong?" Abby asked. Whomever Ben had heard, she hadn't.

Ben put his fingers to his lips, silently asking her to be quiet. The voice came from the direction of the darkened library. "Wait here. I just need to check something out." He sprinted across the road.

A man in old fashioned clothing gestured for him to come closer. "Ben? You're Ben, right?" Joseph was one of the library ghosts, and if he was tied to the building, he wouldn't be able to venture too far from it.

"Yeah. What's wrong?" Ben glanced behind him. Of course, his mother wouldn't stay where he'd left her. She was going to think he was crazy talking to someone she couldn't see or hear.

"You can see me? Bernard thought you'd seen us the other day. Thank God."

"And hear you." Ben lowered his voice, although it was already far too late for that. "What's wrong?"

"It's Josh." Joseph gestured for Ben to follow. "Behind the library. Hurry."

Ben ran after him. "Stay there," he called to Abby.

Josh lay in Cody's arms, groaning. Cody was poking at his phone, almost in tears. Bernard stood next to them, watching the area warily. Once Joseph arrived, both ghosts faded away.

"What happened?" Ben dropped to his knees beside Cody and grabbed his phone. "Shit, no. No ambulance." If they took Josh to a normal hospital and they found out he was a werewolf, all hell would break loose.

"He's hurt, but I can't figure out why." Cody tried to snatch back his phone. "I need to call for help." He stroked Josh's brow. "They didn't hit him that hard. I don't know what's wrong."

Abby knelt down beside Ben, despite him telling her to stay back. "Hi, you're Cody, right?" She kept her tone friendly and non-threatening. "I'm Abby, Ben's mum. I'm a nurse. Let me help."

"Who attacked you?" Ben had a horrible feeling about this. He caught the scent of burning. "Oh shit. We need to find whatever's causing this and quickly."

Josh opened his eyes. "Fuck, it hurts," he muttered. His eyes glowed gold, then he closed them again.

"Where does it hurt?" Ben asked the question too late. "Damn it. Cody, what happened?"

"These men attacked him. They kept going on about werewolves, but he can't be. He can't be." Cody sounded hysterical.

Ben ran his hand over Josh, trying to find the source of the burning. He stopped halfway up Josh's thigh. The denim felt weird, like it was stuck to his skin. "Get his jeans off. Now!" he ordered.

"I can't see any blood," Abby said.

"Whatever did this is still in him." Ben glared at Cody. "Now, or he's going to die. Cody! You with me? Trust me, okay. I've seen this before."

Cody fumbled with Josh's belt, then yanked down Josh's jeans. He winced when part of Josh's skin came away with the denim. "One of them grabbed him. He looked at me and didn't fight them even when they punched him in the gut. Then the other guy pulled out a... it looked like a nail gun, for fuck's sake."

"Silver-coated nails." Ben could see the head of the nail in Josh's thigh, tiny silver lines spreading in all directions around it. "Wankers." He turned to Abby. To hell with keeping secrets. He needed help. The nail head was too small to get his fingers around. "He's been poisoned. We need to get the nail out before the infection spreads. Do you still have tweezers in your bag?"

"I always carry—"

"Good." Ben shuffled back to give her room to work. "This is all going to look weird, but I'll explain later. Get the nail out, and he'll be okay. I promise."

Abby felt Josh's forehead. "He feels very warm."

"That's normal," Ben assured her. Werewolves had a hotter base temperature than humans, while vampires were much colder.

One of the ghosts phased back into being. "The men who did this are long gone. Josh's young man scared them off."

"Great, thanks," Ben said.

The silver in Josh's leg kept spreading. His breathing

didn't sound too great either. Ben turned on his phone's flashlight to give his mother more light.

Abby worked quickly. The nail refused to budge with her first go, and the tweezers slipped. She cursed, changed her angle, and pulled. The nail came out, and Josh started breathing more easily.

Ben sighed in relief. "I think he should be okay now, but he's going to be sore and tired for a few days, like he's getting over the flu." He turned to Cody. "I don't think it's a good idea if he goes home by himself. If you bring him to my granddad's we can—"

"He needs to be looked at by a doctor," Abby corrected him. "Though the wound is closing up by itself, it shouldn't be doing that this quickly."

"Not a hospital." Ben shook his head. "I'll explain once we're home, okay? I can probably arrange a doctor, but it needs to be through a friend."

"Bring him to our place then," Abby insisted. "At least I can keep an eye on him that way." She felt Josh's forehead again. "He's still hot, and I'd like to take his temperature to make sure he's not running a fever."

"His normal temperature is hotter than ours." Ben dug out his phone and rang Simon. "Hey, it's me. Josh is hurt. Silver poisoning. Arseholes attacked him with a nail gun. We got it out. That's all I need to do, right?"

"Yes, that's all you need to do." Simon sounded worried. "They just killed one of their own. A human. Tash and I are waiting for an ambulance, and then we'll be home. Be careful and keep an eye on him until he regains consciousness." He hung up.

"Shit." Ben took a deep breath to steady himself. "Cody, do you have—"

"I can't do this. I'm sorry." Cody glanced at Josh, then at Ben. "Fuck, how could I be so wrong? I didn't know. I swear I didn't know." He pressed his lips to Josh's forehead and pushed him into Ben's arms. "I love him, and I wouldn't hurt him. I promise. I just—" He scrambled to his feet and bolted.

Abby pursed her lips. "Find your friend's car keys. If he doesn't have any on him, phone your father. We're taking him to our place, not Granddad's. I want an explanation for this when we get there. Okay?"

CHAPTER FOURTEEN

"Cody?" Josh tried to sit up. "Where's Cody?" He frowned. "Where am I? What happened?"

"Thank goodness you're awake." Abby was by his side in an instant. "How much do you remember, if anything?"

Josh recoiled, then winced at the sudden movement. "God, I feel like shit."

"You're on the sofa at my parents' house." Ben handed Josh a glass of water. "Drink this. You need to keep your fluids up."

He and Abby had found Josh's car and keys. Ray had helped them settle Josh on the sofa after they arrived home. He agreed to wait for the explanation until Simon joined them, but he didn't look happy with Ben's insistence they not call a doctor. Neither did Abby. In the end, Ben had called Anita and got her to take a look at Josh via an AbenChat call. After a quick introduction, she'd assessed Josh and assured them that the wound closing so quickly meant he was on the mend. They could call her back anytime if they were worried.

Josh took the glass with shaking hands. He'd slept for

over an hour while his body had fought the infection, but he still looked weak, and probably wouldn't feel too good for a few days. The silver threads on his skin had begun to fade once the source of the poison had been removed.

"I should leave." Josh tried to get up, then flopped back down on the sofa.

Abby shook her head. "You're in no fit state to go anywhere," she insisted. "Ben tells me you live alone. I've made up the bed in his old room in case you need it."

"You don't know me." Josh eyed her suspiciously. "Why are you doing this?"

"You're a friend of Ben's, and Ange has spoken of you many times. You've helped her out on a few occasions, so we're returning the favour." Her tone brooked no argument. Ben hoped Josh wasn't foolish enough to try. "However, I do expect an explanation in return."

"I'd better leave then." Josh struggled to his feet again. He shot Ben a look of disbelief. "You know it's against the rules—"

"You were dying of silver poisoning. Mum saved you. I think that cat is already out of the bag." Ben let out a long sigh. Not that casually bringing up the subject of supernaturals over dinner would have worked any better. "She saw your wound close, and your eyes do the glowy thing."

"Shit." Josh bit his lip. "I'm sorry. I didn't mean to drop you in it." He glanced around the room. "Cody?"

"It's way too late for that." Ben studied him, not sure if there was a good way of answering. "Cody left. He said to tell you he loves you." Ben frowned. "He said you were attacked, and you did nothing. Why?"

"And let Cody find out?" Josh rolled his eyes, his tone bitter. "He knows now, I guess. They were going on about werewolves, and they knew what I was."

"This explanation is going to be a doozy," Ray got up to answer the door.

Simon strode across the room and took Ben into his arms. "You're sure you're all right?"

"Yeah, we got there afterwards." Ben leaned into Simon's embrace for a moment. He took a deep breath, taking strength from Simon's presence, as the earlier adrenaline rush started to wear off. "He's okay now. I phoned Anita and got her to take a look as I haven't seen much of this stuff." Anita and Lucas had medical training, and knew far more about werewolf physiology than either he or Simon did. "She said you'd know if we needed to call a doctor."

"A silver coated nail?" Simon gestured for Abby to step aside and took a quick look at Josh's thigh. "I can't see any sign of infection, and it's continuing to heal as I'd expect. You kept the nail?"

"Yeah, it's safely tucked away in a plastic bag."

"Good." Simon took off his coat and turned to Abby and Ray. "I'm very sorry you've had to get involved like this. I had hoped to have this conversation after dinner tonight, and broach one supernatural at a time." He glanced at Tash who had followed him into the house. "Would you mind making some tea? I think we're going to need some."

Abby cleared her throat.

Simon flushed. "My apologies. This is your home, and I've walked in and taken over. Do you want me to start again?"

"Sit down," Ray said, "and start at the beginning. And don't think I didn't hear the word supernatural. Your explanation had better be a good one."

The doorbell rang again.

"I asked Frank to come over early. He can vouch for what we're about to tell you. I thought it might help." Simon grabbed two chairs from the table and gestured for Ben to take one. "Leave your parents the other sofa, hmm?"

At least Tash wouldn't need convincing like their parents that he and Simon weren't crazy. Ben squeezed Simon's hand. Simon slid his free hand around Ben's waist and shuffled his chair over so they sat closer together.

"Do you need me to leave?" Josh looked like he was trying to find a reason to bolt.

"No!" said Ben and Abby at the same time.

"You can walk out that door when you can do it unaided on your own two feet," Abby said. "Can you do that?"

Josh shook his head. He wouldn't have the energy to transform and leave on four legs, either. "No, ma'am."

"That's settled then." Abby settled on the other sofa with Ray. "And you owe me an explanation too. I'm not about to forget that."

Josh nodded and said nothing.

"There's a way bigger world out there than you know about." Ben figured he'd start slow, and that Simon had already had his fill of explanations for the day. "I had no clue until I went to Boggslake."

"That's why it's good to travel," Ray said.

Frank chuckled. "You're just going to have to get to the point."

"Fine." Simon took a deep breath in, then out. "Everything you've heard about us isn't true. Just like humans, we have good and bad within our community. I..." He stopped and bit his lip.

"He doesn't drink human blood anymore," Ben added helpfully.

"I was trying to ease into that part," Simon muttered.

"Human blood?" Abby's eyes widened. "And you said 'we,' like you're not human." She studied him with curiosity rather than fear. "Are you trying to tell us you're some kind of... vampire?"

"That's ridiculous," Ray said. "It's still daylight out, and I've seen you in the sun."

"What is it with your family not believing me? Not some *kind* of vampire. I *am* a vampire." Simon glanced at Josh. "And he's a werewolf."

"It's true," Tash said. "I've seen it. Simon ran after the perp we were chasing this afternoon so fast I couldn't see him and jumped a high fence without breaking a sweat."

"Prove it." Ray crossed his arms, and narrowed his eyes, the expression he used when his children had foolishly tried to lie about something they shouldn't have done.

"Ben, go get a mirror just in case this doesn't convince your father any more than it did you." Simon sighed. His eyes turned fully brown, and he dropped his fangs.

Ben grabbed the hall mirror from its hook and held it up in front of both him and Simon. Only Ben reflected in it.

"The sunlight thing is wrong, but he doesn't reflect." Ben swallowed, his face heating. Vampires reflected when they had an adrenalin rush. Fuck, that had been hot. "Mostly. He doesn't photograph either which is why we don't want any photos at the wedding. Kind of awkward to explain and all that."

"That's how I found out," Frank said helpfully. "I met Simon and his friends in Boggslake when I visited, and took a photograph of Simon. I got one hell of a surprise when I got it developed."

"But that was nearly sixty years ago!" Abby glanced at Simon, then back at the mirror.

"I'm quite a bit older than I look." Simon retracted his fangs. "I'm sorry we kept this from you, but I—"

"We—" Ben interjected.

"No." Simon shook his head. "This is on me. You wanted to do this earlier. I didn't." He ducked his head. "My parents... my father, in particular, didn't take the news well."

"Well, then, he's an idiot. I can't pretend to understand it, but you love my son, and he loves you. Anyone can see that, and you're already a part of this family. We don't judge people because of who they are." Ray frowned. "Does it hurt? The fangs and all that? What about having to drink blood?"

"I think you might regret him knowing what you are for a whole different reason," Frank said. "Ray, let's do the vampire 101 thing later, hmm? These boys have other stuff going on that you need to know about. Like those idiots who attacked young Josh here."

~

"Sorry, I need to sleep." Josh had grown quieter after dinner and hadn't eaten much. "Don't worry if I sleep most of the day tomorrow either. It's normal after something like this." He yawned, his eyes half closed.

Trent glanced at Maddie. They'd walked in on the middle of Josh's brief explanation about Human Destiny and how he'd been attacked. While they'd taken the news in their stride like the rest of the family, Simon suspected once it fully hit home, they'd be asking a lot more questions. "Maddie's getting tired, so we might head off."

"I'm not that tired," Maddie protested.

"Yeah, you are." Trent kissed her cheek, "and you'll need your energy for work tomorrow."

Maddie worked at a local preschool. "The mums keep telling me this tiredness will go, but I don't believe it."

"Get any rest while you can. Your dad and I will walk you to your car." Abby frowned. "We're not in any danger from these people, are we?"

"Whatever they have planned, I doubt they'll want to draw attention to themselves with a random attack." They'd killed to protect their secrets, and the break-in at Frank's had been to find information. Unfortunately, Simon doubted Wayland would see the point of providing any sort of protection for humans. "If you'd like, I can contact a friend and see if I can set something up. In the meantime, lock your doors and don't invite anyone in you don't know. That includes tradesmen."

"That sounded more like a no than a yes," Ray said.

"Simon's just being cautious," Ben said. "If they went after every human who has connections to the supernatural world, they'd risk their agenda."

"So us normal humans should be okay?" Maddie placed a hand on her stomach. "You're sure?"

"Yeah. You normal humans should be fine." Ben stood when they did. "I'll help Josh get settled in my old room. Simon, you want to put the kettle on again?" He gave his sister and brother-in-law a hug. "Being aware of this stuff isn't always scary you know, and we track down guys like this all the time."

"Look after yourself, and don't do anything stupid." Maddie rolled her eyes when Ben grinned. "I know you, remember, and thanks for trying to reassure us like that."

"Love you too, Mads." Ben helped Josh from the sofa, and they headed towards the bedroom.

"They're going to notice Ben's slip, and you haven't told them about *that* yet," Frank said after Abby and Ray left to see Maddie and Trent to their car. "And who are you going to ask for help?"

"Elard should have some connections." Simon busied himself making another pot of tea. He hadn't intended to tell Ben's family about their soulbond. "And I'll try Rupert again. He can't ignore my calls forever."

"I can only stay two nights," Josh said from the bedroom, "and although I'd like to help, right now, I'd probably fall flat on my arse if I tried." He sounded exhausted.

"I'm surprised you're still upright. Don't worry. We'll make sure they don't try for round two." Simon doubted Wayland would do anything to help Josh either.

"Do you think we should stay here tonight?" Frank asked.

"I'm planning to stay over. These guys are human, and Mum and Dad have a security system. We'll be fine." Tash collected the empty cups and took them into the kitchen. "Told us about what yet?"

"Full moon's on Thursday, yeah?" Ben said when he came back into the room.

"Yes." Simon pulled coffee off the shelf. "You'd prefer this?"

Ben grinned. "Yep. I could do with the caffeine hit. Feeling the long day as well." He wandered into the kitchen, slid his arms around Simon from behind, and nuzzled his neck. "See, that wasn't so bad, was it?"

"Considering you haven't told us the whole truth, you mean?" Tash got out of their way and, despite her question, smiled at Ben's open display of affection for Simon.

"Huh?" Ben lifted his head to look at her. "But—"

"*You* normal humans should be okay." Simon waited until Ben took a step back, then handed him his coffee. "You're right about needing caffeine." Usually, Ben was more careful than that.

"Umm... I am..." Ben trailed off.

Simon raised an eyebrow and thought very clearly about what he wanted to do with Ben when they got home.

Ben flushed bright red when Simon's desire flowed through their bond. "Okay. You've made your point." He lowered his voice. "Are you sure this is a good idea? This stuff is private and not that well known outside vampire society."

"You trust them." Simon already knew the answer, so didn't phrase it as a question.

"Yes, if it's okay with you." Ben glanced at his sister. "Sorry."

"Don't mind me." Tash grabbed the teapot and refilled her tea. "I get the feeling I should have brought something stronger than wine to drink once I've finished this round of tea."

"I trust you, but what we've told them so far is about me, not you." Simon met Ben's gaze directly, drinking in the love and trust in his eyes. Although he'd pushed Simon to be honest with his—their—family, he'd still been prepared to keep this last secret if Simon had wanted him to.

"Us. Everything about us, and has been since we..." Ben caressed Simon's cheek. "Till death do us part, and you'd better not go before me."

"I don't want that either." Simon leaned into Ben's touch.

Frank coughed loudly. "Just in case you're distracted, we're not alone."

"Yes, I know that." Simon placed his hand over Ben's. "Yes?"

"Yeah, definitely. I love you." Ben grabbed the tea and pulled Simon back out to the living room. His parents had barely re-entered the house and closed the front door behind them when the words rushed out of him. "Umm, you know what I said earlier about normal humans?"

Ray raised an eyebrow, his expression one Simon had seen on Ben many times. "You forgot to tell us Simon turned you into a vampire too?"

Simon stilled. "No, not—" He wasn't ready to have that conversation with them yet.

"It's okay. No, I'm not a vampire, although Simon and I..." Ben slipped his hand into Simon's. "We're soulbonded. It's a vampire thing. That was how I knew he told me the truth. I... can feel when he's in trouble, and vice versa, although it's much stronger on his side because I'm not a vampire."

"Knew it!" Tash murmured. "Coincidental phone call, my arse."

"Is that all? Thanks for telling us," Ray said, "but it sounds... very personal, so we're not going to ask you to explain."

"We're not?" Abby sounded more curious than concerned.

"No, we're not," Ray reiterated firmly.

"Now that Josh has settled in, is there anything I need to look for that might suggest we need to call in a doctor like your friend Dr Coate?" Abby asked.

"He should be fine," Simon assured her, "although he needs to leave on Thursday evening, no matter how unwell he is."

As Ben hadn't mentioned the rest of what their bond meant, he wasn't going to go into it either. He'd said everything Ben's family needed to know, and that was enough.

"Full moon," Ben added. "All werewolves lock themselves up then. They're dangerous."

Josh hadn't said much about being a werewolf apart from that he was one, could change, wasn't about to, and silver was poisonous. If he wanted to expand on that, it was up to him, although not explaining the danger associated with a full moon would be reckless, not to mention irresponsible.

"What if he turns into a werewolf before then?" Abby asked.

"He'll still be Josh. Just not on a full moon." Simon blew out a breath. "You're taking this surprisingly in your stride. I'm impressed and, to be honest, a bit nervous."

"Don't worry," Ray said. "I'm intending to get very drunk once you've left."

Abby poked him with her elbow. "What are you doing about finding the people who did this to him?"

Simon pulled out the pen he'd found. This wasn't his city,

so any help he could get would be appreciated. "We're hoping this is a clue. Have either of you heard of Fawke Security?"

Ray took the pen and peered at the bird of prey logo. "They installed a new security system last year at the bank I work at." He was a mortgage broker. "The company have only been in Wellington a couple of years, but they've built a solid reputation in Auckland. Australian based, if I remember correctly, and expanded over here about ten years ago."

"That's a lot more information than I expected," Simon said.

"They do home security too, so I looked into them a couple of months ago when we decided to get an alarm put in here." Ray shrugged. "They knew their stuff, and the price was good, but we decided to go for someone more established." He hesitated. "To be honest, something about the guy running the local branch made me uncomfortable. Couldn't say why, but I went with my gut."

"They're definitely worth checking out then." Simon took back the pen and pocketed it. "Thank you. I think tomorrow will be a good day to go shopping for a security system for a new business I'm about to set up."

CHAPTER FIFTEEN

Ange adjusted Ben's tie. "There, that's better."

"It was fine before," he grumbled. "Come on, let's do this." He slipped his hand into hers, then they crossed the road and headed towards the shop front for Fawke Security.

Simon and Garrick hadn't been happy about Ben and Ange running reconnaissance for this part of the investigation, but Ben had pointed out that they were the more sensible choice. Human Destiny already knew who Simon was, and probably Garrick too, and Tash had been at the latest crime scene. They hadn't seen Ange, and hopefully had no clue what Ben looked like.

They paused in front of the shop window and talked in low voices as though they were discussing something important.

"You haven't been to see Dax yet," Ange reminded him. She pointed at the sign that talked about the importance of having a good fire sprinkler system and turned back to him like she was making a point.

Which she was, just not the one she was pretending to.

"She probably doesn't remember me." Ben wanted to see

his cat again, although she was no longer his. He'd been gone a long time in animal years, and he didn't want her to treat him like a stranger.

"I bet she does." Ange squeezed his hand. "Once we've caught these people, you and Simon should still come around for coffee like we planned. You can even meet the cat from next door. She and Dax are good friends."

They'd decided it was safer not to lead the bad guys to Ange's door in the meantime. Her flatmates had no clue about the weirder side of Wellington, and if Fawke was connected to Human Destiny, it was more sensible to approach them in their shopfront on a busy street.

"Catsby, right?" Ben bit his lip. Great, then he could have two cats ignore him. "Yeah, sounds good." He glanced across the street but, although he could sense Simon, he and Garrick were well hidden. "One of the shop assistants is staring at us, so we'd better get in. You have our cover story down pat?"

Ange raised an eyebrow. "Hey, I'm not new to this undercover lark, you know." She pushed open the door, leaving Ben to follow. "Oh look, this could be exactly what we need."

A man at least ten years younger than either of them approached them. "Welcome to Fawke Security. How can I help you today?"

"My brother and I have just started our own business." Ange stuck to the plan and took point. She handed him the business card they'd mocked up and printed out that morning. "Dax Computing. We've been talking about it for years, and now we have a house with a front room that's perfect to work out of. It makes sense to make sure our premises are secure." Ange paused to take a breath. "We've got insurance, of course, but it's easier to be proactive rather than reactive, don't you think?" She smiled. "And our premium will be cheaper once we have an alarm system installed, so it's a sensible move all round."

"Oh definitely." The sales assistant—Rodney, according to his name badge—grabbed the bait like a hungry shark.

"We don't have many clients yet, but as our business is going to grow, it's better to get everything in place before that happens." Ange beamed at him. "Oh goodness me, I'm sorry, where are my manners?" She held out her hand. "I'm Angela Duncan, and this is my brother Benjamin."

Ben winced at the use of his full name. The last time he'd been called Benjamin, he'd been a child, and his parents had caught him in the hallway trying to hide a lamp he'd broken with his cricket bat.

Once Rodney let go of his hand, Ben walked over to one of several different alarm systems displays and pretended to study the specs. He didn't like the way the guy was looking at Ange or fawning over her. "This square one looks like what we're looking for. Straightforward with a keypad so should be easy to programme to do what we need. What do you think, Angela?"

"That's our starter package. It's a basic alarm system, but you also have the option to arm or disarm through an app on your smartphone." Rodney rattled off a price excluding tax. "Monitoring is extra, but we have a deal going currently if you add a fire sprinkler system at a reduced price. A residential property doesn't need one, per se, but you're using at least part of your premises for a business."

"Water or some other kind of suppression solution?" Ben had scanned their website earlier that morning, so he didn't sound completely like he was pulling information out of his arse.

"Huh?" Rodney looked blank for a moment, confirming Ben's suspicion the guy was inexperienced and quoting the training manual.

"For the sprinklers." Ben said. "Water and electronics don't mix."

"Of course, we will work with you to ensure you get the right system for your needs."

"Do you have some brochures we can take with us?" Ange asked. "We're still window shopping and we need to discuss any plans with our business partner before making any decisions."

Rodney's expression soured. "You could always bring him or her into the shop if you see something you like, so we could discuss possible options."

So, you get the sales commission, you mean.

"My husband's busy all day with a client," Ben said, "so sorry, that's not going to happen. We'll be sure to tell him how helpful you are, though."

"Oh, I see. Yes, of course." Rodney didn't miss a beat. He walked behind the counter and pulled some brochures from a rack, then found a folder to put them in.

Ben wandered around the shop, stopping at intervals so he could pretend to be interested in the different displays. He picked up a brochure listing some of the firm's major clients. Many of them had written glowing testimonials.

Considering the size of the building, the shop front wasn't that big, although the website suggested they did most of their business online, and usually met with clients at their homes or business premises to confirm and arrange installation. A storeroom beckoned from the back of the shop, its door ajar. Ben glanced at Rodney to make sure he was busy with Ange, then glanced inside. Several boxes of office water cooler bottles lined the walls.

An older man, about Ben's father's age, entered the shop. "Is there a problem here, Rodney?" He spoke with an Australian accent and frowned when he saw Ben and Ange.

"No, sir." Rodney averted his eyes. "I was just telling them about the special we're running at the moment."

"Rodney's been very helpful," Ange said. "We were hoping to get some information to take with us. A ballpark figure for what it will cost, and what you can offer us. That kind of thing."

"Of course." The man's gaze lingered on Ben, then he looked away. "Malcolm Wright. I'm the Wellington area manager for Fawke Security. Sorry, I didn't catch your names."

"Angela Duncan, and this is my brother Benjamin. We're looking for security for our business premises."

"You seem familiar," he said to Ben. "Have you used our firm before or worked somewhere that might have? We provide security guards for several local businesses and some private customers."

"I don't think so." Ben hoped Wright hadn't figured out who they were. "My dad looked into one of your systems a while back," he added. "Perhaps it's the family resemblance you're remembering."

"Perhaps." Malcolm smiled. "Please come into my office, and we can talk through a plan that will benefit both of us."

"That sounds wonderful, thank you," Ange said.

A chill ran up Ben's spine. This guy was making him very uncomfortable, yet he couldn't figure out why. "Excuse me a moment, first. Sorry." He made a show of taking his phone out of his pocket and checking it. "Actually, perhaps we can just take some brochures. Sorry. Something's come up with a customer and we need to cut this short."

"Of course. Not a problem." Malcolm handed Ben his card. "If you or your husband want to discuss your security needs with us, I'm very happy to meet with you personally."

"Thanks. We appreciate the service. Good day, Mr Wright."

Malcolm nodded. "And to you, Mr... Duncan."

Ben hurried Ange out of the shop and didn't stop walking until they'd reached the crossing a few metres away.

"What was that about?" Ange asked.

"He was definitely onto us. I think he recognised me." Ben hoped if that was the case, Simon had managed to get hold of either Elard or Rupert to organise some security of their own. "And what kind of security firm has a storeroom full of water cooler bottles?"

Ange frowned. "Hold up. Wright came in after you told Rodney about having to check with our other partner, right?"

"Right. But what—" Ben glanced behind them. "Oh shit. He mentioned my husband, but he couldn't have heard that bit. I'm wearing a wedding ring, but why presume I'm married to a man?" Wright definitely wasn't a vampire or werewolf. Ben had got good at spotting those.

"He wouldn't." Ange crossed the road, heading towards the café where they'd arranged to meet Simon and Garrick afterwards. "I think there's a good chance Fawke Security is connected to who we're looking for."

"Except if they are, they now know we're onto them too."

"Damn it." Garrick finished his telephone call and drained the rest of his coffee. "Wayland wants to talk to me urgently."

"You mean, he's summoned you." Simon had tried not to listen in to the conversation, but he'd heard enough of it to know Wayland wasn't happy.

Garrick growled. "Yes. I explained we're following a lead, but when he wants a meeting, he doesn't give a damn what I'm doing." He glanced at his watch. "I'll be in touch. Hopefully, Wayland's contacted me because he has information, not because he's getting impatient."

"Or a mix of both? Do you think he knows we're looking into Fawke?" Simon didn't bother lowering his voice. Instead, he gave a curt nod to the two werewolves sitting a couple of tables away. The woman narrowed her eyes while the man grinned.

"Of course, he does. Nothing much happens in this city he doesn't know about."

"Not knowing who is behind Human Destiny must be very frustrating for him."

"Quite." Garrick pushed back his chair. "Keep an eye on your husband and his friend." He nodded towards the couple when he passed their table and, unsurprisingly, they got up and followed him.

"Not even subtle," Simon murmured, partly amused and annoyed that Wayland had sent werewolves to spy on them. It figured he'd only trust a vampire so far. Simon waited a minute for Garrick and the other werewolves to be clear of the café, then shoved on his sunglasses and walked out into the spring morning.

The wind had come up a little, so he pulled his coat collar up over the top of his scarf. The seasons here changed several times a day, but the mild, weather suited him for the most part. His dislike for extreme temperatures was a preference he'd carried with him from before he was turned.

He set a brisk pace, intent on intercepting Ben and Ange before they reached the café, then slowed to watch them cross the road up ahead. He frowned, then waited a few moments to confirm his suspicions. The man following them had also been hanging around the shop opposite Fawke Security. He'd glanced in Ben and Ange's direction when they'd left, then mirrored their action when they'd walked to the crossing, although he'd stayed on this side of the road when they'd crossed. For now, he was keeping a decent distance behind, but how long would that last?

Simon's phone buzzed, informing him he had a text. He ignored it.

"For goodness sake, pick up your phone."

Simon turned at the sound of Rupert's voice, but his friend was already on an intercept course for Ben, Ange, and the man following them. Simon fished out his phone and read the message.

I've got this. My office. One hour.

He didn't bother arguing, having learnt the hard way that attempting to change Rupert's mind when he'd already set a plan in motion was a waste of time. Instead, he texted Ben. *Change of plan. I'll meet you at the cable car.*

Ben pulled out his phone immediately, read the text, then turned and headed back down Willis Street towards Lambton Quay. Once he'd changed direction, Rupert bumped into his target, nearly knocking the man to the ground.

"I'm so sorry. I wasn't looking where I was going." Before the man could reply, Rupert took a step back. "Oh, I say, Morton Pringle, isn't it? You were in my medieval literature class six years ago, weren't you?" He shook the man's hand as Simon walked past. "I never forget a student, especially the ones who never paid attention during my lectures."

Simon chuckled. He knew exactly the type of student Rupert referred to. He also had a few who were obviously only there to fill in time. The rubbish they wrote in their assignments more than verified his impression of them. His students had quickly learnt not to argue with him about what life was like in Britain during the 1930s, and quote some obscure, poorly researched book to prove their point. Simon had been there. They hadn't.

He kept enough distance behind Ben and Ange to hear

their conversation but not so close anyone would notice he was following them. Ben paused in front of a jewellery shop on the corner, glanced in Simon's direction, and smiled, but didn't meet his gaze.

Ange grabbed Ben's arm and pulled him along until they reached one of the local bookshops. "So, have you read the latest in this series yet?" She pointed to a book on display. "It picks up straight after the one we read together last year."

"I started it on the flight over." Ben grinned. "Hey, no spoilers. I'm only at the bit where the dragon accidentally burns down the village."

"I *loved* that scene, and what happens next is sweet as. Those guys are so cute together." Ange lowered her voice, and Simon strained to hear. "Have you had any luck getting Simon hooked on comics yet?"

"Nope, but I caught him flipping through that Midnighter and Apollo title you put me onto. He was totally checking out Midnighter's arse, though he denied it."

He totally had *not* been doing that. The book had fallen on the floor and opened at that page when he'd picked it up.

Ange laughed. "Of course he did." She gave Ben a brief hug.

"Hey, what was that for?"

"I miss you, and the conversations we used to have. Aben-Chat calls are okay, but it's not the same. Meeting in person is so much better."

"I miss you too, but I'm happy with Simon and we've made our home in Boggslake together." Ben's voice softened. "Sometimes, when we have evenings when no one's trying to kill us, we curl up on the sofa together. Simon grades assignments and reads out some of the unintentionally funny comments his students write, and I share a line or two from whatever I'm reading. It's comfortable, and we fit, you know?"

"Yeah, I know. I see you and Simon together and wish I could have that." Ange sounded wistful. "Maybe one day, but not seeing it right now." She elbowed his side. "But, anyway, we need to get moving, or Simon will be waiting for us, instead of the other way round."

"We're here for another month yet," Ben said. "Plenty of time for us to do the stuff we used to. I'm playing in a darts match next week, like old times. You should come and hang out for the evening. I'd like that. We'd both like that."

"Sure, sounds good. We should sort out an evening for D&D too. Zeke and Olly both have some free evenings next week, so we could make it work. The campaign isn't the same without you." Ange started back down the street.

Ben turned, caught Simon's eye again, mouthed the words "I love you," and then sprinted to catch up with her.

Simon waited until they'd walked a decent distance ahead before following. He enjoyed the quiet evenings he and Ben shared too. Although Ben had a reputation for being loud and always having something to say, he had a knack for knowing when he didn't need to fill the silence between them. He also didn't talk very often about how much he missed his family and the friends he'd left behind when he'd decided to make his home in Boggslake with Simon. Their soulmate bond wasn't the only reason they'd stayed together. Ben's love for Simon humbled him. Ben knew everything about Simon, and all the terrible things he'd done in his life, yet never judged or held it against him.

Watching Ben interact with his family brought home to Simon how much Ben had given up for their life together. It wasn't easy to start afresh in a new country, even with the support of friends who were more like family. Did Simon have the right to drag Ben away from his family again? Seeing Ben helpless and hurt in his hospital bed a few months ago had brought home how dangerous their life was, especially for Ben if he remained human. Once they returned to Boggslake, when would he have the opportunity to spend time with his family again? His sister was expecting, and Ben would make a great uncle. But he wouldn't get to see the children grow up.

Family was important. And family who accepted you for who you were without blinking an eye like Ben's had done, needed to be embraced like the precious jewel they were.

"Everything okay?" Ben asked when Simon caught up to them as they boarded the cable car.

"Yes." Simon kissed Ben on the cheek. "Just thinking about how lucky I am to have you in my life."

Ben chose a seat, then shuffled over to give Simon room to sit next to him. "I love you." He took Simon's hand in his, squeezed it, and then looked at their rings side by side. "I don't need a ring to remind me of that, but I'm proud to wear yours." He lowered his voice so only Simon could hear. "Ditto for your mark."

"Once this case is over, we'll have a proper honeymoon and spend some time together as we planned." Simon wanted to give that to Ben, and more.

"You really think we have a chance of that?" Ben chuckled. "I thought coming here would be very different from Boggslake, yet it's turned out to be much the same." He raised Simon's hand to his lips and kissed his ring. "It's weird, but I'm used to chasing bad guys, and all the crap that goes with that."

Ange rolled her eyes from her seat across the aisle but, instead of commenting, turned away to give them some privacy.

"I've been doing this a lot longer than you have, but getting used to it doesn't mean we can't take at least a few days off." Simon glanced out the window. The view of Wellington from the cable car was breathtaking. "This is still your home, and I want you to be able to show it to me." He swallowed. "To be able to pretend, at least for a while, that we're a normal couple, doing all those things that come with that."

Ben didn't answer immediately. Instead, he cupped Simon's chin, turned him so they were facing, and studied him. "You don't need to give me that, or feel you need to. I love our life, and that means *every* part of it. And yeah, this is where I grew up, and my family is here, but home isn't just a place. If we're together, it doesn't matter where we live or what we do with our lives. You're my home." He smiled. "Not only that, but you have my heart and half my soul. No matter what our future holds, I wouldn't have it any other way."

CHAPTER SIXTEEN

Simon glanced at his watch. "We have fifteen minutes to get to Rupert's office. He dislikes tardiness, so we shouldn't be late." He drained the rest of his coffee. "Thanks for recommending this café," he told Ange. "Not only is the coffee decent, but the ambience is something I could get used to."

He didn't recognise the jazz music playing in the background, but had been caught up in it quickly. He'd ask what it was and add it to the list of CDs he wanted to look for to take back to Boggslake.

"If we have time afterwards, we can swing by the history department if you'd like," Ben said. "You could talk shop with some of the staff here, or make an appointment to meet up before we go home."

"I'd like that."

Simon was keen to take a look at the curriculum to see what courses the university offered. It never hurt to make connections with faculty in different cities either.

"If you're coming back, you need to try the kumara wedges here," Ange said. "It's one of their specialities.

Although the ones at the other campus cafés aren't bad, they have nothing on these."

"We could get them to go and eat them at the rose gardens if you'd like," Ben suggested. "Make a day of it, if the weather cooperates. I need to introduce you to Dax too, so perhaps we can visit Ange for coffee afterwards."

"Sounds like a plan." Ange leaned in closer and lowered her voice. "I still can't believe Professor Milne is the 'you know what'. He was the last person I suspected."

"That's rather the point." Simon wondered how many of the faculty she'd photographed in an attempt to figure out who the vampire was on staff.

"He was also the only one I didn't manage to pin down for a photo."

"Of course, he was." Simon grinned. "He's very experienced at dodging cameras, although he always has the latest model."

"He does?" Ben's eyes gleamed with excitement. "Very cool, although I still love the one you gave me. I forgot to take some shots of the university buildings with it the last time we were here. I got some good photos of the rose gardens, then got distracted by what we found in Rupert's office."

"Then I'll be sure to remind you to bring it with you before we set off next time. You can take some photographs while I'm waxing lyrical about history." Simon loved seeing Ben so enthused about his photography. He'd insisted Ben bring the Brownie camera to New Zealand with him, although he hadn't had much opportunity to use it here yet. "Uncle Edwin would have loved to have seen the photographs you've taken with it."

"I wish I could have met him." Ben took Simon's hand in his. They headed towards Rupert's office, Ange trailing behind them.

"So do I." Simon was glad Ben hadn't met his parents. He would have given them a piece of his mind, and Simon's father would have retorted in kind. "He would have loved you."

Rupert's door was shut. "Come in," he called before Simon had the chance to knock.

"Thank you for intervening." Simon waited for Rupert to tell him to sit. Despite having been Rupert's student nearly a hundred years ago, standing in front of his desk made it feel like yesterday.

"That boy could never think for himself." Rupert glanced up at them, then opened his laptop. "Miss Duncan, please shut the door and take a seat. The spare one is for Detective Frater. He'll be along shortly."

Ben's eyes widened. "I didn't think that laptop model was on the market yet."

"It's not." Rupert grinned. "At least four months away from what I gather."

"Rupert loves technology and always gets the latest of everything before they're officially available." Simon had never seen the appeal and only used new-fangled devices when he didn't have a choice.

"Unfortunately, there are so many more choices now than there used to be." Rupert sighed. "Not so long ago I didn't have to make those kinds of decisions. Although, of course, they'd give me whatever I asked for."

"You must have one hell of a lot of connections." Ben whistled.

Rupert frowned. "Well yes, of course. What's the point of watching trends if you don't become acquainted with the person behind the next big thing before they're famous? Despite that, there are few of us who aren't enamoured with technology." He gave Simon a pointed look. "Apart from needing to move with the times to survive, I don't see the point in being gifted with a long life if you don't use it to your full advantage." He scrolled up the page on his laptop. "As I said to Ernest that time..."

"Ernest?" Ange asked.

"Here we go," Simon murmured. Rupert loved to name drop, and considering his age, encouraging him was never a good idea.

"Rutherford of course." Rupert glanced at Simon and rolled his eyes. "But anyway, enough chit chat. I'm not surprised that Fawke Security has its finger in this particularly distasteful pie. I've had my eye on Malcolm Wright since he arrived in the area. He's a nasty piece of work, although he's given the illusion of keeping his opinions to himself over the past few years. That's suspicious in itself."

"Meaning he didn't before?" Simon asked.

"Exactly." Rupert rested his elbows on his desk and steepled his fingers. "He had quite the reputation in Brisbane for reporting to the police anyone who did anything that didn't mesh with his ideals. More often than not, the people he targeted were supernaturals. If he knew about us, he didn't confirm it, although I always thought his actions were a thinly veiled threat."

"Brisbane?" Ange moved her chair closer to the desk. "Josh is from there. It's where his pack was slaughtered."

Rupert smiled grimly. "Exactly. I doubt it's a coincidence, or that he left his business there in the hands of his brother, who is the other company director, and moved here to manage the expansion himself, only a few weeks later."

"When did Josh move here?" Ben frowned. "He started working at the library a couple of months before I left for Boggslake."

"He came to New Zealand nearly ten years ago," Ange confirmed. "He moved around the country a lot and worked in a few different libraries in fixed term positions before settling in Wellington and getting the job he has now."

"If Wright came to the country shortly after Josh, the two are most likely connected." Simon didn't like the dots he was connecting. "If you're responsible for a massacre but no one can prove it, you'd want to clean up afterwards. Even if Josh doesn't know Wright, he seemed very certain Human Destiny was responsible. If he can tie the two together, that makes him a very dangerous loose end."

"Wright might not have personally killed those werewolves, but I wouldn't be surprised if he ordered it. If I was your friend Josh and I knew someone was following me, I wouldn't stay too long in one place either. Not only that, but I'd make sure I'd find out everything there is to know about whoever was after me."

"Do we have anything tying Wright to them?" Simon asked.

"Not yet. He's good at covering his tracks." Rupert turned his laptop around so they could see the screen. "I can't find anything to link him to that organisation, or much of anything about them, but I did find something very interesting about Fawke Security."

"That's a list of their managing directors." Ben glanced at Simon, then back at the screen. "Malcolm Wright and... I thought you said his brother was the other company director."

"Shit, no. That can't be right." Ange looked and sounded horrified. "This has to be a coincidence. It's a very common last name, right?"

"I assure you the information here is quite correct," Rupert confirmed. "I spent an interesting morning calling in a favour with someone who works at Births, Deaths, and Marriages."

"And?" Simon didn't wait for Rupert to continue building suspense. He enjoyed that a little too much too.

"Malcolm and his brother aren't full siblings. Malcolm kept his father's name when their mother remarried. His brother Gordon's father, is her second husband." Rupert brought up a birth certificate. "Gordon married a New Zealander. I believe you've met their son."

"Cody," Ange whispered. "No. It can't be." She bit her lip. "I know him. He's a good guy. He can't be involved in this."

Ben gripped Simon's hand. "When Josh was attacked, Cody kept going on about werewolves and how he didn't believe it, and how wrong he'd been. I thought it was because the guys who poisoned Josh said something but... fuck, we need to warn him. What if Wright *is* Human Destiny, and Cody leads them right to Josh?" He paled. "He's still at my parents. They could all be in danger."

"I've already contacted the vampire Elard sent to watch them. He'll keep an eye on Josh too." Rupert turned the screen back towards him. "At present, we still have no proof that these people are the ones we're looking for."

"If they're not, why send someone to follow Ben and Ange?" Simon wasn't about to take any chances.

"Well then, that's the question we need answered, isn't it?" Rupert looked up at the same time Simon smelt the familiar scent of werewolf approaching their door. "And if I'm not mistaken, Detective Frater is about to join us. Let's hope he has that missing puzzle piece we need, hmm?"

Ben's phone vibrated in his pocket. "Sorry." Normally he'd ignore it, but with everything going on he couldn't afford to. He'd never forgive himself if something had happened and his family were trying to get hold of him.

Weirdly, the number wasn't one he recognised, and the message made little sense either. Unless...

"You didn't give my number to Wright or his sales assistant, did you?" he asked Ange.

"No, of course not. I just took some brochures. Why?"

"Just got a weird message. Looks like spam." Ben read out the message. "Sprinklers."

"They're not the only firm selling them," Simon said, "and I thought mobiles didn't usually get those annoying telemarketing calls."

"Some of those people can be very persistent, and if you've given your number out recently, I wouldn't put it past them to try." Garrick strode into the office without waiting for an invitation. "It's surprisingly easy to find a mobile number online."

"Yes, but I've only used this number for a short time. I got a New Zealand sim card while I'm here." Ben glared at his phone, then pocketed it. "Never mind. We have more important things to think about." He'd turned the GPS off on his phone immediately after Rupert had told them about Human Destiny. Bad enough they knew where he lived, but he wasn't about to give them the opportunity to track his movement too.

"How did the meeting with Wayland go?" Simon asked.

Ange moved her chair over to give Garrick some space to sit between her and Ben. He smiled, and she returned it, then quickly averted her gaze. Ben raised an eyebrow but said nothing. He'd tease her about her reaction later.

"Not any better than I'd expected." Garrick took a long drink of the takeout coffee he'd brought with him. "Wayland isn't happy and wants us to prove or dismiss our theory that Fawkes could be a front for Human Destiny as soon as possible."

Ange dug into her bag and pulled out the folder Rodney

had given her. She flipped through the fliers then handed Garrick one of them. "According to this, Wayland Real Estate is one of their biggest clients. They haven't just installed security for the firm's business premises, but also provide security patrols for empty properties."

Garrick's expression turned grim while he read through the testimonials. "Some of these other businesses are pack too. No wonder Wayland is worried." He frowned. "About six months ago, Fawke offered Wayland a deal for anyone interested in residential security, and a lot of the pack signed up for it. I thought about it, then decided against it. I've been a cop for too many years, I guess. Although the offer was only a basic alarm system, and sprinklers, I would have had to let someone I didn't know into my house."

"I'm surprised Wayland let Wright into the building to talk to him," Ben said. "The guy's a creep."

"Malcolm Wright didn't deal with Wayland, or any of the pack directly. He sent his nephew to do the sales spiel on his behalf. The man was very personable and almost got through to me too." He shrugged. "Whatever he said to the pack's head of security must have resonated, though. When I was at an event at the pack community hall a few weeks ago, I noticed new alarms and sprinklers."

A chill went down Ben's back. "Community hall?"

"Most packs here have them," Garrick said. "We use them for big social gatherings like the pack dinners on the full moon nights. Those of us who live near human populations have locked ourselves away on the full moon for a very long time."

"*Most* of you lock yourselves away. About twenty years ago, a group of humans were torn apart by werewolves who didn't follow the rules." Rupert shook his head. "The pack had the nerve to try to blame us for it. We wouldn't risk drinking human blood when there's a good supply of the alternative."

"Once you get a taste for it, the temptation is always there." Simon bit his lip.

Ben squeezed his hand.

"My apologies," Rupert sighed. "The last time we crossed paths was before that... incident. I shouldn't have been so insensitive."

"The pack has safe rooms attached to the community halls so everyone gathers for dinner a few hours before the full moon. It's a huge social event." Garrick moved the conversation on before Ben could. "And before you ask, there are shelters for werewolves who aren't associated with the pack, and some of the older pack members who have been here for decades have saferooms built into their houses. It's part of the Supernatural Treaty, and Wayland has enforcers to make sure anyone caught in werewolf form outside on a full moon won't be again."

"I've heard about his so-called enforcers." Rupert sounded like he'd tasted something unpleasant. "They can be a little too... enthusiastic. I've always made it a point to stay out of their way."

"We don't have time for all the politicking you all love so much." Ben interrupted before the conversation took another nosedive. "This guy who talked the pack into installing alarms... what was his name, and do you remember what he looked like?" He still didn't want to think that Cody was a part of this, but targeting the pack with a tempting deal wasn't helping prove his innocence.

"Cody Prentice," Garrick said without hesitation.

"Bastard said he worked as a sales rep," Ange muttered. "Hang on, I have a photo somewhere if you could confirm it's him." She scrolled through her gallery, then handed her phone to Garrick.

Ben leaned over to get a closer look. Josh and Cody sat on a bench at one of the local beaches. Both looked unaware they were being photographed. Josh rested his head on Cody's shoulder. Cody had his fingers threaded through Josh's hair and gazed at him with an expression Ben had seen on Simon many times.

"He's in love with Josh." Ben doubted Cody was faking his feelings. The couple of times he'd seen Cody and Josh together confirmed it. "What the hell?"

"I don't think he knew what Josh was until that evening he was attacked," Simon said. "I suspect he's trying to marry whatever he's been told and what his heart tells him to be true."

Rupert cleared his throat. "We're missing something very important here. We're presuming Fawke and Human Destiny are connected, but we don't have any proof. Until we have the fact, we can't accuse this young man of anything. It's too easy to weave our own narrative into a situation. Not only easy, but dangerous. I remember those poor young women at Salem only too well. We do not want a repeat of that."

"You were at Salem?" Ange asked.

Ben elbowed her. While Simon hadn't been forthcoming about how old Rupert was, he'd learned not to ask about that kind of thing. Some vampires said straight up how old they were. Others didn't.

"How old do you think I am, young lady?" Rupert raised an eyebrow.

"Umm." Ange flushed. "Five hundred?"

Rupert chuckled. "An interesting guess, but you're not even close. Anyway, we're digressing. We've linked young Mr Prentice to Fawke Security, but not to Human Destiny, so we're still no further ahead."

"Back up." Ben thought back to the text he'd received. "Garrick, you said you wouldn't let anyone into your house.

What about the rest of the pack? They might not want security, but what about a sprinkler system? A lot of older houses don't have them installed, and if Fawke was offering a good deal, it might have tempted someone who hadn't thought of it before."

"Right." Garrick frowned. "I don't think the shelters would have installed them, but I can check."

"Can you also ask Wayland how many of the pack had sprinkler systems installed in their houses?" Simon had obviously come to the same conclusion.

"Sure. Give me a minute." Garrick stepped out of the room.

Ben pulled out his phone and called the number that had sent the text. It rang for a few minutes and then clicked over to an answering service.

"Hi, you've reached Cody Prentice. I'm not able to take your call at present..."

Ben hung up without leaving a message, then he rang Josh. "Hey, it's Ben. Have you heard from Cody? I got this weird message from him, so wondering if he'd said anything to you."

"What? Yeah, a brief call about an hour ago." Josh sounded groggy from sleep. "It didn't make much sense, but some of that might have been because I was out of it."

"What did he say?" Ben paused. "If you don't mind me asking?" He had to trust his gut that no matter what Cody had done, he wouldn't deliberately hurt Josh.

"No, of course not." Josh paused. "He told me to be careful, that he loved me, he didn't know, and he's sorry and is trying to put things right."

"Nothing about sprinklers?"

"No. Why would he ask about that?" Josh sounded puzzled. "Now you're sounding weird too. Is there something you're not telling me?"

"He—" Ben stopped himself in time. He'd wait for proof before he risked Josh thinking the man he loved had betrayed him. "Hey, do you have a sprinkler system installed in your house?"

"No. I know a few werewolves who do, though. Most of them avoid me, but there are a couple I meet up with from time to time. They got it through some deal through the pack, but I'm not pack..." Josh lowered his voice. "Do your parents know the nice young man your Mum invited in for a cuppa is a vampire?"

"She invited him in?" Ben groaned. "I told her not to—"

"I introduced Elard to your parents this morning," Rupert said, "and told him to let them know who was watching them so they wouldn't be concerned."

"Right," Ben sighed. His mother wouldn't let someone sit outside for hours without offering them a cup of tea. "Umm, I'm not sure, so I guess that's up to him to let them know? Thanks, and we'll talk later, okay?"

"Okay." Josh hung up.

"Elard also has someone temping at the preschool where your sister works," Rupert said, "and another watching your brother-in-law's place of work. Natasha insisted she'd be fine, but he organised that too."

"I'm sure Tash will give whoever that is a piece of her mind when she finds out," Ben said. "And thanks. I appreciate it."

Garrick walked back into the room. "Okay, not good news with the full moon tomorrow night, but this could be the break we needed. Although we do have a serious problem if it is."

"Oh?" Simon asked.

"Wayland's confirmed they had sprinklers installed in their offices, and in the pack community hall. There aren't any in the shelters, though."

"Shit, that's still a lot of werewolves at risk." Ben hoped the dots he'd put together were way off.

"I'm not seeing the connection." Simon frowned. "How are fire sprinklers putting the pack at risk?"

"It's the way they work," Ben explained. "When I was undercover with Ange, I asked Fawke Security for some brochures. The systems they use have a sensor that's set off by a glass bulb filled with a glycerine mix. Once it gets to a certain temperature, it explodes. There's often a water reservoir sitting behind that. If it burst, and it wasn't just glycerine in there—"

Garrick looked sceptical. "Would they do something that complicated?"

Ben snorted. "We worked a case with aconite-laced ultrasound gel. After that, this wouldn't surprise me at all."

"Oh, crap." Garrick paled. "If something like aconite or silver was added to the mix, and they were set off when everyone was gathered for the full moon dinner, most of the pack could be killed or badly injured. It would weaken those who escaped enough that they'd be no match for anyone waiting outside to pick them off or hunt them down later. And there aren't many who don't use the shelters. Mainly lone wolves like Josh."

"They tortured the werewolves they killed using aconite and silver," Rupert said. "What if they weren't just random murders, but tests for their mode of attack? And that would explain why they've suddenly gone quiet. With the full moon not far off, they only need to sit and wait for the werewolves to gather like they do every month."

"Rodney very helpfully told us that an app could arm and disarm their systems," Ange added. "I'm guessing it wouldn't take much to send a signal to the sensor and fool it into thinking the air was much hotter than it actually is."

Garrick let out a long breath. "But how the hell do we prove it in time?"

"Check the sensors, of course." Ben wondered why Garrick hadn't thought of the obvious. "If we check half a dozen and they're fine, then we know we're wrong. Isn't it better to do that than find out in a couple of days that we weren't?"

"It's not that simple." Garrick frowned. "If we're right, and I hope we aren't, it's a huge risk taking something apart that might be filled with one or more lethal substances."

Ben rolled his eyes.

"You're thinking like Wayland, Garrick," Simon said. "*We* don't have to take them apart. Humans aren't affected by silver, and although they are by aconite, it's not to the extent you are. They use minute traces in their herbal medications. If Ben wears gloves so he doesn't touch whatever is in the bulb and doesn't breathe in any fumes, he'll be fine."

Garrick stared at him in disbelief. "You're suggesting Ben do this?"

"Well, yeah." Ben grinned. He was going to enjoy this a little too much. "I'm thinking it's time your alpha figures out that we humans can be useful in an alliance after all."

CHAPTER SEVENTEEN

"Be careful." Simon held the ladder steady while Ben eased the bulb from the sprinkler.

Holt Wayland and Garrick watched from a safe distance away. Silence hung heavy between them. Wayland's expression was grim. He hadn't wanted to believe their theory, but couldn't afford to ignore it. Simon had volunteered to stay with Ben. Silver would burn, but wouldn't kill him, and aconite wouldn't affect him like it did the werewolves.

Besides, he wasn't about to let Ben do this alone, and had insisted he wear a visor and gloves.

"Nearly got it." Ben cursed under his breath when the bulb stuck. He gave it another yank and it popped out intact into his hand. "I'm really hoping I'm wrong about this."

"All of us are, Mr Leyton," Wayland said. "Despite needing to find these people, making sure my pack isn't at risk takes priority."

"They're still at risk whether or not this pans out." Ben climbed down the ladder, holding the bulb.

Garrick took it in a gloved hand, placed it in an evidence

bag, and sealed it. "I'll take this to the lab immediately, sir." He strode out of the hall, leaving Simon and Ben alone with Wayland.

"We have a medical facility on the premises," Wayland said. "They'll be able to open it safely and check the contents." He gave Ben a nod. "Would you both like to join me for coffee while we wait?"

"You're asking *me* for coffee?" Ben peeled off his gloves and removed his protective visor.

"Thank you, we'd appreciate that." Simon gave Ben a warning glance. Wayland was offering an olive branch, and refusing it wouldn't be sensible. "Traditions are often difficult to break. It takes a wise man to know when it's time to do just that."

"Exactly," Wayland said. "If you'll leave your equipment here, someone will fumigate it before we use the hall again."

Ben raised an eyebrow.

"In case there are any traces of poison on it," Wayland added hastily. "I owe you an apology. Both of you. As Professor Hawthorne says, it is not always easy to adjust one's thinking. Despite living and working amongst humans since our arrival here, most of our pack haven't taken the time to get to know you socially. We tend to be somewhat insular, and although many of our young have studied at your universities in recent years, they still tend to come back to their families and follow the paths chosen for them."

"It's not always easy to separate work from the rest of your life," Simon said as they followed Wayland down a long corridor.

"It does tend to bleed over," Wayland agreed, "and more often of late. We are trying to move with the times, despite some of our elders not being enamoured by the thought of it."

"Like middle management stuck between the top brass and the workers," Ben said. "Thanks for the apology. I—we appreciate it."

Wayland smiled, showing his teeth. "I have watched you both work well with Detective Frater. I am interested to see how his working relationship with Detective Leyton progresses."

"You're not the only one," Ben murmured, but didn't elaborate when Wayland raised an eyebrow.

Simon cleared his throat.

"Tash is a good detective, and she'll work until she solves a case," Ben added. "She's always been like that."

Wayland looked pleased with his response. "Right answer."

Simon laid a warning hand on Ben's shoulder. "It must have been difficult for Garrick working with humans so closely, especially without being able to reveal what he is. Given he's the only one investigating supernatural incidents in the city, I'm presuming there are no other werewolves on the force?"

"Garrick is a relative newcomer to our pack. He is originally from Dunedin." Wayland walked up to the counter of the communal dining room and ordered coffee. The server looked past him at Ben and Simon and frowned. "Is something the matter, Noellene?"

"No, sir, of course not, sir." The server swallowed. "I've never seen you order coffee here before, that's all."

"I could have sworn I had. Oh well." Wayland looked around the room and raised his voice. "These gentlemen are my guests."

Every werewolf in the room turned to look at him, then lowered their gaze after a moment's silence, and continued with their conversations.

Wayland gestured for them to sit at a table in the far corner. Despite the distance between them and the other werewolves, their enhanced hearing meant their conversation would not be private. "The server will bring our coffee over. Once Garrick has the test results, we will move to another location to discuss our next move. We'll need to test the contents of the water reservoir behind the bulb too."

Simon nodded. Although Wayland was making an effort to build bridges, how long would that last if they weren't able to get the results he wanted? "Good idea. Ben noticed several boxes of water cooler bottles at their offices."

"Garrick tells me you haven't taken the opportunity to find a suitable property yet." Wayland gave the server a nod when he delivered the coffee, then took an appreciative sip. "Let me know when you're ready. I have several properties that I'm certain would exactly meet your needs."

"We're not staying," Ben said. "This is a holiday, not a permanent—"

Simon placed his hand over Ben's. "Thank you. That would be appreciated." Telling Wayland they weren't interested wouldn't be a good idea, although Simon did not intend to owe him any favours either. Not that they were staying...

"Not a rental obviously." Wayland sounded amused. "It makes more sense to invest, yes?"

"Yes." Simon wished Garrick would hurry up before this conversation got any more awkward.

"Of course, the council now has a—" Wayland's telephone rang. "Yes?"

Garrick didn't sound happy, although Simon only caught a few of the words. He glanced at Ben and nodded, silently warning him their brief respite from the case was over.

"Recruit however many we need. I will be there in a few

minutes." Wayland hung up, his expression grim. "Unfortunately, your suspicions were correct. I don't see the need to waste time confirming anything else. We need to move, and now, to wipe out this threat." He pushed back his chair. "I'm presuming you wish to be present for the hunt?"

Although he asked a question, the expectation they would be was implicit.

"Hunt?" Ben asked.

Wayland smiled. "If someone threatened your family, you'd act quickly and use any means at your disposal to protect them, yes?"

"Within the law, yeah."

"Of course." Wayland's eyes flashed gold. "The laws are there, so justice will be served."

"We'll be there." Simon doubted Wayland referred to human law. He'd have to move quickly to ensure the right kind of justice was served to the humans who were part of this organisation.

These humans had gone after, and killed, supernaturals. The Supernatural Treaty was very clear about the fate of those who crossed that line.

Especially this close to a full moon.

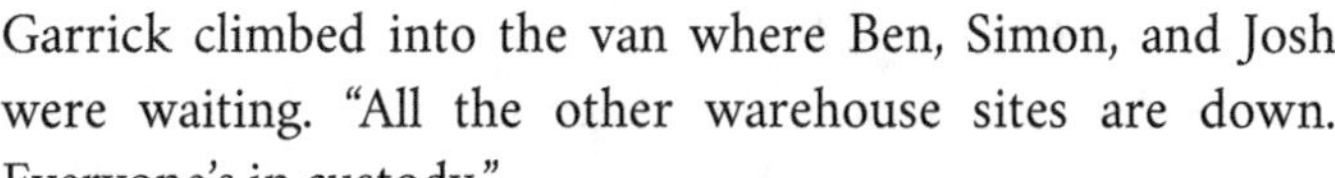

Garrick climbed into the van where Ben, Simon, and Josh were waiting. "All the other warehouse sites are down. Everyone's in custody."

"Police or pack custody?" Ben hadn't missed the underlying threat in Wayland's words when he'd talked about justice within the law. Human law was way more lenient compared to what the council would dish out if they got their hands on these guys.

"Police for now, and Tash will make sure it stays that way." Garrick lowered his voice. "I suspect most of Fawke's employees have no clue the supernatural community exists."

"I agree." Simon had shown his vampire nature to a couple of the men they'd taken into custody, and they'd nearly peed themselves. They'd been not only scared but surprised too. "We'll need to make sure those complicit in this crime don't try to escape justice by pretending ignorance."

"Don't worry." Garrick smiled thinly. "Wayland knows what he's doing. By the time he's finished, we'll have a list of everyone involved and exactly where to find them."

Josh shivered. He'd contacted Garrick directly a few hours ago and asked to be a part of the operation. "Is it bad that I'm glad Ange didn't hang around to see this?" She'd dropped him off at Wayland's building on her way to work as he'd not been up to driving.

"Then I'm bad in thinking it too." Ben had seen a lot of stuff over the last few years he wished he could forget. The longer he could shield Ange from most of it, the better.

"Are you sure you're all right doing this?" Simon asked Josh. "You're still shaky from the silver."

"No, I'm not all right." Josh stuck out his chin in a stubborn gesture, "but I'm doing it anyway." He crossed his arms across his chest and refused to meet Simon's eyes. "I still can't believe Cody could be a part of this."

"We don't know what he's been taught to believe." Ben wanted to think that Cody had given him the information about the sprinklers when he'd realised people would die, but couldn't dismiss his suspicions that he'd known about it way before he'd found out Josh was a werewolf. "He saved a lot of people today."

"His family killed my pack!" Josh growled low in his throat, and his eyes glowed gold. "I don't give a rat's arse that he finally decided to play the good guy. There's no coming back from that." His voice broke. He grabbed his water bottle from his pack and gripped it tight enough to dent the metal shell.

Ben winced. "I'm sorry."

"Yeah," Josh took a deep breath, then let it out again. "Surely your people are in place by now?" he asked Garrick.

Garrick checked his phone. "Yes. I don't want any of you playing hero, got it? This is police and pack business."

"They killed a vampire too," Simon reminded him. "That makes it council business."

"Do we really want the pack and the council fighting over who gets these guys?" Ben wanted this done and dusted, although the ringleaders being tossed into a cell and forgotten about for a few months, while the council worked through its incessant red tape sounded appealing too.

"Not going to happen." Garrick headed for the van door. "Simon, with me. Ben, watch Josh. He can't identify anyone if he's dead. I'll call you when it's safe."

He jumped out of the van, Simon behind him. Ben would have usually protested and gone after them anyway, but Josh looked like he was barely keeping it together.

"I thought you found your pack afterwards?" Ben turned to Josh once they were alone. "Simon and Garrick will take care of these arseholes. You're not in any state to—"

"I didn't lie." Josh bit his lip. "But... it was the full moon, and I snuck out before the change. I was young and an idiot, and I didn't want to be locked up. I came home in the morning expecting my dad to rip shreds off me for disobeying him. I could deal with that. I'd been careful. I'd got away from any humans before I had to change." He sat down on the bench seat with a thump.

"But?" Ben prompted.

"I didn't sneak out alone. A couple of friends dared me.

They got back first." Josh took a chug of water. "I heard a werewolf howl. Then another. They'd found all the bodies. One of the men responsible was still there. He took advantage of their grief and slaughtered them. I... froze. I watched from the shadows while he shot them full of silver, then butchered them. I could have saved them, don't you see? But I did nothing."

"You did *something*." Ben put his arm around Josh. "You survived, so you can stop it happening again. If you'd gone after this guy, he might have killed you too. Ten years ago, you would have been a kid. Yeah, okay, a werewolf and all the stuff that goes with that, but still a kid against an adult who knew who and *what* you were, and how to take you down." He hated asking but needed to be sure. "You got a good look at the guy?"

"Yeah. I made a noise. He turned and looked at my hiding place but didn't see me." Josh dropped his water bottle to fall with a clunk to the floor. "I've seen him every time I close my eyes. He haunts me, more than any fucking ghost. I need to end this. Not just for my pack, but for me." His shoulders slumped. "God, I'm sorry. I've never told anyone this before. I..." He bit his lip. "I nearly told Cody everything about a month ago. I came this close..."

Josh gasped for breath, his complexion grey.

"Come on, let's get some fresh air." Ben helped Josh to his feet. They were a block away from the warehouse, so all the bad guys would be distracted. "You don't want to give them any satisfaction when you see them, yeah?" He'd have a word to Garrick to hold whoever this guy was in custody until Josh was ready. "I figure even without your testimony, they're going down for a long time."

If Wayland let them survive that long.

Ben grimaced, preferring not to think about that. These guys had tried to play judge, jury, and executioner, but if they got the same in return, how did that make any of it right?

"I hope so." Josh stumbled when they climbed out of the van.

"There's a bus stop bench over there. Do you think you can make it?" Ben helped Josh right himself. "Sitting on the side of the road in the gutter probably isn't a great idea, and won't be very comfortable."

"Okay." Josh gritted his teeth until they were sitting down. "Fuck, I should have stayed in bed. Full moon's tomorrow night too." He laughed hoarsely. "Bloody thing isn't helping. I've been on edge since this morning. I usually deal with it better than this."

"It's not just the moon. It's the memory of the night your pack died." Ben could understand that. Simon's nightmares were always worse around anniversaries too.

"Yeah, ten years ago this month." Josh grew silent and stared ahead, although his eyes seemed unfocused.

Ouch. Ben didn't answer him. Better to let Josh sort through his thoughts for a bit. "I'm going to go grab your water, okay? You look like you could use it." That way he'd be able to give Josh a few moments' privacy yet be close enough to keep an eye on him.

Josh didn't acknowledge him.

Ben placed a hand on Josh's shoulder, squeezed and then sprinted back to the van. The bottle had rolled under one of the seats, so it took him longer to find. He glanced over at Josh sitting with his head in his hands. Ben bent to pick up the bottle, and grabbed the collapsible police baton shoved between the seat and the chassis, hooking it into his belt, just in case.

Josh looked up when Ben jumped down from the van and got to his feet. He started walking towards Ben, then froze. "Look out!"

Ben turned too late. Pain shot through his head. He lost his footing. Something heavy collided with him, shoving him on his back onto the pavement. His vision darkened. He pulled out the baton and raised his hands to defend himself.

A man loomed over him. "You're not the werewolf my son's gone soft on."

He slammed down his fist on Ben's knuckles. Ben gritted his teeth against the pain, but the baton fell from his grip and rolled into the gutter.

"Oh shit." Ben backpedalled, his arse hitting the kerb. He blinked, his head clearing enough to see the guy who'd attacked him. "You're Cody's dad."

Josh skidded to a halt. "You're Cody's father?" He growled, his face sprouting fur. "You fucking bastard!"

"Well, well." Prentice smirked. "All these years looking for you, and Cody found you for us. He'll make me proud yet."

"You killed my pack." Josh shoved Prentice away from Ben. "Give me one good reason why I shouldn't kill you." He dropped to the ground and howled, sounding more werewolf than human.

Prentice took a step back. Then another. "You don't scare me."

"Then you're an idiot." Ben crawled towards the baton and struggled to his feet while Prentice was distracted.

Josh leapt, now fully werewolf, tackling Prentice to the ground. Josh snarled, held Prentice still with one paw, and swiped at him with the other.

"Josh, stop! You don't want to do this." Ben couldn't let Josh kill the guy. "You're not a killer. You're better than them."

The huge werewolf, similar in size to Lucas, but with blond fur speckled in a lighter shade of grey, glared at Ben, as though considering, then sat on Prentice, his tail in the man's face.

"Get off me!" Prentice fought to escape, but Josh held him firmly in place.

"Ben!" Simon blurred to Ben's side and lifted him into his arms. "Did that bastard hurt you?"

"I'll be fine." Ben collapsed into Simon's embrace. "Josh took him down. He totally kicked arse."

CHAPTER EIGHTEEN

"Let me help with that." Simon stepped between Ben and the mirror, redid the knot in his tie, then took a step back to take a look. "My word, you look fabulous in a suit."

They had two hours before their family and friends arrived for their exchange of vows and had retreated to Ben's old bedroom to stay out of Abby's way while she made sure everything was perfect.

The pack had checked every sprinkler system that had been installed, and the full moon had passed without incident. Only Wright and Cody had evaded capture, and if they had any sense, they'd be long gone. Simon and Ben had survived another case, and most of Human Destiny were behind bars awaiting sentencing. Everything else paled in comparison, but Simon wasn't about to tell Abby that. Better to let her fuss and be happy.

"You say that every time I wear one." Ben flushed.

"I can count on one hand the number of times you have since we met." Simon chuckled at Ben's reaction, then licked his lips. He swallowed, already growing hard at the vision before him. Ben's dark hair and eyes set off nicely against the midnight grey of the fabric, which clung to his muscled thighs and buttocks in all the right places. "Although I must admit I'm very tempted to rip it off and have my wicked way with you."

"My parents are in the next room!"

"Well, then, I'll just have to hold that thought until later, won't I?" Simon threaded his fingers through Ben's hair holding him close, then kissed him long and hard.

Ben groaned into the kiss.

Simon broke it, let his eyes go fully brown, and dropped his fangs.

Ben groaned louder. "Fuck, not helping. You know what that does to me." He wrapped his arms around Simon and met his gaze. Ben's eyes were wide with desire, his mouth partly open, his breathing, hard.

Simon reached for Ben's belt, then took a couple of breaths to calm himself. "Your parents are in the next room."

"The door locks." Ben swallowed. His flushed skin highlighted the still healing scrape on one cheek.

Simon blurred to the door, locked it, then walked slowly back to the bed. His mouth was dry. Hunger rose in him. "Knowing we could get caught makes me want you more."

"Fuck yes. Me too." Ben hooked his finger in a come here motion. "I can be quiet if you can."

Simon snorted. "You're never quiet." He shrugged out of his suit jacket, started to undo his shirt, then changed his mind. "I want to undress you first."

He loosened and removed Ben's tie, and then the top button of his shirt, his mouth watering at the dark hair underneath. He forced himself to unwrap each part of his present slowly, instead of ripping the buttons off like he usually did. With each button, he dipped his head and licked the newly revealed skin. Ben's breathing sped up. He groaned loudly.

Simon silenced him with a kiss. "Quiet," he murmured in Ben's ear, and nipped at the shell with his fangs. He backed Ben towards the bed.

Ben's heart thumped. He swallowed. Once, then again.

The shirt unbuttoned, Simon eased it over Ben's shoulders, then yanked it down, careful not to rip the material and laid it on the chair. He undid Ben's belt, pulling it just enough from his trousers so they'd open. He knelt in front of Ben, then took the zipper in his mouth and eased it down.

Ben swayed. He placed his hands on Simon's shoulders and squeezed hard. Raw need flooded their bond.

Simon growled and pushed down Ben's trousers and underwear. He licked the tip of Ben's cock, swallowing the precum already pooling there. "My God, you're so beautiful," he murmured.

To hell with going slow. He wanted Ben, and now.

Ben kicked off his shoes and stepped out of his trousers. "Now. Please." He grabbed Simon's tie and pulled him onto the bed with him. "And get rid of your clothes." Ben licked his lips. "Except for your tie. That's hot." He undid Simon's shirt buttons, except the top one. "Yeah. Perfect."

Simon shimmied out of his trousers and grabbed the lube from his pocket before Ben threw them on the floor. He'd barely got rid of his underwear before Ben opened his legs, inviting him in. "Need to prep." Simon ground out the words, barely finding the control to think clearly, but not wanting to risk hurting Ben.

"Hurry up." Ben picked up the lube when Simon dropped it after prepping him. He smeared it over Simon's cock, each touch sending jolts of fire through his body. Ben wrapped Simon's tie around his fingers, then used it to pull Simon close to him. "Want you." His eyes darkened. He arched his hips off the bed. "Want you now."

Simon caught Ben's mouth in a searing kiss as he slid into

him. Ben wriggled up the bed, bringing Simon with him, then wrapped his legs around Simon, pulling him in deeper. He tightened around Simon's cock, and started rocking.

"Fuck yes." Ben kissed Simon again, their tongues stroking each other's, their bodies moving in synch.

Instead of their usual slow dance, Simon shoved harder into Ben, needing to feel him physically and through their bond. Ben groaned loudly. He tightened his legs around Simon and arched up, meeting Simon's thrusts. Simon broke the kiss and scraped his fangs down Ben's neck. Ben went rigid. Simon silenced his scream with his mouth, pumped into him, and then let go, dragging them both into a whirlpool of mutual pleasure.

The bond between them burned white, and for a moment Simon saw himself through Ben's eyes, his body slick with sweat, a mix of human and vampire, reflected in the mirror at the end of the bed. His vision shifted and Ben went limp under him. He collapsed on top of Ben, panting.

"Bloody hell." Simon caressed Ben's cheek, rolled them so they were facing, and buried his head on Ben's shoulder, breathing in his scent. "I think we'll need another shower after that."

"Yeah, or everyone will know what we just did." Ben furled his fingers through Simon's hair.

"That horse has already long bolted its stable. Your parents know exactly what we just did." Simon leaned into Ben's embrace, basking in contentment.

"Shit, what?" Ben struggled to sit up.

Simon held him tightly. "We have time, and I don't want to move just yet." He trailed kisses across Ben's bare shoulder. "And yes, expect some teasing from your father at least. He's most amused." Ben always promised to be quiet. He always failed. And right now, Simon didn't care. He loved that Ben let go so totally when they made love.

"I saw something." Ben let go of Simon's hair, then spooned around him. "The moment we both came. I saw myself like I was looking through your eyes for a moment." He linked their fingers together. "Like I did when we first bonded and I saw your life. You reflected in the mirror too."

Vampires usually didn't reflect, but heightened adrenaline could cause a shimmer, creating a temporary reflection, and making it possible for them to be photographed. They had a mirror at the foot of their bed at home for that reason, but Simon had so far managed to persuade Ben that a photograph like that was never going to happen.

"I know." Simon grew quiet for a moment. "I saw myself through your eyes too. That's never happened before." When two vampires bonded, they saw each other's lives. Ben, being human, had seen Simon's, but Simon had only seen his own played back like highlights of everything he'd wanted so badly to forget.

"It's not the vow thing. We're already married, and I invited you in when we bonded." Ben shrugged. "Not going to diss it, but it was kind of weird."

Simon raised an eyebrow.

"In a totally cool way, of course." Ben grinned and stretched. "I wanted to talk to you about something while there's just us here. Once the others arrive, any kind of private conversation will have to wait until later."

"What did you want to talk about?" Simon propped himself up on one elbow.

"You know how Wayland started talking about us buying a house the other day?" Ben loosened Simon's tie and threw it towards the chair. "I felt your reaction. Are you thinking about it? Staying here a while, I mean."

"What would you like to do?" Simon chose his words carefully. "You miss your family and your friends here. We can visit more often if you'd like, but it's not the same as experiencing everyday life with them." He traced Ben's lips with one finger.

"Our home is in Boggslake. You have a job there you love, and I'm just starting to get my photography business off the ground."

"Rupert said the university here is looking for a new head for their history department. He rang me yesterday while you were visiting Maddie. I've lived in Boggslake for decades." Simon shrugged. "You dragged me into the twenty-first century, which I'd never thought was possible—"

"You still have a foot firmly in both centuries," Ben kissed Simon's finger, "but I like that old fashioned vibe you have. I don't want you to get rid of it completely." He grew silent, so instead of finishing what he'd been about to say, Simon waited for him to continue. "You'd really be okay with moving here? It doesn't have to be forever, and we can go home if it doesn't work out."

"You gave up a lot to stay in Boggslake for me. Let me do this for you." Simon smiled at Ben's growing excitement. "If this job at the university turns out to be viable, you can set up your photography studio here too." The way Rupert had spoken made it sound like the position was Simon's if he wanted it. He'd investigate further before their planned picnic at the rose gardens early the following week if this was what Ben wanted. "The house Wayland mentioned is not only close to the university, but it has space downstairs with a separate entrance that would be perfect for a studio."

"You've already looked into all of this." Ben frowned. "You've been thinking about this for a while, and you didn't mention it?"

"Only since I saw you and Ange together after your visit to Fawke Security. And I didn't look into it." Simon caressed Ben's cheek. "I wouldn't keep anything from you, even without our bond. Wayland dropped the information off this morning while you were in the shower. He said the house is ours if we want it, and for a good price." Simon took a deep breath. "But if you don't want this, that's fine too. I haven't given either of them an answer. I wouldn't do that without talking to you. It's one of the reasons I suggested we have some time before our vows."

"I know you wouldn't." Ben kissed Simon on the lips. "Yes."

"Yes?"

"Yes, I want this. Yes, I want to make a life here with you." Ben sighed. "Damn it. I'm not worried about leaving Boggslake in capable hands. Anita and Charlie totally rock, and you know Anson will join their team once it's official."

"Charlie's girlfriend, Lily, helped us out on that case earlier in the year too, and she's an IT major. She'd also jump at the opportunity." Simon grinned. "Can you imagine Jacob's reaction?"

"Totally worth it," Ben agreed. His expression sobered.

"Yes?" Simon hadn't missed Ben's earlier concern before his thoughts had derailed about their friends filling the breach they'd leave.

"We can talk to Anita and Charlie over AbenChat, but what about Mr Boggs? He's part of our family too, and I don't want to leave without properly saying goodbye. Sure, he'd hear us, but I want to know he's okay with this."

Simon smiled. "He and I had an interesting conversation before we left. I thought at the time it was a little... strange... but you know how he can be." He squeezed Ben's hand. "He told me he'd miss us, but we had to do what was right for us. I reminded him that we were only going for a short time, and he smiled and said, we'll see."

~

Ray wore a huge grin when Ben and Simon finally made their way out into the garden. Ben returned the grin, then flushed when Ray winked.

Abby rolled her eyes. "Am I the only one here approaching this day with the seriousness it deserves?"

"Everything looks perfect," Simon reassured her, "and the important thing is that we're exchanging our vows in front of family and friends. The details don't matter."

"The afternoon tea spread looks great," Ben added. "And you've outdone yourself with the wedding cake."

Although they'd insisted on keeping everything low key, Abby had been equally firm in making sure the cake was just right. She'd made this same fruit cake for Maddie's reception, so it was only right that Ben had it too. Ben didn't dare remind her that this was a formality, and they were already married.

"You both look very handsome." Abby wiped a tear. "Such a shame we can't take a photograph."

"You could still take one of Ben," Simon suggested.

She shook her head. "No, that wouldn't be right."

"You've told Uncle Martin no photographs, right?" Ben's uncle was the only one coming who didn't know Simon was a vampire, and Ben wanted to keep it that way. He'd caved into Ray's wishes that his brother should be invited, but that didn't mean he was going to share anything he didn't need to.

"Of course." Abby chewed on her lower lip. "I'm going to put on some coffee. I need a clear head before I start drinking."

"Your mum's on edge about our wedding," Simon said. "After the way she took the news about me, I wasn't expecting her to be."

"You didn't see her when Maddie and Trent got married." Ben shrugged. "She hit the coffee first thing and was jittery as hell most of the day. Weddings do this to her for some reason."

"I like your mother." Simon smiled. "She's like you, fiercely protective of those she cares about. I feel honoured to be included in that."

"You don't want to get on her wrong side either." Ben led them over to the apple tree, wondered if the grass would stain his trousers, then settled for leaning against the trunk.

A dozen or so chairs were laid out in rows in front of the climbing rose trellis, with space in front for Simon and Ben to stand to exchange their vows. The trellis had the added advantage of providing enough shade so Simon wouldn't have to wear his glasses. Elard had offered to preside over the ceremony, but hadn't turned up yet, despite his promise to be there ten minutes ago. Josh and Ange were running late too.

Simon pulled Ben into a loose embrace. "You're still nervous, though calmer than you were earlier."

"You were way tenser when we got married in Boggslake." Ben kissed the tip of Simon's nose. "Although I still can't believe we got through that day without anything happening."

"About that..." Simon tightened his grip around Ben's waist. "Anita talked Jacob into having the council take care of the ghoul who threatened to gatecrash. He refused to tell me the details of their conversation, but said it was a one-off wedding present and wouldn't be happening again."

"Seriously?" Ben narrowed his eyes. "And we don't owe them anything?"

"Apparently not." Simon didn't sound convinced despite his words. "We've done our bit in keeping Boggslake safe. It wouldn't have hurt the council to step up for one day." He frowned. "Apart from your uncle, we're not expecting any uninvited guests today, are we?"

"No. Why?"

Simon let go of Ben and sprinted towards the back fence. Ben jogged to keep up with him. The section was fenced on all sides, although a gate led through to the several metres of native reserve at the rear of the property.

"That's odd. I could have sworn I heard something." Simon peered through the gate. A large bird with distinctive blue and green feathers flew out of the trees towards them. They both ducked, although it changed direction when it approached the gate.

"Bloody wood pigeon," Ben said.

"It wasn't a bird I heard." Simon tilted his head to one side, listening.

Ben caught a glimpse of sun on metal on top of one of the trees. "Get down," he yelled, tackling Simon to the ground.

A wooden projectile hit the grass where Simon had stood a moment before. Ben climbed to his feet and yanked it free. The tip was coated in what looked like silver. These arse-holes were making sure they played for keeps.

"Fuck no." Ben muttered. "No one's staking you today of all days."

Simon stood and spun, so they were back to back. "We have company."

Three men climbed over the side fence, all armed with crossbows and stakes, and with what looked like super soakers on their belts. They strode towards Ben and Simon.

Ray walked out the back door and froze on the back deck. "Seriously? Have you guys heard of overkill?"

"We don't mean *you* any harm," one of the men said.

"Funny way of showing it. Looks like Wright isn't happy we took down his operation." Ben took a step towards them, keeping Simon behind him. "Get out. The cops are already on their way." He shifted the weight of the stake in his hand.

"Let them come," the man who had obviously decided to

be their voice said. "See how they react when they find out they have a vampire in their midst." He grinned at Ray, and then at Abby who had joined her husband on the deck.

"You need to leave." Abby drew herself up to her full height. "We also have security cameras which would have already sent very clear photographs of you to the authorities. This is your last warning." She handed Ray the old cricket bat they kept behind the back door by the sports equipment cupboard.

The man's grin grew wider. He seemed amused. "And this is a warning for you." He glanced at Simon, then spat in the grass like he'd tasted something nasty. "Your son is married to a vampire, and keeps company with werewolves. Those abominations are real, and they'll kill you without hesitation."

Ray blinked. "We already know who Simon is, thanks all the same." He glared at them. "He's family, and you're on our property. Get out."

"Wright is the gift that keeps on giving," Simon murmured. "Do you want me to deal with these trespassers?"

"Nah, I've got this." Ben didn't want to risk whatever was in those soakers. The sprinkler water reservoirs in the pack safe rooms had contained traces of aconite, and the boxes of water coolers from Fawke's shop had disappeared with Wright. He caught Ray's eye, and nodded. Ray raised his right eyebrow in response to the code they'd used when they took the rest of the family on in their modified rules of back-yard cricket.

Ben threw the stake at the nearest man, then ran at him when he ducked to avoid it. He hit the man full on, and slammed him to the ground.

A cricket ball whizzed past him and hit the man next to him. Ray slammed another ball after the first, and the man collapsed, holding his stomach, and groaning.

The third man fell to the ground with a thud. Trent stood behind him brandishing a frying pan. "Good thing we brought that spare you wanted, Abby. Didn't get an answer at the front door, so I came around the side to see what was up."

"I'll grab some rope," Abby said.

"No need for that," Tash pushed past her, Garrick bringing up the rear. "Garrick's called for backup. They can take these idiots into custody." She grinned at Ben. "We got a tip that Wright was going to out Simon because of the part you both played in taking down his organisation."

Ben got out of the way so Tash could handcuff the guy he'd subdued, then brushed off his trousers. "Is Wright in custody?"

"Not yet, unfortunately." Garrick handcuffed the other two men while being careful to avoid their weapons. "Still no sign of Cody either, but hopefully this is the last of it for a while." He gave Ray a nod. "Nice batting there, sir."

"Thanks. I like to keep in practice." Ray held out his hand. "You must be Garrick. And it's Ray, not sir." Once they'd shaken, Ray retrieved the soakers and weapons. "You'll need these as evidence."

Garrick took a step back, keeping his distance from them.

"Thanks, Dad." Tash stepped up to take them.

Ray hadn't asked what Garrick was, but must have noticed his caution around the soakers and stakes. "Trent, do you want to give Tash a hand with these? Good to get them out of the way before our guests arrive."

"Is this a normal day for you boys?" Abby picked up the cricket balls. "I was impressed with that tackle, Ben."

"Yeah, nah." Ben didn't want to scare his mother, yet he couldn't lie either. "Yeah, it is kind of what happens a lot, except Simon usually goes all vampire and kicks their arse too."

"Succinctly put as always." Simon flicked a spot of dirt

from Ben's tie. "I'm impressed with how calmly you handled this situation," he said to Abby.

Abby shrugged. "No one threatens my family." She kissed both their foreheads. "And that includes both my sons."

Simon swallowed. "Thank you. That means a lot." He glanced at the house. "I didn't realise your security cameras covered the back garden."

"They don't." Abby grinned. "But given they didn't install them, I figured they wouldn't know that." She ushered them inside. "I don't know about you, but after that, I need something stronger than coffee before everyone else arrives. Join me?"

Simon caught Ben's arm, holding him back to let Abby into the kitchen first. "Thank you."

"I'll protect you with my life," Ben reminded him. "You're mine, and no arsehole is going to take you from me."

"Not just for that." Simon brushed his lips against Ben's. "For convincing me to come here, and giving me the gift of being a part of your family."

CHAPTER NINETEEN

"Ben!" Ange sprinted into the kitchen, her posture relaxing when she saw Ben and Simon sitting at the breakfast bar. "You're okay, yeah? We got here as fast as we could."

"Yeah." Ben hugged her. "Where's Josh? And hold up. How did you know what happened?"

"He's talking to Garrick." Ange slid into the empty chair. "Frank's running interference to let them have some privacy." Maddie and Trent had offered to give Frank a ride so Ben and Simon could use his car.

Abby poured her a glass of wine. "I need to make sure everything is under control outside and that your grandfather isn't trying to reorganise anything." She disappeared out the door before anyone could protest.

"She's giving us some time to talk." Simon waited for Ange to take a few sips of wine and calm down. "Josh called Garrick. He was the tip."

"How did you—" Ange's eyes widened.

"He's listening to their conversation." Ben rubbed his foot against Simon's.

"It's a little difficult to miss," Simon admitted. He wasn't deliberately eavesdropping. "Josh is a little... heated." He reached for the bottle and emptied it into another glass. "As he's going to be walking in the door in three... two..."

"Hey, Josh," Ben said. "Everything okay?"

Josh sighed. "Yeah. Kind of." He looked much better than when they'd seen him a couple of days ago, although the dark smudges under his eyes suggested he hadn't slept much. "Fuck, this is such a mess."

"What happened?" Simon pushed the glass towards him.

"Cody." Josh scowled, then took a gulp of wine. "He texted me."

"I thought you told him you didn't want to hear from him again?" Ben asked.

"Yeah, but he ignored me." Josh ducked his head. "Probably the last time, though. I was... I'm not going to repeat what I said to him. That bridge is well and truly burnt."

"But?" Simon prompted.

"He warned me that his uncle was sending someone after you. I let Garrick know once I read the text, I swear." Josh rubbed at his eyes. "Fuck it. He'd sent one a couple of hours ago, and I ignored it, so he kept resending it until I answered. If something had happened to you, I'd never forgive myself." He took another gulp of wine.

"We're fine, and the men responsible are in custody." Simon took Josh's glass and placed it out of reach. "Wine is meant to be sipped, not gulped. If you want to get drunk, I'll supply whatever you need, but I'd prefer you keep a clear head in the meantime."

"Half a glass isn't..." Ben started to say, then trailed off when Simon squeezed his knee.

"Why did Cody warn you?" Simon asked. "He must still be with his uncle, or he wouldn't have known, and his actions don't sound like someone who believes in what their organisation is doing."

Josh reached into the messenger bag he carried and pulled out a thick notebook. He gave it to Simon. "He says he's trying to make amends, and that he can help more by staying with them. Shit, I don't know what to believe anymore. At first, I thought he was just trying to make excuses, but then he warned Ben about the sprinklers, and now this."

The notebook looked old and well worn. The shape and feel of it reminded Simon of his family bible. He opened it cautiously and raised an eyebrow. The pages were ruled into columns with lists of names, dates of birth, and addresses. He flipped through it, unsurprised when the neat handwriting changed at intervals, prefaced with a short introduction explaining why the book's guardian had changed.

"This is the missing werewolf register."

"That's got to be a good thing, right?" Ange put her arm around Josh. "He's trying to help."

"How do you know it's from Cody?" Ben asked.

Josh shrugged. "He left it at work for me to pick up. The bag had a note on it. Not obviously signed by him, of course, but I knew it was." He bit his lip. "He remembered the lyrics of the song he was playing when we first met." His voice softened. "I've never forgotten them."

"I'll give this to Garrick," Simon said. "He'll make sure the new councillor gets it."

"Yeah." Josh gripped the edge of the breakfast bar. "I thought he sent the warning because he owed me. That's why I replied the way I did. He didn't owe me anything. I don't want his pity. I never did."

"Owe you for what?" Ben asked.

Josh refused to look at any of them. "I warned him. That's why he wasn't there when we took them down. I only wanted to save him. I'd convinced myself he wasn't really one of the bad guys." He sounded hoarse. "I'm an idiot. Of course, he told his father and his uncle. How else would they have known we were coming? I put you all in danger because I trusted my instincts. Never again. I'm done with all of this. You need someone you can trust. I don't even trust myself at the moment."

"We all berate ourselves at some time for following our hearts," Elard said from the doorway.

"Good afternoon, Elard." Simon had felt his presence around the same time Josh and Ange had arrived, and figured he'd join the conversation when he was ready.

"Simon." Elard nodded. "And Ben. Nice to see you again." He walked over to the counter. "Good to finally meet you, Mr McKenna. Ms Duncan."

Josh hesitated for a moment, then shook Elard's hand. "I've heard about you," he said slowly. "Mostly good things."

"That's always encouraging." Elard smiled with a hint of fang. "If you need someone impartial to talk to at any time, please ask."

"I'm a werewolf," Josh said. "Why would you want to want to listen to me?"

"And I'm a vampire." Elard seemed amused. "So? If this has shown us anything, it's that we are stronger against our enemies if our community works together, rather than in factions." He placed a brief hand on Josh's shoulder. "I'm also a priest, and I've been told I'm a good listener. My offer doesn't have a use by date."

"Josh has the werewolf list," Simon said, "although you already know that."

Elard chuckled. "Of course." He glanced at it. "He needs to keep it too."

"Garrick—" Josh started to say.

"Will be in touch about it later. In the meantime, put it back in your bag out of sight, hmm?" Elard lowered his voice. "I've found the missing vampire list too. It turns out Victor hid it with the one person who had protected his secret all her life."

"His wife?" Ben asked.

Elard's smile broadened. "Yes. Her urn is a lot fuller now we've added Victor's dust to the ash. Together for always, and perhaps that is for the best." He glanced towards the front door at the same time Simon did. "I believe it's time to get the reason we're all here underway. I'll see you in the garden shortly."

"He burnt the list?" Ben said after Elard had left.

"I'm not sure that's a bad thing." Simon hadn't been happy about the council's insistence that they register supernaturals, and this case showed that having them in physical form was no safer than having them online.

"Do you think we should burn the werewolf one too?" Ange asked. "What if Wright has already made a copy of it?"

"We can't prove what he has, so until we learn otherwise, we'll have to hope for the best. I'm sure if there are copies out there, it won't be too long before we're made aware of them." Simon stood. "Victor is out of the council's reach now, but unfortunately, we are not, so we need to be more vigilant about keeping the werewolf list safe."

"You trust me with it?" Josh sounded surprised.

"You are still a member of this team," Simon reminded him. "If you still want to be, that is?"

"Yeah, I'd like that." Josh shrugged. "After all, if you're going back to Boggslake soon, it won't be for much longer, right?"

"We'll see." Simon ushered them out of the kitchen. "Ben, your uncle has arrived. Could you introduce us, please?"

"Sure." Ben slipped his hand into Simon's and led them outside.

A man a little older than Ray was talking animatedly with Ben's parents. He glanced up when Ben and Simon approached and smiled. Simon would have recognised him as part of their family immediately. He had the same dark hair as Ben, although while Ben's expression was usually open, something about Martin gave the impression he was a man used to keeping secrets.

"I knew it!" Martin said.

Ben cleared his throat. "Uncle Martin, this is my husband, Simon Hawthorne. Simon, Martin Leyton."

"Yes, yes, I saw you kissing outside the church. I figured he must be." Uncle Martin grinned, although his right eye twitched. His heartbeat sped up when he held out his hand to Simon. "Pleased to finally meet you, my boy."

Simon forced a smile. "I assure you I'm much older than I appear." He shook hands for as long as deemed polite. "I've heard a lot about you."

"Good things, I hope." Martin glanced at Ben. "Thanks for inviting me today. Family's important, don't you think?"

Ben put his arm around Simon. "I wouldn't be without mine."

"It looks like our final guest has arrived," Abby said. "Martin, I'm sure you'd like to meet Professor Milne. He's a colleague of Simon's." She led him away.

"Poor Rupert," Ben murmured once they were out of earshot.

"Rupert can look after himself. He's been dealing with obnoxious people for years." Simon spoke without thinking. "Bloody hell. I'm sorry."

"Don't worry about it. Uncle Martin has that effect on most people." Ben lowered his voice. "Not just me then, huh? He's always given me an off vibe, but I don't know why, but he's my uncle, so..."

Elard spoke over their conversation. "We're gathered today to celebrate the love between Ben and Simon." He looked up at the sky. "And in true Wellington tradition, we're probably about to swap this beautiful day for rain, so I suggest we get on with it."

His audience laughed.

Ben kissed Simon's cheek. "Ready?"

"Yes." Simon's mouth suddenly felt dry. He squeezed Ben's hand. Although this was their second time exchanging their vows in front of family, it didn't make it any the less heartfelt. Or nerve wracking.

Ben met his gaze. "I love you. We're doing this together. You'll never face anything alone again. I promise."

"I know." Simon blinked back tears. "I love you too."

"Let's go do this." Ben kept his voice light and steady. Simon's emotions flowed through their bond. It wouldn't take much for Ben to lose it too, and they needed to get through their vows first.

Elard cleared his throat. "If you gentlemen are ready?" Of course, he would have overheard their conversation. No privacy in a community of supernaturals.

"Yeah, definitely." Ben linked hands with Simon, and they walked together to stand in front of Elard. Despite Abby's comments about walking down the aisle, Ben had told her early on that wasn't something they would do. Although Simon was old fashioned as hell, he'd agreed with Ben, so she'd backed down.

"Thank you for inviting me to be a part of this today." Elard smiled. "Is there anyone who wishes to stand by you or say a few words before we begin?"

Ben frowned. That last bit hadn't been part of what they'd arranged, and Simon didn't have any family to stand for him.

"Let this take the path it wants, my love," Simon said softly.

"I stand by Ben." Ange joined them to stand on Ben's left. "Of course, that means I have a few words to say."

Ben groaned. "I thought you'd wait until afterwards for that."

She smiled at him, then winked. "Hey, you didn't think you were going to get away from me doing this by having your first ceremony somewhere else, did you?" Ange leaned in and kissed Ben on the cheek. "This is the brief bit. I'll spill all the dirt on you later," she whispered before raising her voice. "As you know, Ben and I have been friends for years. We've been through a lot together and shared everything." She paused. "Except Simon, of course." The audience laughed. "Seriously though, the first time I saw Simon and Ben together, I could see how much they love each other. Not just that, but they respect each other too. Their connection isn't just emotional but something deeper. I wish them all the best for a long future together."

Simon blinked rapidly and tightened his grip on Ben's hand. His eyes reflected his vampire for a moment, an outward sign of his struggle to contain his emotions.

Ray stood and walked up to stand by Simon's right. He placed a hand on Simon's shoulder.

Surprise and shock flared through their shared bond. Ben let out a long breath. He hadn't known about this either. He flashed his father a smile. One of the reasons they hadn't wanted to do the full ceremony like they had in Boggslake was that Simon didn't have anyone here.

"I stand by Simon," Ray said in a clear voice. "I must admit I was a little taken aback when Simon phoned me and asked for my permission before asking Ben to marry him. Amused too, and yet very happy that Ben had found someone who valued the importance of family like we do. We hadn't had the opportunity to get to know Simon very well before they arrived here, despite them being together for a while." He shrugged. "But we trusted Ben's judgement and could tell by the way he talked about Simon that they were a good match. Meeting Simon and seeing them together confirmed that almost immediately." He smiled. "Abby and I are very proud to welcome another son into our family."

Simon bit his lip. A tear escaped from one eye. He nodded, yet said nothing.

"Thanks, Dad," Ben said. "This means a lot. To both of us."

It wouldn't make up for the way Simon's father had treated him, but it came damn close.

Ray shrugged. "I tell it how I see it. Always have. Always will."

"Just like your son," Simon said hoarsely.

"Can we leave any more speeches until later?" Ben asked. "Or Simon and I will lose it before we get through our vows."

"As long as I get to second everything Ray just said," Abby called out.

"I think you just did, Mum." Tash pulled Abby down into her seat again.

"Do you need a moment?" Elard asked.

"Simon?" Ben met Simon's gaze, then leaned in and kissed him softly on the lips. Simon wasn't one for showing his emotions in public, and although he was pulling himself together, he hadn't totally regained his composure.

"I'm fine." The bond between them flared in a burst of emotion, tendrils merging together. Simon took a deep breath. "I'm fine," he repeated.

"Right then." Elard sounded suspiciously choked. "I do so love this part."

Ben took a deep breath, and placed his and Simon's joined hands over his heart. They'd agreed he'd speak first, given Simon had taken the lead the first time.

"I, Benjamin Francis Leyton, take you, Simon Edwin Hawthorne, to be my husband. You are my heart, half my soul, and I love you with everything I am. I will do whatever it takes to keep you safe and stick with you no matter what. I accept you for who are and promise to kick your arse when you need it. You're mine. I am yours. And that's forever." He kissed Simon's ring. "You're my soulmate, and whatever life brings, we'll face it together."

Simon bit his lip. When he took Ben's hand in his again, he was trembling. He cleared his throat and placed their hands over his heart.

"I, Simon Edwin Hawthorne, take you, Benjamin Francis Leyton, to be my husband." Simon paused. Love flowed through their bond, and he smiled. "You are my heart, half my soul, and I love you with everything I am. I am privileged to have you in my life. I promise to stay by your side while we grow older together. You've reminded me how to live again and given me a future to look forward to. You're mine. I am yours. And that's forever." He kissed Ben's ring. "You're my soulmate, and whatever life brings, we'll face it together."

Ben swallowed. The bit about growing older together was new. He threw his arms around Simon's neck and hung on tightly. "I love you."

Simon carded his fingers through Ben's hair. "How did I get so lucky?" he whispered. "I love you too."

Ben looked up at Simon and smiled. "I'm the lucky one. You waited for me for so long."

"So totally worth it."

Simon's words, sounding more like Ben's but in a very clipped British accent, made him grin. He brushed his lips against Simon's. Simon met him halfway, and leaned into the kiss, adding his promise to Ben's for a shared life and a future together full of love, and whatever other shit came their way.

EPILOGUE

"This is very nice." Simon took another kumara wedge from the paper cup, and dipped it in the pottle of sour cream. He was slowly getting used to the differences between the States and New Zealand. Ben had found that he'd had to think twice about the little things when he'd first come to Boggslake too, like a pottle being the Kiwi name for a disposable condiment cup.

"Knew you'd like them." Ben grinned and stretched his legs out over the blanket they'd spread over the grass.

"I didn't just mean the wedges." Simon leaned in and stole a kiss.

The wind he was growing used to had eased down to a breeze that morning, and the storm of the last few days dissipated into a beautiful sunny day. The roses were beginning to bloom, their perfume permeating the air. They'd found a private spot at the side of the public gardens and set up a picnic with food and coffee from the university café.

He'd spotted a few rose variations he hadn't noticed before and planned to find out from Abby where he could source them. Once she'd discovered his love of roses, they'd spent an hour or so in her garden and she'd loaned him one of her books about the local varieties.

"How did your meeting with the history department go?" Ben covered another wedge in sour cream and popped it into Simon's mouth.

Simon nodded, chewed, and washed the food down with coffee. "It wasn't only an opportunity to look around. Rupert has been busy. I suspect it was actually a wedding present." Not that Rupert would ever admit that, of course.

"Oh?" Ben raised an eyebrow.

"The meeting was a job interview." Simon hadn't time to prepare because it had been sprung on him, but he'd been teaching the subject so long his reputation had preceded him. "I suspect they were more interested in how good a fit I'd be for them than my credentials. They were already more than aware of those."

"Well, you did build the Lakeview history department from the ground up." Ben didn't hide the pride in his voice. "Though you couldn't exactly say that, considering how old you're *supposed* to be."

"Something like that, yes."

"And?"

"The job is mine if I want it. They did have a couple of other applicants whom they've already interviewed, so that part of the process is already done."

"Well, of course, you want it." Ben frowned. "You haven't changed your mind about staying, have you?"

"No. Have you?" Simon had to ask, in case. "I told them I'd talk to you about it first and I'd let them know after we'd discussed it."

"That's a yes to the job then." Ben grinned. "You'd better tell Wayland we're taking the house too." He let out a long breath. "Shit, and then we'd better tell everyone else. And start organising everything. God, they'll be so much to do. When do you—"

"Slow down." Simon silenced him with a kiss, then leaned their foreheads together. "We have plenty of time. It's October, and I don't start until the first semester of next year, although I can teach a couple of summer papers if I want to." He caressed Ben's cheek. "Once it's official, we'll sit down and figure out what we want shipped from Boggslake, and I can help you set up your business too." He smiled, already picturing them in their new home.

"Mum will want to help you set up your rose garden." Ben grinned. "And don't deny you'll want one. You've been itching to get your hands on all the varieties you don't already have since we got here."

"You know me too well." Simon paused. "Did you say anything to Frank about us staying?"

"No. Why?"

"He told me his cat needs a proper home, and he's even less subtle than you are." Simon had grown attached to the little black cat, and Ben missed Dax, although he denied it. "I figured we might adopt her, although she still needs a name. We can't keep referring to her as that cat."

"Selina," Ben said without skipping a beat. "He had that conversation with me too, and I know Granddad well enough to know when he's up to something." He rolled his eyes. "Although yeah, I totally missed that he was trying to set us up when he suggested I visit Boggslake for my OE."

"Selina..." Simon tried the name aloud. "It fits her. It's a reference to something though, isn't it? I'm sure I should know, but it escapes me."

"Catwoman." Ben grinned. "Batman's cat thief nemesis, although they do end up on the same side, and romantically involved. Kind of. It's complicated."

"Of course it is." Simon laughed.

Ben swatted him with an empty paper bag. "Don't diss the comics."

"I wouldn't dream of it." Simon tried and failed, to keep a straight face.

He stilled and glanced around the gardens. The other visitors had left them alone for the most part, apart from a group of ladies who had smiled when they'd passed by. "Are you expecting someone?"

"No. Why?" Ben looked up and followed Simon's gaze. "That guy is heading straight for us, isn't he?"

"Yes." Simon stood and brushed the crumbs from his trousers. "Pack up the blanket, and get ready to leave." The man approaching them looked very familiar, yet Simon couldn't quite place him. Wellington appeared to be tarred with the same brush as Boggslake in its views on privacy and time off. A couple of days had passed since they'd closed the case for the council and had yet to hear from them about it.

He suspected the long overdue other shoe was about to drop.

By the time the man strode over to their corner, Ben had already packed their belongings into his backpack, and they'd retreated to the nearby bench seat.

"Mr Hawthorne?" The man's tone was polite. He held out his hand in greeting. "I'm Erik Sedway. The council sent me to talk to you."

"Of course, they did." Ben moved to stand next to Simon.

"*Professor* Hawthorne." Simon corrected him and shook his hand.

Sedway had a firm grip, and laughter lines around his eyes, although his expression was sombre. He was tall and lean and looked every year of his late fifties.

"And you must be Mr Leyton." Sedway offered his hand to Ben. "My nephew said you'd been in the shop looking for me."

"Everyone's been looking for you," Ben said after shaking Sedway's hand. "Kind of convenient being out of mobile range, yeah?"

Sedway ducked his head. "Yes, well. That wasn't very clever of me, was it? I was feeling a little stressed with everything going on, so figured I'd take some time out. I didn't expect to get hauled back to civilisation by a group of werewolves, that's for sure."

"You're here on council business," Simon said. The council never bothered with small talk, unless it was to their advantage. Looking for Sedway had muddied the investigation and would have been time better spent saving lives.

"Why yes." Sedway indicated the seat. "Can we sit?"

"We'll stand, thank you all the same." Simon kept his tone pleasant. "How can we help you, Mr Sedway? We've done what the council requested. Most of Human Destiny is in custody, and the missing registers have been recovered."

"Mostly recovered," Sedway corrected. "I believe the vampire list is still missing?"

"If we can't find it, I doubt anyone else can either." Simon wasn't about to tell the council the entire truth. Victor's wife should be allowed to rest in peace, and he wouldn't put it past them to confiscate her urn in an attempt to retrieve the list. "And the werewolf list?"

"That's in the hands of the new werewolf councillor." Sedway looked suspiciously smug. "He took a bit of convincing to take the role, but in the end saw the benefits of taking it on. After all, we're all capable of minor discrepancies, aren't we?"

"You threatened him?" Ben asked.

"Oh goodness no." Sedway smiled. "I don't see the point in threats when it's so much easier to appeal to someone's better nature. And with all the pack politics, it makes more sense to build a wider community by having someone who isn't affiliated with them take on the role, don't you think?"

Simon and Ben exchanged a glance.

"Josh?" Ben asked.

Sedway nodded.

"Shit." Ben shook his head. "He's got enough crap to deal with without shoving that on him. You people have no empathy at all."

Simon laid a warning hand on Ben's arm. Considering they were planning to make their home here, angering the council wouldn't be a good move. He'd heard enough to read between the lines and guess what Sedway wasn't saying. The council had found out that Josh had warned Cody, which had allowed Wright to escape. Josh wouldn't care about politics and all that other garbage Sedway was spouting, but he did feel bad about that, and it getting out wouldn't earn him any favours.

"My list is also safe," Sedway added, "although I have added your name to it, Mr Leyton."

"Why?" Simon asked sharply. "Ben's human. He shouldn't be on your bloody list."

"He's married to you. You're a vampire." Sedway tilted his head to one side and studied Ben. Simon growled. "My vampire colleagues inform me that brings with it a risk of some kind of bond, so, until we're certain that hasn't happened, we will be keeping an eye on him." He paused. "On both of you."

"Like hell you will." Ben took a step forward. "Are you threatening us?"

"Of course not." Sedway's smile widened. "We were very pleased to learn you're planning to stay in Wellington instead of returning to Boggslake."

Bloody hell, here it comes.

"No," Simon said before Sedway could ask. "No way in hell."

"Think about it, *Simon*. And, given we'll be working together, I'm sure we should drop the formalities too." Sedway cleared his throat. "It's a great opportunity to influence the future direction of our community not only in Wellington, but the entire country. You're not coming in with any preconceptions—"

"Ask Rupert," Simon said.

Ben's eyes widened. "He's asking you to be the next vampire councillor? Fuck."

Sedway chuckled. "Professor Milne has already made himself scarce. With his history of disappearing when trouble rears its head, do you really think he'd be a good fit for the role?"

"How is that different from you going fishing?" Ben asked.

"Being on the council would also give you an insight into our plans, and the opportunity to oppose..." Sedway gave Ben a long hard look. "... or endorse them."

"Are you threatening my husband?" Simon removed his sunglasses, let his eyes change to show his vampire, and dropped his fangs.

"Of course not." Sedway's innocent act wasn't convincing in the slightest. "You can either give me your answer now, or later." He handed Simon his card. "I assure you I will be easy to contact from now on. No fishing for a while. I've had my hand slapped for it." He sighed. "What's the world come to that a man can't go fishing in peace."

"I'll do it until you can find someone else."

"Simon, you can't—"

"Wonderful." Sedway gave them both a nod. "I'll be in touch with the details. I do so look forward to getting to know you better. Both of you."

"Bollocks," Simon exclaimed once Sedway was out of earshot.

"You're not seriously going through with this." Ben scowled. "You know what they're like. Shit, they threatened you in Auckland so you'd take this case. You give in now and it's only going to get worse."

"I know exactly what they're like." Simon hugged Ben tightly. "That's why I'm doing this." He let go of Ben and met his concerned, angry gaze. "We want to stay here, and that means we'll end up dealing with all the supernatural trouble in the area. We need the council on our side, rather than dealing with their bullshit on top of whatever else we're facing." He kissed Ben hard, needing to connect with him physically as well as through their bond. "This way, I have some control. Turning them down means I don't."

"I hate that you're right." Ben's anger faded, but his concern didn't. "Don't do this just to keep me safe, okay?"

"If the situation were reversed, you'd do it for me."

"Yeah, I would." Ben sighed. "I had hoped we could have a normal life here."

Simon rolled his eyes. "I'm a vampire, and we've only been here a few weeks, none of which has been the relaxing honeymoon we'd planned. Do you really think the rest of our life together is going to be any different?" He brushed a strand of hair from Ben's face. "I meant what I said in our vows about staying by your side while we grow older together. I was going to talk to you about this tonight, but this feels like the right time for this conversation."

"We can wait—" Ben's heart sped up. "Hold up. Vampires still age, but slowly. When you said that, you *did* mean what I thought you did, yeah?"

"Yes." The item Simon had been waiting for had been delivered that morning. Lucas had asked some friends from The Vampire Guard to arrange it. "I was waiting for this to arrive from Lucas first." He placed the small metal vial in Ben's hand. "Vampire blood," he explained. "Or, more specifically, mine, taken when I was contagious. The human operatives for The Guard carry them in the field."

Ben turned it over in his hand. "In case of death, break glass?" He glanced at Simon, then at the vial. "I'm not going to ask how Lucas got this, or what magical properties it contains, so it doesn't spoil."

"I've learnt not to ask about a lot of things where Lucas is concerned, and The Guard has their own secrets I don't particularly want to know either." Simon hesitated, then dropped a fine gold chain next to the vial in Ben's hand. "I thought... after thinking I was going to lose you a few months ago... I won't be able to change you until I'm contagious again next July, but with the dangerous lives we lead, you could wear this around your neck in case..."

"Yes," Ben leaned in and kissed Simon. "And this way, if something does happen before we're ready, you'll still be my maker. I wouldn't want anyone else." He threaded the vial onto the chain, slipped it around his neck, then tucked it under his shirt out of sight.

"We still need to talk to your family about this," Simon reminded him, "and I'd like your turning to be a good thing." He wouldn't want his experience for Ben. "A celebration of the beginning of a long life together, rather than—"

"We're doing this together and because we *both* want it." Ben had grown quiet. When he spoke, tears filled his eyes. "I want to spend the rest of my life with you however long that is, and to leave it with you, whatever happens."

Simon wiped Ben's tears. "That's what I want too. You've given me a future, and the courage to put my past behind me."

"You've always had that strength inside you. I just nudged it a bit." Ben leaned into Simon. "And on that subject, don't expect me to stay quiet and not call the council out on their bullshit if they try to get you to do anything else, okay?"

Simon smiled. "Of course not. You wouldn't be you otherwise, and I love that part of you too." He licked his lips and showed Ben his vampire. "We should go home and tell your family we're staying. And then I'm going to take you to bed and show you just how much I love you."

"I'd like that." Ben swallowed. "And then I intend to show you how much I love you too."

ABOUT THE AUTHOR

CONNECT WITH ANNE
Contact me at:
annebarwell.wordpress.com
darthanne@gmail.com

Anne Barwell lives in Wellington, New Zealand. She shares her home with Kaylee: a cat with "tortitude" who is convinced that the house is run to suit her; this is an ongoing "discussion," and to date, it appears as though Kaylee may be winning.

In 2008, Anne completed her conjoint BA in English Literature and Music/Bachelor of Teaching. She has worked as a music teacher, a primary school teacher, and now works in a library. She is a member of the Upper Hutt Science Fiction Club and plays violin for Hutt Valley Orchestra.

She is an avid reader across a wide range of genres and a watcher of far too many TV series and movies, although it can be argued that there is no such thing as "too many." These, of course, are best enjoyed with a decent cup of tea and further the continuing argument that the concept of "spare time" is really just a myth. She also hosts and reviews for other authors, and writes monthly blog posts for Love Bytes. She is the co-founder of the New Zealand Rainbow Romance writers, and a member of RWNZ.

Anne's books have received honourable mentions five

times, reached the finals four times—one of which was for best gay book—and been a runner up in the Rainbow Awards. She has also been nominated three times in the Goodreads M/M Romance Reader's Choice Awards—twice for Best Fantasy, once for Best Historical, and once for All-Time Favourite M/M Author.

READ BEN AND SIMON'S ORIGIN STORY

The Sleepless City Book 1
Shades of Sepia

To be soulmates they first have to survive.

A serial killer stalks the streets of Boggslake, Ohio. The victims are always found in pairs, one human and one vampire.

Simon Hawthorne has been a vampire for nearly a hundred years, and he has never seen anything like it. Neither have the other supernaturals he works with to keep the streets safe for both their kind and the humans.

One meeting with Simon finds Ben Leyton falling for a man he knows is keeping secrets, but he can't ignore the growing attraction between them. A recent arrival in Boggslake, Ben finds it very different from his native New Zealand, but something about Simon makes Ben feel as though he's found a new home.

After a close friend falls victim to the killer, Simon is torn between revealing his true nature to Ben, and walking away to avoid the reaction he fears. But with the body count rising and the murders becoming more frequent, either, or both of them, could be the killer's next target.